DOCTOR WHO
THE TERRESTRIAL INDEX

DOCTOR WHO
THE TERRESTRIAL
INDEX
by
Jean-Marc Lofficier

TARGET

First published in 1991 by Doctor Who Books
An imprint of Virgin Publishing Ltd
338 Ladbroke Grove
London W10 5AH

Printed and bound in Great Britain by
Cox & Wyman Ltd, Reading, Berks.

ISBN 0426 20361 5

CONTENTS

Acknowledgements
Table of Stories   2
1 History of Mankind According to *Doctor Who*   22
2 Who's Who in *Who*   78
    The Actors   78
    The Creative Team   103
    Key Technical Personnel   109
    The Novelization Writers   116
3 Which *Who* Is What   118
    The Missing Season   119
    The Motion Pictures   120
    The Stage Plays   122
    The Radio Plays   125
    Records and Tapes   126
    Video   128
    Games   128
    The Novels   130
    The Short Stories   134
    Miscellaneous Fiction   157
    The Comics   159
    Index of Fiction   225
4 Addendum to *The Programme Guide*   239
    Twenty-Sixth Season Story Summaries   239
    Episode Titles for Stories A–Z   241
    Errata   244

To Terrance Dicks

ACKNOWLEDGEMENTS

First and foremost, I must acknowledge the constant help and support of my wife Randy, who has been the uncredited co-author of this book since its inception in 1980.

I am also deeply grateful for the help of those devoted *Doctor Who* scholars without whom this book could never have been put together, and who deserve a good share of the credit for their unswerving dedication to the common cause: Jeremy Bentham, who among other things helped compile the section devoted to comics; Eric Hoffman, who kindly loaned me his extensive collection of *Doctor Who* material; Shaun Ley, who provided numerous corrections and suggestions; John and Nan Peel, ever true friends and cartographers of the Whoniverse; and finally, David J Howe, whose labours have always been a precious source of information. Thank you all!

J-ML

TABLE OF STORIES

CODE	STORY TITLE	EPISODES	COMPANIONS	GUEST STARS	VILLAINS
First Doctor					
First Season					
A	An Unearthly Child (The Tribe of Gum)	4	Susan Ian Barbara	None	Kal
B	The Daleks	7	Susan Ian Barbara	Thals	Daleks
C	The Edge of Destruction	2	Susan Ian Barbara	None	None
D	Marco Polo	7	Susan Ian Barbara	None	Tegana
E	The Keys of Marinus	6	Susan Barbara Ian	None	Yartek The Voord
F	The Aztecs	4	Susan Ian Barbara	None	Tlotoxl

CODE	STORY TITLE	EPISODES	COMPANIONS	GUEST STARS	VILLAINS
G	The Sensorites	6	Susan Ian Barbara	None	Administrator
H	The Reign of Terror	6	Susan Ian Barbara	None	Colbert
Second Season					
J	Planet of Giants	3	Susan Ian Barbara	None	Forester
K	The Dalek Invasion of Earth	6	Susan Ian Barbara	None	Daleks
L	The Rescue	2	Ian Barbara Vicki	None	Bennett (Koquillion)
M	The Romans	4	Ian Barbara Vicki	None	Nero
N	The Web Planet	6	Ian Barbara Vicki	None	Animus Zarbi
P	The Crusade	4	Ian Barbara Vicki	None	El Akir

CODE	STORY TITLE	EPISODES	COMPANIONS	GUEST STARS	VILLAINS
Q	The Space Museum	4	Ian Barbara Vicki	None	Lobos Moroks
R	The Chase	6	Ian Barbara Vicki Steven	None	Daleks Mechanoids
S	The Time Meddler	4	Vicki Steven	None	Monk
Third Season					
T	Galaxy Four	4	Vicki Steven	None	Maaga Drahvins
T/A	Mission to the Unknown	1	None	Marc Cory	Daleks
U	The Myth Makers	4	Vicki Steven Katarina	None	None
V	The Daleks' Masterplan	12	Steven Katarina	Sara	Daleks Monk Mavic Chen
W	The Massacre	4	Steven Dodo	None	Abbot of Amboise
X	The Ark	4	Steven Dodo	None	Monoids

CODE	STORY TITLE	EPISODES	COMPANIONS	GUEST STARS	VILLAINS
Y	The Celestial Toymaker	4	Steven Dodo	None	Toymaker
Z	The Gunfighters	4	Steven Dodo	None	Clantons Johnny Ringo
AA	The Savages	4	Steven Dodo	None	Elders
BB	The War Machines	4	Dodo Polly Ben	None	WOTAN War Machines
Fourth Season					
CC	The Smugglers	4	Polly Ben	None	Captain Pike
DD	The Tenth Planet	4	Polly Ben	None	Cybermen
Second Doctor					
Fourth Season continued					
EE	The Power of the Daleks	6	Polly Ben	None	Daleks Bragen
FF	The Highlanders	4	Polly Ben Jamie	None	Gray

CODE	STORY TITLE	EPISODES	COMPANIONS	GUEST STARS	VILLAINS
GG	The Underwater Menace	4	Polly Ben Jamie	None	Professor Zaroff
HH	The Moonbase	4	Polly Ben Jamie	None	Cybermen
JJ	The Macra Terror	4	Polly Ben Jamie	None	Macra
KK	The Faceless Ones	6	Polly Ben Jamie	None	Chameleons
LL	The Evil of the Daleks	7	Jamie Victoria	None	Daleks Maxtible
Fifth Season					
MM	The Tomb of the Cybermen	4	Jamie Victoria	None	Cybermen Klieg
NN	The Abominable Snowmen	6	Jamie Victoria	Travers	Intelligence Yeti
OO	The Ice Warriors	6	Jamie Victoria	None	Varga Ice Warriors
PP	The Enemy of the World	6	Jamie Victoria	None	Salamander

CODE	STORY TITLE	EPISODES	COMPANIONS	GUEST STARS	VILLAINS
QQ	The Web of Fear	6	Jamie Victoria	Lethbridge-Stewart Travers	Intelligence Yeti
RR	Fury from the Deep	6	Jamie Victoria	None	Weed
SS	The Wheel in Space	6	Jamie Zoe	None	Cybermen
Sixth Season					
TT	The Dominators	5	Jamie Zoe	None	Dominators Quarks
UU	The Mind Robber	5	Jamie Zoe	None	Master-Brain
VV	The Invasion	8	Jamie Zoe	Lethbridge-Stewart Benton	Cybermen Tobias Vaughn
WW	The Krotons	4	Jamie Zoe	None	Krotons
XX	The Seeds of Death	6	Jamie Zoe	None	Slaar Ice Warriors
YY	The Space Pirates	6	Jamie Zoe	None	Caven
ZZ	The War Games	10	Jamie Zoe	Time Lords	War Lord War Chief Security Chief

CODE	STORY TITLE	EPISODES	COMPANIONS	GUEST STARS	VILLAINS
Third Doctor					
Seventh Season					
AAA	Spearhead from Space	4	Liz	Lethbridge-Stewart	Nestene Autons
BBB	The Silurians	7	Liz	Lethbridge-Stewart	Silurians
CCC	The Ambassadors of Death	7	Liz	Lethbridge-Stewart Benton	Carrington
DDD	Inferno	7	Liz	Lethbridge-Stewart Benton	Stahlman Primords
Eighth Season					
EEE	Terror of the Autons	4	Jo	Lethbridge-Stewart Yates Benton Time Lords	Master Nestene Autons
FFF	The Mind of Evil	6	Jo	Lethbridge-Stewart Yates Benton	Master (Professor Keller) Parasite
GGG	The Claws of Axos	4	Jo	Lethbridge-Stewart Yates Benton	Master Axos
HHH	Colony in Space	6	Jo	Lethbridge-Stewart Time Lords	Master IMC

CODE	STORY TITLE	EPISODES	COMPANIONS	GUEST STARS	VILLAINS
JJJ	The Daemons	5	Jo	Lethbridge-Stewart Yates Benton	Master Azal
Ninth Season					
KKK	Day of the Daleks	4	Jo	Lethbridge-Stewart Yates Benton	Daleks Ogrons
MMM	The Curse of Peladon	4	Jo	Ice Warriors Alpha Centauri	Arcturus Hepesh
LLL	The Sea Devils	6	Jo	None	Master Sea Devils
NNN	The Mutants	6	Jo	None	Marshal
OOO	The Time Monster	6	Jo	Lethbridge-Stewart Yates Benton	Master (Professor Thascales) Kronos
Tenth Season					
RRR	The Three Doctors	4	Jo	Lethbridge-Stewart Benton Time Lords	Omega
PPP	Carnival of Monsters	4	Jo	None	Kalik Drashigs

CODE	STORY TITLE	EPISODES	COMPANIONS	GUEST STARS	VILLAINS
QQQ	Frontier in Space	6	Jo	None	Master Daleks Ogrons
SSS	Planet of the Daleks	6	Jo	Thals	Daleks
TTT	The Green Death	6	Jo	Lethbridge-Stewart Yates Benton	BOSS
Eleventh Season					
UUU	The Time Warrior	4	Sarah	Lethbridge-Stewart	Linx Sontarans
WWW	Invasion of the Dinosaurs	6	Sarah	Lethbridge-Stewart Benton	Sir Charles Grover Yates
XXX	Death to the Daleks	4	Sarah	None	Daleks
YYY	The Monster of Peladon	6	Sarah	Alpha Centauri	Azaxyr Ice Warriors Eckersley
ZZZ	Planet of the Spiders	6	Sarah	Lethbridge-Stewart Benton Yates Time Lords (K'Anpo)	Spiders
Fourth Doctor					
Twelfth Season					
4A	Robot	4	Sarah Harry	Lethbridge-Stewart Benton	SRS Miss Winters

CODE	STORY TITLE	EPISODES	COMPANIONS	GUEST STARS	VILLAINS
4C	The Ark in Space	4	Sarah Harry	None	Wirrn
4B	The Sontaran Experiment	2	Sarah Harry	None	Styre Sontarans
4E	Genesis of the Daleks	6	Sarah Harry	Thals Time Lords	Davros Daleks
4D	Revenge of the Cybermen	4	Sarah Harry	None	Cybermen
Thirteenth Season					
4F	Terror of the Zygons	4	Sarah Harry	Lethbridge-Stewart Benton	Broton Zygons
4H	Planet of Evil	4	Sarah	None	Anti-Matter
4G	Pyramids of Mars	4	Sarah	None	Sutekh
4J	The Android Invasion	4	Sarah	Harry Benton	Styggron Kraals
4K	The Brain of Morbius	4	Sarah	None	Morbius Solon
4L	The Seeds of Doom	6	Sarah	Beresford	Krynoids Chase

CODE	STORY TITLE	EPISODES	COMPANIONS	GUEST STARS	VILLAINS
Fourteenth Season					
4M	Masque of Mandragora	4	Sarah	None	Mandragora Helix
4N	The Hand of Fear	4	Sarah	None	Eldrad
4P	The Deadly Assassin	4	None	Time Lords (Bonusa)	Master Goth
4Q	The Face of Evil	4	Leela	None	Xoanon
4R	The Robots of Death	4	Leela	None	Taren Capel (Dask)
4S	The Talons of Weng-Chiang	6	Leela	None	Magnus Greel (Weng-Chiang) Li H'Sen Chang Mr Sin
Fifteenth Season					
4V	Horror of Fang Rock	4	Leela	None	Rutan
4T	The Invisible Enemy	4	Leela K9	None	Nucleus
4X	Image of the Fendahl	4	Leela K9	None	Fendahl
4W	The Sunmakers	4	Leela K9	None	Collector Usurians

CODE	STORY TITLE	EPISODES	COMPANIONS	GUEST STARS	VILLAINS
4Y	Underworld	4	Leela K9	Minyans	Oracle Seers
4Z	The Invasion of Time	6	Leela K9	Time Lords (Borusa) (Andred)	Stor Sontarans Vardans Kelner
Sixteenth Season (The Key to Time)					
5A	The Ribos Operation	4	Romana 1 K9	White Guardian	Graff Vynda-K
5B	The Pirate Planet	4	Romana 1 K9	None	Captain Queen Xanxia
5C	The Stones of Blood	4	Romana 1 K9	None	Vivien Fay (Cessair) Ogri
5D	The Androids of Tara	4	Romana 1 K9	None	Count Grendel
5E	The Power of Kroll	4	Romana 1 K9	None	Thawn
5F	The Armageddon Factor	6	Romana 1 K9	Time Lords (Drax)	Black Guardian Shadow
Seventeenth Season					

CODE	STORY TITLE	EPISODES	COMPANIONS	GUEST STARS	VILLAINS
5J	Destiny of the Daleks	4	Romana 2 K9	None	Davros Daleks Movellans
5H	City of Death	4	Romana 2 K9	None	Scaroth
5G	The Creature from the Pit	4	Romana 2 K9	None	Lady Adrasta Huntsman
5K	Nightmare of Eden	4	Romana 2 K9	None	Tryst Mandrels
5L	The Horns of Nimon	4	Romana 2 K9	None	Nimon Soldeed
5M	Shada (not televised)	6	Romana 2 K9	Time Lords (Salyavin)	Skagra
Eighteenth Season					
5N	The Leisure Hive	4	Romana 2 K9	None	Pangol West Lodge Foamasi
5Q	Meglos	4	Romana 2 K9	None	Meglos Gaztaks
5R	Full Circle	4	Romana 2 K9 Adric	None	Marshmen

CODE	STORY TITLE	EPISODES	COMPANIONS	GUEST STARS	VILLAINS
5P	State of Decay	4	Romana 2 K9 Adric	None	Great Vampire Zargo, Camilla and Aukon
5S	Warriors' Gate	4	Romana 2 K9 Adric	None	Rorvik Gundans
5T	The Keeper of Traken	4	Adric Nyssa	None	Master (Melkur)
5V	Logopolis	4	Adric Nyssa Tegan	Watcher (Doctor)	Master
–	K9 and Company (50-minute special)	1	Sarah K9	None	Pollock Lily Gregson

Fifth Doctor

Nineteenth Season

CODE	STORY TITLE	EPISODES	COMPANIONS	GUEST STARS	VILLAINS
5Z	Castrovalva	4	Adric Nyssa Tegan	None	Master (Portreeve)
5W	Four to Doomsday	4	Adric Nyssa Tegan	None	Monarch Urbankans

CODE	STORY TITLE	EPISODES	COMPANIONS	GUEST STARS	VILLAINS
5Y	Kinda	4	Adric Nyssa Tegan	None	Mara
5X	The Visitation	4	Adric Nyssa Tegan	None	Terileptils
6A	Black Orchid	2	Adric Nyssa Tegan	George Cranleigh	None
6B	Earthshock	4	Adric Nyssa Tegan	None	Cybermen
6C	Time Flight	4	Nyssa Tegan	None	Master (Kalid)
Twentieth Season					
6E	Arc of Infinity	4	Nyssa Tegan	Time Lords (Borusa)	Omega Hedin
6D	Snakedance	4	Nyssa Tegan	None	Mara
6F	Mawdryn Undead	4	Nyssa Tegan Turlough	Lethbridge-Stewart	Black Guardian Mawdryn

CODE	STORY TITLE	EPISODES	COMPANIONS	GUEST STARS	VILLAINS
6G	Terminus	4	Nyssa Tegan Turlough	None	Black Guardian Terminus
6H	Enlightenment	4	Tegan Turlough	White Guardian	Black Guardian Captain Rack Eternals
6J	The King's Demons	2	Tegan Turlough	Kamelion	Master (Sir Gilles Estram)
6K	The Five Doctors (90-minute special)	1	Tegan Turlough Sarah K9 Romana 2 Susan Liz Jamie Zoe	Lethbridge-Stewart Yates Colonel Crichton Time Lords (Rassilon) (Flavia)	Borusa Master Cybermen Dalek Yeti
Twenty-first Season					
6L	Warriors of the Deep	4	Tegan Turlough	None	Silurians Sea Devils
6M	The Awakening	2	Tegan Turlough	None	Malus
6N	Frontios	4	Tegan Turlough	None	Gravis Tractators

CODE	STORY TITLE	EPISODES	COMPANIONS	GUEST STARS	VILLAINS
6P	Resurrection of the Daleks (45-minute episodes)	2	Tegan Turlough	Lytton	Davros Daleks
6Q	Planet of Fire	4	Turlough Peri	Kamelion	Master
6R	The Caves of Androzani	4	Peri	None	Morgus Sharaz Jek

Sixth Doctor

Twenty-first Season continued

| 6S | The Twin Dilemma | 4 | Peri | Time Lords (Azmael) | Mestor |

Twenty-second Season

6T	Attack of the Cybermen (45-minute episodes)	2	Peri	Lytton	Cybermen
6V	Vengeance on Varos (45-minute episodes)	2	Peri	None	Sil Quillam
6X	The Mark of the Rani (45-minute episodes)	2	Peri	None	Rani Master
6W	The Two Doctors (45-minute episodes)	3	Peri Jamie	None	Stike Sontarans Chessene Shockeye

CODE	STORY TITLE	EPISODES	COMPANIONS	GUEST STARS	VILLAINS
6Y	Timelash (45-minute episodes)	2	Peri	None	Borad
6Z	Revelation of the Daleks (45-minute episodes)	2	Peri	None	Davros (Great Healer) Daleks

Twenty-third Season (The Trial of a Time Lord)

7A	The Mysterious Planet	4	Peri	Time Lords (Inquisitor) Glitz	Valeyard Drathro
7B	Mindwarp	4	Peri	Time Lords (Inquisitor) Yrcanos	Valeyard Kiv and Sil Crozier
7C1	Terror of the Vervoids	4	Melanie	Time Lords (Inquisitor)	Valeyard Vervoids Dolland
7C2	The Ultimate Foe	2	Melanie Peri	Time Lords (Inquisitor) Glitz Yrcanos	Valeyard Master

Seventh Doctor

Twenty-fourth Season

7D	Time and the Rani	4	Melanie	None	Rani

CODE	STORY TITLE	EPISODES	COMPANIONS	GUEST STARS	VILLAINS
7E	Paradise Towers	4	Melanie	None	Kroagnon
7F	Delta and the Bannermen	3	Melanie	None	Gavrok Bannermen
7G	Dragonfire	3	Melanie Ace	Glitz	Kane
Twenty-fifth Season					
7H	Remembrance of the Daleks	4	Ace	None	Davros (Emperor Dalek) Daleks
7L	The Happiness Patrol	3	Ace	None	Kandy Man Helen A
7K	Silver Nemesis	3	Ace	None	Cybermen Lady Peinforte De Flores
7J	The Greatest Show in the Galaxy	4	Ace	None	Gods of Ragnarok Chief Clown
Twenty-sixth Season					
7N	Battlefield	4	Ace	Lethbridge-Stewart Bambera	Morgaine Mordred Destroyer
7Q	Ghost Light	3	Ace	None	Light Josiah Smith

CODE	STORY TITLE	EPISODES	COMPANIONS	GUEST STARS	VILLAINS
7M	The Curse of Fenric	4	Ace	None	Fennic Haemovores
7P	Survival	3	Ace	None	Master Cheetah People

1: HISTORY OF MANKIND ACCORDING TO DOCTOR WHO

The following essay is a creative exercise in retroactive continuity. It presupposes that the Earth on which the Doctor's adventures take place (which is obviously not to be confused with our Earth) is a single world with a straightforward, linear history. If you cannot agree with this premise – if you prefer to think that the Doctor is visiting alternative realities or, in spite of his claims to the contrary, rewriting history as he goes – then read no further.

As usual, there are a few exceptions: alternative time lines (such as these explored in *Day of the Daleks*, *Battlefield* and so on) are all clearly identified as such; but for the purpose of this chapter, Earth-Who has otherwise been treated as the same planet.

During its lifetime, the programme has contradicted itself many times. How could it be otherwise considering the number of writers, story editors and producers who have worked on it? No one familiar with the demands of television could realistically expect perfect continuity of a programme that spans twenty-seven years. This chapter is an exercise in retroactive continuity precisely because it tries to look retroactively at all the Earth-related *Doctor Who* stories and make them fit into a coherent continuity.

'Impossible,' some people might say. Indeed, it would be if one were to adhere strictly to every bit of conflicting and contradictory information generated by and during *Doctor Who*'s existence. Because the aim of this essay is to make this impossible premise come true, however, creativity needed to be called into play no matter what.

To establish a coherent history of mankind, some choices have had to be made – certain clues have been selected to the detriment of others – to provide a vision of what that history might be.

About The Past
Whenever possible the programme's information has been reconciled with historical accuracy and up-to-date scientific evidence. Indeed, a brief listing of other, relevant anthropological and geological (for the prehistoric ages) and scientific and political (for the modern ages) events have often been provided to give added context to the stories.

Whenever a date was known, that is if it were clearly mentioned in the broadcast or a novelization, that date has been used unless it obviously conflicted with the above evidence. If it conflicted, then the two have been reconciled.

Where a specific date was not mentioned, but the context of the story gave a good idea of when it was supposed to have taken place, either about or the abbreviation for circa (c) has been used next to the best guess, based on a myriad of small clues. Readers should feel free to disagree with these guesses.

Lastly, I have not taken into account the Doctor's mentions of his alleged encounters with numerous historical figures, listing 'unrecorded' adventures only when there was irrefutable third-party evidence that they did indeed take place.

About The Present
Although the UNIT stories were supposed to have taken place during the 1980s, these stories started being referred to as having taken place in the past when reality (the real 1980s) caught up with the show's producers. For instance, it was relatively clearly established in *Mawdryn Undead* that the Brigadier had retired in 1977.

To find a way out of this conundrum, the somewhat arbitrary decision has been made that each modern-day story took place either in the year of its broadcast or, in the case of the UNIT stories, the year afterwards. This approach is probably in accord with the intention of the producers who, for obvious reasons of credibility at the time, meant these stories to take place in an unspecified 'near future'.

The result is a universe that closely parallels ours, but which, even if one ignores the various alien invasions that obviously have not taken place on our Earth, still diverges on crucial background elements such as the manned Mars space probes launched in 1971 and the South Pole space tracking station of 1986. Educated guesses have been made about the most remarkable divergences between Earth-Who and our Earth, again to give added context to the stories.

Obviously, this approach will continue to lead to greater divergences, not only with our reality but within the programme itself, if the show continues and generates more modern-day stories that take place in the 1990s and beyond.

About The Future

Many readers may well disagree with this essay's view of the future at one point or another. As with the past, whenever an actual date or time period was specified on the show (or its novelization), that date has been used unless it conflicted with the rest of the programme. In that case, an attempt has been made to reconcile conflicting information and to come up with explanations for what happened on screen.

Otherwise, levels of science and technology, sociological data and so on have been used to estimate when a story took place. There are millions of ways of arranging the *Doctor Who* future, and it would be unconscionably foolish to believe that this way is the correct or only one.

One might question the purpose of this exercise. First, I have always had a fondness for vast, sprawling historical sagas, and preparing this document was fun. Then, one also hopes that this chapter will be of some use, not as much as a reference tool (it is too subjective properly to function as such) but more as a springboard, to future *Doctor Who* writers who choose to locate their stories in the future.

Or, to quote the Seventh Doctor, 'Time will tell. It always does.'

Jean-Marc Lofficier

THE PAST

PREHISTORY

5.5 billion BC
Earth was formed. The oldest rocks so far studied by science are more than three and a half billion years old. It has therefore been theorized that Earth is four to six billion years old. Because the maximum time required for the formation of all the elements of the Earth's crust has been determined by the latest scientific evidence to be about five and a half billion years, this is the date adopted here.

The first four-fifths of the estimated five billion years of Earth's history is recorded in rocks that contain no fossils. Adequate fossil records exist for only the past 600 million years, probably because the earliest lifeforms were soft-bodied: the hard body parts necessary for preservation did not develop until the Cambrian period.

This division has conveniently enabled science to separate Earth's span of existence into two main periods: the Cryptozoic (meaning 'hidden life') or Pre-Cambrian Age, and the Phanerozoic (meaning 'obvious life') or Cambrian Age.

The Cryptozoic
5.5 billion to 570 million BC
The crippled spaceship of Scaroth, a Jagaroth, exploded while taking off c3.5 million BC. The radiation caused by the ship's explosion triggered a mysterious biological mutation in the amniotic primordial soup, thereby creating life on Earth. The explosion also split the alien into twelve segments scattered across different time periods between then and AD 1980. Scaroth attempted to return in time to prevent the explosion, but his efforts were thwarted by the Fourth Doctor, Romana and Duggan (5H).

(The events described in this story were incorrectly reported as having happened four hundred million years ago. Yet, the earliest known forms of life on Earth are single-celled forms resembling modern bacteria (procaryotic cells), and these date from three and a half billion years ago, hence the decision to recast the date of 5H. Also, there was no breathable atmosphere on Earth at that time. Being Time Lords, the Doctor and Romana – and presumably Scaroth too – could survive such an absence, but the fact that Duggan did so would indicate that he, at least, would need to have been encased in some form of portable force field.)

The procaryotic cells were anaerobic. During the next two billion years, these cells evolved through amalgamation to produce more advanced cells, the eucaryotic cells. About 1.5 billion BC, these cells developed the more complex modes of living and advanced types of reproduction that eventually led to the appearance of multicellular plants and animals.

Finally c700 million BC, the first invertebrates appeared on Earth, thereby implying the presence of at least moderate levels of free atmospheric oxygen and a predictable supply of food plants.

The Paleozoic
570 to 225 million BC
The Paleozoic is divided into six sub-divisions: Cambrian, Ordovician, Silurian, Devonian, Carboniferous and Permian.

The Cambrian (570 to 500 million BC): During the next 130 million years, the basic body plans of modern animals developed during a remarkable burst of evolutionary change.

Beginning 570 million years ago, skeletons developed independently in a number of animal lineages. One wormlike lineage that swam evolved a stiff dorsal cord, and eventually an articulated internal skeleton that supported the body to improve swimming efficiency. Thus, fish (chordates) arose from early invertebrates.

A characteristic animal of the Cambrian Period is the trilobite, a primitive form of crustacean, which became extinct during the Permian Period. Snails and molluscs also appeared during this period. Flora was entirely confined to seaweed and lichens.

The Ordovician (500 to 430 million BC): The first primitive fish and the earliest corals appeared during the Ordovician

Period. The largest animal of the period was a cephalopod mollusc that had a shell about three metres long.

The Silurian (430 to 395 million BC): Land-based plants began to appear during the Silurian Period. Arthropods (some evolving into insects) and other invertebrate groups followed them. The first recorded air-breathing animal was the scorpion.

(The saurian lifeforms mistakenly known as Silurians and Sea Devils did not exist during this period, but made their appearance much later, during the Mesozoic.)

The Devonian (395 to 345 million BC): Land vertebrates, amphibians at first, evolved from freshwater fish. In the sea, sharks, lungfish, and other armoured fish thrived. Lower lifeforms of this period included the starfish and the sponge. The first woody plants, such as ferns, appeared on land.

The Carboniferous (345 to 280 million BC): The progress of land vertebrates made them increasingly mobile. In the sea, the cestraciontes (a group of sharks) were the dominant creatures. On land, the dominant lifeforms were the stegocephalia, lizard-like amphibians that evolved into the first reptiles. Other land animals included spiders and more than 800 species of cock-roaches.

The Permian (280 to 225 million BC): This period, the last of the Paleozoic, saw the disappearance of many forms of marine animals and the rapid spread of evolution on land, especially of reptiles. A comparatively small group of reptiles that evolved during the Permian were the theriodontia, from which mammals would later spring.

The Mesozoic
225 to 65 million BC
The Mesozoic is divided into the Triassic, the Jurassic and the Cretaceous.

The Triassic (225 to 195 million BC): The Triassic heralded the age of reptiles, the dominant lifeforms of this period. The dinosaurs – aquatic ichtyosaurs and flying pterosaurs included – ruled the Earth, first as comparatively slender animals that ran on their feet and balanced their bodies with their tails. The first mammals, however, also made their appearance: small, nocturnal creatures with reptilian looks.

The Earth's land mass which, until then, had been welded into a single area known as Pangea, split into a northern landmass, known as Laurasia, and a southern one, called Gondwana.

The Jurassic (195 to 136 million BC): The evolution of the dinosaurs continued, producing the brontosaurus, the tyrannosaurus, the trachodon, the stegosaurus and so on. The first true bird, the archeopteryx, evolved from other reptiles. The mammals remained smaller than modern-day dogs. New insect lifeforms also appeared: the moth, the beetle, the grasshopper and the termite.

Geologically, Gondwana was ripped apart to make room for the Atlantic Ocean.

It was during the Jurassic that the petrified hand of the Kastrian Eldrad landed on Earth and became a fossil. It was dug up in AD 1977 and used Sarah Jane Smith to facilitate its regeneration. Eldrad's plans to return to Kastria and rule the planet were ultimately foiled by the Fourth Doctor (4N).

Also, one may suppose that the various reptiles scooped up by Professor Whitaker's time device, and brought back to AD 1975 to help Sir Charles Grover's Operation Golden Age, were taken from the Jurassic. Sir Charles's plan was thwarted by the Third Doctor, Sarah Jane Smith and UNIT (WWW).

According to the TARDIS's evidence, it was 140 million years ago, towards the end of the Jurassic, that the Fifth Doctor, Tegan and Nyssa fought the Master (disguised as Kalid) for control of the powerful alien Xeraphin, and the return of a Concorde aeroplane hijacked from AD 1983 through a time corridor (6C). (In spite of occurring 140 million years ago, this incident was incorrectly recorded as having taken place during the Pleistocene, which began 138 million years later. It has now been restored to the correct time.)

The Cretaceous (136 to 65 million BC): Reptiles remained the dominant lifeform on Earth until the end of the Mesozoic: the triceratops as well as snakes and lizards appeared. Among the mammals, the first marsupials arose. In the plant kingdom, the first flowering plants evolved, leading to the beech, the holly, the laurel, the maple, the oak, the walnut and so on.

It was during the Cretaceous that the (misnamed) Silurians

(BBB) and their aquatic brethren the Sea Devils (LLL) ruled the Earth.

(It is interesting to remark that mammals must already have evolved into some kind of early primate, because on several occasions members of both reptilian races indicated they were familiar with this type of creature during the period. It is also possible that the Silurians used advanced genetic technology to accelerate the evolution of primitive mammals to create those primates, which they more or less regarded as pets. Fossil evidence so far uncovered, however, has not confirmed the existence of any Cretaceous primates.)

The Silurians and the Sea Devils were eventually driven underground by some, as yet unknown, cosmic event. Members of the Silurian species encountered by the Third Doctor blamed it on a sudden change in the Van Allen radiation belt (BBB). Some theories include other cosmic phenomena such as movements of the Moon or of Earth's twin planet, Mondas (DD). Lastly, it is a possibility that the Silurians somehow became aware of the forthcoming crash of a space liner from the future (6B).

In any event, the Silurians and the Sea Devils disappeared from the surface of the Earth, but survived underground in suspended animation. They were to return in AD 1971 (BBB), 1973 (LLL) and 2084 (6L), when they met defeat at the hands of the Third and Fifth Doctors.

Sixty-five million years ago, a space freighter from the 24th century crashed on Earth. The Cybermen had meant the ship to crash on the planet to destroy the galactic alliance against them, but Adric successfully diverted it into the past. The ship crashed with the young Alzarian on board (6B).

The cloud of dust caused by the explosion brought about the end of the Mesozoic and the extinction of the dinosaurs.

The Cenozoic
65 million BC to present
The Cenozoic is divided into the Paleocene, Eocene, Oligocene, Miocene, Pliocene, Pleistocene, Paleolithic, Mesolithic, and Neolithic.
The Paleocene (65 to 54 million BC): With the dinosaurs

extinct, seven groups of mammals developed in Northern Asia. They then migrated to other parts of the world. All were four-footed and five-fingered, walking on the soles of their feet, and none exceeded the size of a modern-day bear. They had slim heads, narrow muzzles and small brain cases.

Geologically, North America's land-ties to Europe were finally broken, but its ties to South America were forged.

The Eocene (54 to 38 million BC): The first monkeys made their appearance, as well as the horse, the camel, the rhinoceros, the eagle and the vulture.

The Oligocene (38 to 26 million BC): Most of the archaic mammals disappeared to be replaced by their modern versions. The first anthropoid apes, as well as dogs and cats, began to evolve.

The Miocene (26 to 12 million BC): The first appearance of grasses helped boost the development of mammals, encouraging grazing animals, and ultimately carnivores, who preyed on herbivores. In Europe and Asia the *Dryopithecus* - a gorilla-like ape - became quite common.

The Pliocene (12 to 2.5 million BC): The Pliocene was the culmination of the age of mammals, setting the stage for the appearance of man, with early hominids such as the *Ramapithecus* (c7-12 million BC) and the *Australopithecus* (c4 million years BC).

It was near the beginning of this period that the Fendahl skull, which originated on the fifth planet of the solar system, landed on Earth, in the country that would one day become Kenya, and began to influence man's evolution. It would eventually be destroyed, thanks to the efforts of the Fourth Doctor and Leela, in AD 1978 (4X).

(The five periods listed above are also known as the Tertiary. The Quaternary, which followed and continues today, heralded the age of man.)

The Pleistocene (2.5 million to 650,000 BC): The first actual humans emerged during the latter part of the Pleistocene. The *A Africanus* (a sub-species of the *Australopithecus*) evolved into the first *Homo erectus* between 2 million and 1.5 million BC.

The Pleistocene also saw the emergence of animals such as

the mammoth, the sabre-toothed tiger and the mastodon, all of which became extinct before the end of the Pleistocene. But the badger, the fox, the lynx, the otter, the skunk, the puma and the bear, which also appeared during this period, did not die out.

Towards the end of the period, men began using crude stone tools, ushering in the Paleolithic.

The Paleolithic (650,000 to 8000 BC): Also known as the Stone Age, the Paleolithic began when stone tools were first used by *Homo erectus*. The story of human evolution now encompassed most of the world: Asia (Peking and Java Man), as well as Europe and Africa.

Sometime about 400,000 BC, *Homo erectus* began slowly to evolve into the early form of *Homo sapiens*.

Towards 150,000 BC, the first Neanderthals appeared. In c100,000 BC, the First Doctor, Susan, Ian Chesterton and Barbara Wright helped a tribe of Neanderthal cavemen rediscover the secret of fire (A).

About the same time, the alien being known as Light visited the Earth, intending to catalogue its evolution. He rescued Nimrod, a Neanderthal. Trapped in his spaceship, Light was eventually brought to England in AD 1883 by explorer Redvers Fenn-Cooper, only to meet defeat at the hands of the Seventh Doctor and Ace (7Q).

Around 100,000 BC, the aliens known as the Daemons arrived on Earth. Between 50,000 BC and 30,000 BC, the Neanderthals became extinct and were replaced by early modern humans, very likely because of the Daemons' intervention.

There is still considerable disagreement whether the Neanderthals were a step in the evolutionary process leading to modern humans, or were simply an offshoot branch that became extinct, while modern humans evolved in parallel.

In any event, as a result of their intervention, the Daemons made a deep and everlasting impression on the native cavemen and shaped their mythology. From then on, man's collective unconscious would remember with dread the powerful image of great, horned creatures.

The Third Doctor even surmised that the Daemons sometimes

revisited Earth to check the results of their evolutionary experiments, but in the absence of irrefutable evidence of further Daemon interventions, such a hypothesis cannot be substantiated.

What is known, however, is that the Daemons left one of their own, Azal, behind in suspended animation, as well as in a miniaturized state. Azal was summoned back to life by the Master in AD 1972, but was defeated by Jo Grant's willingness to sacrifice her life to save that of the Third Doctor (JJJ).

(The Fendahl (4X) would certainly have had no objection to the Daemons' tampering with man's evolution, and may even have pushed things along in the same direction.)

In about 20,000 BC, two alien vegetable Krynoid pods landed in the Antarctic and buried themselves into the permafrost. They were eventually dug up in AD 1977 and, aided by the mad millionaire Harrison Chase, threatened to destroy the Earth. They were defeated by the Fourth Doctor and Sarah Jane Smith (4L).

It was during that later part of the Paleolithic (20,000 to 8000 BC) that Earth was first visited by two alien races with which mankind would have numerous encounters in the future.

First, the Mondasians, from Earth's twin planet, visited our world before finally deciding to leave the solar system with their entire planet. They left behind legends of Space Gods and Giants Who Walked The Earth. They would return in AD 1986 in the guise of the dreaded Cybermen, to be defeated by the First Doctor, Ben Jackson and Polly (DD).

Second, it is likely that during the last of the prehistoric Ice Ages, a Martian ship visited Earth and became buried and frozen in a glacier. Its crew, led by Varga, was to be rediscovered only in AD 3000. Brought back to life, the so-called Ice Warriors threatened Earth, but were beaten by the Second Doctor, Jamie and Victoria Waterfield (OO). It is possible that, not seeing Varga return, the Martians concluded that Earth was unsuitable for colonization. In any event, soon afterwards, they decided to evacuate their dying homeworld to relocate elsewhere in the galaxy.

The Mesolithic (8000 to 6000 BC): During the Mesolithic, Paleolithic tools were adapted to the greater availability of food, leading to the development of agriculture. By 6000 BC, agricultural villages began to develop, ushering in the Neolithic Age.

The Neolithic (6000 to 2000 BC): During this period, mankind began to settle into permanent enclaves.

It was sometime between 6000 and 3000 BC – the estimated date of the beginning of the First Dynasty – that the powerful alien Osirians visited Ancient Egypt, creating a new pantheon of gods in their image.

Led by Horus, the Osirians fought the evil Sutekh, and left him imprisoned inside a hidden pyramid. He was accidentally released in AD 1911, however, by Egyptologist Marcus Scarman and would have destroyed the world if not for the Fourth Doctor and Sarah Jane Smith (4G).

Another of the so-called Egyptian gods was, in reality, a splinter of Scaroth of the Jagaroth. Unlike the Osirians, Scaroth fostered the development of sciences, trying to help mankind acquire the technological knowledge that would someday enable the alien to build a time machine to return to 3.5 billion BC (5H).

In c3000 BC, the alien villainess Cessair of Diplos, fleeing the Megara justice machines, landed on Earth. It was the time of the erection of the great Neolithic stone monuments and, with the help of her monolith-shaped servants, the Ogri, she succeeded in impersonating a Druidic goddess, the Cailleach. She would be unmasked by the Fourth Doctor and Romana in AD 1979 (5C).

The alien Urbankans visited Earth for the first time c2800 BC and kidnapped an Australian aborigine named Kurkutji. They would return (5W).

(The dating of the Urbankan visits to Earth poses a problem. The Fifth Doctor, who met their leader, Monarch, towards the end of the 20th century, guessed that the Urbankans' visits had taken place every four thousand years, based on the time he supposed it took the aliens to travel between their world and Earth. According to this method, the approximate dates of the Urbankans' visits would be 10,000 BC, 6000 BC, 2000 BC, Year 0, and AD 2000 (half-a-trip). However, the nature of the native Earth people taken by the aliens (Kurkutji; Lin Futu, a Chinese mandarin from the so-called Futu dynasty; Villagra, a

33

Mayan princess and Bigon, a Greek philosopher) contradicts these dates. We know that the fifth Urbankan visit took place in about AD 2000, that the Mayan civilization ruled Central America between AD 250 and AD 900, and that Greek philosophers flourished about 400 BC. There is no trace of a Futu dynasty in China; however the Shang Dynasty (18th to 12th centuries BC) would be consistent with Lin Futu, based on archaeological discoveries made at the burial site of Fu Hao, a royal member of that dynasty. Lastly, Australian aborigines are estimated to have first populated Australia between 40,000 BC and 25,000 BC, thus Kurkutji could have been taken at any time before the Lin Futu visit. Therefore, we estimate that it is more likely that the time it took for the Urbankans to travel between their planet and Earth was not four thousand but twelve hundred years, and their visits occurred in 2800 BC, 1600 BC, 400 BC, AD 800 and AD 2000.)

At the time of the construction of one of the Great Pyramids of Egypt, c2500 BC, the First Doctor, Steven Taylor and Sara Kingdom faced the Daleks and the Meddling Monk (V).

The Neolithic ended with the discovery of bronze. Thus, the Bronze Age marked the end of Prehistory.

ANTIQUITY

The Urbankans returned c1600 BC and kidnapped a Chinese nobleman of the Shang Dynasty, named Lin Futu (5W).

The volcano on the island of Thera in the Aegean Sea erupted, c1500 BC, in a violent explosion, one of the most stupendous of all times. According to ancient Egyptian records later rewritten by Plato, this was the site of a flourishing civilization, known as Atlantis, that perished in the cataclysm. What is now known is that the eruption was triggered when the Master released – in spite of the Third Doctor's intervention – the time-devouring entity known as Kronos, which the Atlanteans had trapped in a crystal (OOO).

(The inhabitants of a lonely Atlantean outpost located south of the Azores in the middle of the Atlantic Ocean were cut off from civilization and forced to eke out a miserable underground existence for nearly thirty-five centuries. They were discovered by Professor Zaroff in AD 1968 and used in his insane plans to destroy the world. Fortunately, Zaroff was ultimately defeated by the Second Doctor, Jamie, Ben Jackson and Polly (GG).)

About 1200 BC the First Doctor became involved in the near-legendary Trojan War. Mistaken for Zeus, the Time Lord gave the crafty Greek warrior Odysseus the idea for the Trojan Horse. After Troy's fall, the Doctor's companion, Vicki, left with Trojan warrior Troilus to become Cressida, while a young Trojan girl, Katarina, helped Steven Taylor get back to the TARDIS (U).

The Trojan War itself may have been triggered by the Rani, who had come to Earth to steal the brain fluid which promotes sleep, thereby increasing the potential for aggression in human beings. She would eventually be defeated by the Sixth Doctor and Peri in AD 1825 (6X).

1000 BC marked the beginning of the Iron Age and the decline of Egypt and Babylonia, which were replaced by a period of Assyrian expansion.

It was about 1000 BC, during the Chavin period, that the alien Exxilons visited Ancient Peru, leaving behind more legends of Space Gods (XXX).

From 500 to 323 BC, the date of Alexander the Great's death, Greek civilization dominated the Mediterranean Basin.

In c400 BC, the Urbankans returned a third time, and kidnapped a Greek philosopher named Bigon (5W).

This period was the time of the rise of the Roman Republic. With the defeat of Carthage in 207 BC, Rome emerged as a first-rate power.

About the time of Julius Caesar, 50 BC, a Roman legion was kidnapped by the alien Warlords using time technology stolen from the Time Lords. These Romans took part in the War Games until these were brought to a stop by the Second Doctor's intervention (ZZ).

More warfare may have been fostered by the Rani, who had again appeared on Earth to steal brain fluid (6X).

The Roman Empire was in full bloom, c30 BC, with Augustus. The birth of Christ, which occurred during the reign of Emperor Tiberius, marks the beginning of modern history (*anno Domini*).

MODERN HISTORY

The Roman Empire

In AD 64, the First Doctor and his companions Ian Chesterton, Barbara Wright and Vicki visited Imperial Rome. The Doctor inspired mad Emperor Nero to set fire to the city (M).

About AD 240 in an unrecorded adventure in Ancient China, the Doctor defeated the ageless, immortal evil known as Fenric and imprisoned it in a flask. Fenric began to shape events through time and space to create human pawns (dubbed 'wolves') who would one day secure his release (7M). (Another version of the same events placed the Doctor's first battle with Fenric in Arabia around the 7th century.)

AD 395 is one of the dates commonly accepted as marking the fall of the Roman Empire. In the East, it was replaced by the Byzantine Empire, which would rule until AD 717. In the West, various Germanic successor states such as the Franks, who conquered Gaul about AD 500, would become christianized.

The Middle Ages

On an alternate timeline, in England about AD 500, a future incarnation of the Doctor became known as Merlin. This incarnation buried the body of King Arthur inside a spaceship, which eventually landed beneath the lake of Cadbury on the regular Earth timeline. On that alternate Earth, the sorceress Morgaine went on to become the ruler of her world. She eventually came to our Earth where she fought the Seventh Doctor for the possession of Excalibur (7N).

The Urbankans appeared for the fourth time about AD 800, and kidnapped a Mayan princess named Villagra. They would return one final time towards the end of the 20th century, and be defeated by the Fifth Doctor (5W).

About AD 1000, the flask containing the evil Fenric was stolen by a crew of marauding Vikings and brought to the shores of Northumbria. Fenric escaped his prison and confronted the Seventh Doctor in 1943 (7M).

In 1066 the First Doctor, Steven Taylor and Vicki battled with the renegade Time Lord known as the Meddling Monk, in Northumbria. The Monk sought to defeat a Viking invasion to ensure King Harold's victory. Troops would be fresh and therefore able to prevent the Norman conquest of England (S).

About that time, a medieval knight was snatched through time by the Master who, with the power of the Kronos crystal, used it in his attempts to stop the Third Doctor, Jo Grant and Mike Yates in 1973 (OOO). The Rani appeared once again during the Dark Ages to steal more brain fluid (6X).

A Sontaran commander, Linx, whose spaceship was crippled in a battle with the Rutans, made an uneasy alliance with Irongron, a medieval warlord, c1190. Using rudimentary time technology, Linx kidnapped scientists from 1975, but was ultimately defeated by the Third Doctor, Sarah Jane Smith and a Wessex archer named Hal (UUU).

In 1192, the First Doctor, Ian Chesterton, Barbara Wright and Vicki saved the life of King Richard the Lionheart in Palestine during the Third Crusade, and defeated the evil El Akir (P). A British peasant of that period was scooped up by Professor Whitaker's time device and brought forward to 1975 (WWW).

In 1215, the Fifth Doctor, Tegan and Turlough stopped the Master from using the shape-changing android Kamelion to impersonate King John and prevent the signing of the Magna Charta (6J).

In 1289, the First Doctor, Susan, Ian Chesterton and Barbara Wright met Marco Polo in Tibet. They followed the Venetian adventurer to the court of Kublai Khan in China, where they prevented Tegana from assassinating the Great Khan (D).

From 1337 to 1475, the Hundred Years War raged between France and England.

The Renaissance and the Scientific Revolution
In 1430 the Aztec High Priest Yetaxa died. In 1480 the First Doctor, Susan, Ian Chesterton and Barbara Wright visited the Aztecs. Mistaken for the reincarnation of Yetaxa, Barbara tried but failed to stop their practice of human sacrifices (F).

In about 1478, the Fourth Doctor and Sarah Jane Smith defeated the Mandragora Helix in the Dukedom of San Marino, Italy, and thus helped save the Renaissance (4M).

The Fourth Doctor met one of Scaroth's twelve splinters,

Captain Tancredi, in Leonardo Da Vinci's house c1505. The Jagaroth had commissioned the painter to paint more than one Mona Lisa to enable his future self in 1980 to raise money to finance his time travel experiments (5H).

1543 marked the death of Copernicus and the beginning of the Western scientific revolution. By the end of the first quarter of the 17th century, new scientific evidence by Galileo (1564 to 1642) had laid the basis for a new cosmology.

In 1572, the First Doctor and Steven Taylor were almost caught in the bloody events leading to the infamous Massacre of Saint Bartholomew's Day in Paris (W).

During an unrecorded adventure c1630, the Doctor spent some time in Tibet, where he met and befriended the future High Lama of Det-Sen, Padmasambhava. The Second Doctor returned in 1935 to confront the evil Great Intelligence (NN).

In November 1638 at Windsor in an unrecorded adventure, the Doctor fought Lady Peinforte, who had found the deadly living metal validium that had crashed on Earth and had shaped it into a silver statue which she had dubbed Nemesis. The Doctor eventually sent the Silver Nemesis into space, in an orbit that would bring it close to Earth every twenty-five years. Soon afterwards, Lady Peinforte hired a mathematician to calculate the exact time of the statue's return to Earth. Then, she used the power of the Silver Nemesis' arrow, which she had managed to retain, to travel through time to 1988 (7K).

In 1643, the English Civil War came to the village of Little Hodcombe, where an ordinary human named Will Chandler was drawn through time to 1984 by the evil Malus (6M).

About the same time, a squadron of roundheads was snatched through time by the Master who, with the power of the Kronos crystal, used it in his attempts to stop the Third Doctor, Jo Grant and Mike Yates in 1973 (OOO).

About 1650, the First Doctor, Ben Jackson and Polly fought Captain Pike's pirates and a ring of smugglers on the Cornish coast (CC). In 1657, Richard Maynarde died (7K).

In 1663, the Silver Nemesis came close to Earth, possibly heralding the Great Plague of 1665 (7K).

In 1666, the Fifth Doctor, Adric, Tegan and Nyssa of Traken, as well as out-of-work actor Richard Mace, fought the alien Terileptils, who plotted to use the black plague to depopulate the Earth and take over the planet. In the resulting confrontation, the Doctor accidentally started the Great Fire of London (5X).

The crippled spaceship of the Zygons landed in Loch Ness c1676. The Zygons' monstrous pet, the Skarasen, would become known as the Loch Ness Monster. The Zygons re-emerged in 1976 with the intention of conquering Earth, but were defeated by the Fourth Doctor and UNIT (4F). (The Loch was, at the time, already inhabited by the Borad (6Y). One can surmise that either the Zygons, or the Skarasen, killed him.)

Isaac Newton's *Principia*, a breakthrough in the advancement of physics, was published in 1687.

The 18th Century

In 1688 and 1713, the Silver Nemesis came close to Earth, perhaps influencing the warlike policies of France's Sun King towards the Austro-Prussian Empire (7K). In 1738, the Silver Nemesis approached Earth once more, possibly heralding the first great Irish famine (7K).

In 1746, the Second Doctor, Ben Jackson and Polly met young Jamie McCrimmon soon after the battle of Culloden. The Time Lord and the young Scot then put an end to the evil solicitor Gray's slave traffic (FF).

There is also evidence that Redcoat soldiers were kidnapped by the alien Warlords, using time technology stolen from the Time Lords. These men went on to take part in the War Games until these were brought to a stop by the Second Doctor's intervention (ZZ).

In 1763, the Silver Nemesis came near Earth, possibly heralding a war between Turkey and Russia (7K). Approaching Earth again in 1788, the Silver Nemesis possibly heralded the French Revolution. Also, the statue's bow, which had become the Queen of England's property and was kept at Windsor Castle, was mysteriously stolen (7K).

In 1794, the First Doctor, Susan, Ian Chesterton and Barbara Wright were caught up in the events of the French Revolution, a period which the Doctor visited before in various unrecorded adventures. The time travellers helped British master-spy James Stirling escape the guillotine (H).

In 1798, Sir Percival Flint attempted to open the barrow known as Devil's Hump (JJJ).

The 19th Century

Napoleon proclaimed himself Emperor of France in 1804.

In 1813, the Silver Nemesis came close to Earth, maybe exacerbating the warlike policies of Napoleon's First Empire (7K).

During Napoleon's ill-fated Russian campaign, French and Russian troops were kidnapped by the alien Warlords, using time technology stolen from the Time Lords. These men went on to take part in the War Games, until these were brought to a stop by the Second Doctor's intervention (ZZ).

In 1820, according to Reuben, the Beast of Fang Rock was seen. Two men died; another was driven insane.

The Sixth Doctor and Peri, c1825, fought both the Rani and the Master. The Rani was engaged in another attempt to collect brain fluid. The Master was trying to stop the advent of the Industrial Revolution (6X).

The 1838, the Silver Nemesis approached Earth, possibly heralding the Chinese–British Opium Wars (7K).

In 1859, Charles Darwin's *On The Origin of Species by means of Natural Selection* was published, introducing the theory of evolution.

In 1860, Professor Litefoot's father was Brigadier-General on a punitive expedition to China. He remained in Beijing as palace attaché.

An American Confederate army was kidnapped by the Warlords, c1862, using time technology stolen from the Time Lords. These soldiers went on to take part in the War Games, until these were brought to a stop by the Second Doctor's intervention (ZZ). That same year, the Jameson boys went out on Tulloch Moor cutting peat when the mist came down. One, Donald, disappeared, kidnapped or killed by the Zygons. Robert, the elder, was found two days later, clearly insane.

The American Civil War was possibly fostered by either the Silver Nemesis (7K), which came near Earth in 1863, or the presence of the Rani, who had come to Earth to steal brain fluid

(6X), or both. (Although this is historically posterior to the events taking place in 1825, in her own timeline, the Rani's visit to 1862 occurred before her encounter with the Sixth Doctor.)

In 1866, the Second Doctor and Jamie met Victoria Waterfield and, with her father's help, fought an attempt made by Daleks from the future to infect mankind with the Dalek factor (LL).

French and Prussian troops fighting in the Franco-Prussian War, c1870, as well as Mexican rebels (including a man named Villar) fighting Emperor Maximilian, were kidnapped by the alien Warlords, using time technology stolen from the Time Lords. These soldiers went on to take part in the War Games, until these were brought to a stop by the Second Doctor's intervention (ZZ).

In 1872, the First Doctor, Ian Chesterton, Barbara Wright and Vicki, fleeing the Daleks, arrived on the *Mary Celeste*. Soon afterwards, the aliens from Skaro caused the ship's crew to jump overboard (R).

Magnus Greel, the infamous criminal from the 51st century, and his nefarious Peking Homunculus, arrived in China in a time cabinet c1880. His body crippled by the Zigma Experiment, Greel was taken in by a Chinese peasant named Li H'Sen Chang, who mistook him for the god Weng-Chiang. The cabinet, however, was confiscated by the Emperor's men and given to Professor Litefoot's mother (4S).

In 1881, the First Doctor, Steven Taylor and Dodo Chaplet almost took part in the famous gunfight at the OK Corral in Tombstone, Arizona (Z). That same year, Inspector Mackenzie of Scotland Yard investigated the disappearance of Sir George Pritchard, owner of Gabriel Chase (7O).

In 1883, the Seventh Doctor and Ace arrived in a mysterious house in Perivale, where strange events led to the reawakening of the powerful alien known as Light. Confronted by the inevitability of evolution, Light chose to commit suicide. The woman known as Control, explorer Redvers Fenn-Cooper and Nimrod the Neanderthal left Earth in Light's spaceship (7Q).

In an unrecorded adventure that took place later in her life, Ace left the Doctor to settle permanently in France in this time period, where it is rumoured she eventually married one of Sorin's ancestors (7K).

In 1888, the Silver Nemesis approached Earth, possibly heralding the Boer War and numerous other wars which occurred towards the end of the 19th century (7K).

With Li H'Sen Chang's help, Magnus Greel and his Peking Homunculus (known as Mr Sin) moved to London c1890 in an effort to recover Greel's time cabinet, now in the hands of Professor Litefoot. Greel, who by then needed to absorb the lifeforce of young women to survive, was eventually defeated by the combined efforts of the Fourth Doctor, Leela, Professor Litefoot and Henry Gordon Jago (4S).

c1891, the Sixth Doctor met the young HG Wells, who helped him and Peri defeat the Borad on the planet Karfel (6Y).

Early 20th Century

Troops fighting in the Boxer Rising in China and the Boer War in South Africa, c1900, were kidnapped by the alien Warlords using time technology stolen from the Time Lords. These men went on to take part in the War Games, until these were brought to a stop by the Second Doctor (ZZ).

The Fourth Doctor and Leela defeated a shape-changing Rutan, c1904, on the lonely island of Fang Rock (4V).

In 1905, physicist Albert Einstein (at one time briefly kidnapped by the Rani (7D), but restored to his proper place in time and space, his memory erased) enunciated his Theory of Relativity.

In 1911, the Fourth Doctor and Sarah Jane Smith fought the merciless Osirian Sutekh the Destroyer, whose hidden pyramid had been excavated by Egyptologist Marcus Scarman. Sutekh forced the Doctor to take Scarman to Mars to destroy the Eye of Horus, but eventually fell victim to the Doctor's superior cunning (4G). By then, Mars was a dead world, having already been evacuated by the Ice Warriors.

In 1913, the Silver Nemesis circled near Earth, heralding the approach of the First World War (7K).

British and German soldiers were kidnapped, c1917, by the Warlords using time technology stolen from the Time Lords. These men went on to take part in the War Games, until these

42

were brought to a stop by the Second Doctor's intervention (ZZ).

In 1922, a man was kidnapped by the Zygons on Tulloch Moor (4F).

In 1925, the Fifth Doctor, Adric, Tegan and Nyssa of Traken solved the mystery of the Black Orchid at Cranleigh Halt, unmasking the pitiful figure of George Cranleigh, a British explorer horribly disfigured two years before by South American Indians (6A).

In 1926, the SS *Bernice*, a steam ship travelling on the Indian Ocean, was snatched out of time and space to become part of a Scope – a peepshow owned by Vorg, a galactic showman from the future. The device had been outlawed by the Time Lords. The *Bernice* was later restored to its proper location owing to the efforts of the Third Doctor and Jo Grant (PPP).

While on the run from the Daleks, c1928, the First Doctor and his companions briefly visited Hollywood (V).

The Fourth Doctor and Romana, c1934, briefly visited Brighton Beach before going to the Leisure Hive (5N).

In 1935, the Second Doctor, Jamie and Victoria Waterfield fought the evil Great Intelligence and its robot Yeti, which threatened the Det-Sen Monastery in Tibet. The Doctor was unable to save his friend Padmasambhava's life, but defeated the Intelligence. He also befriended Professor Travers (NN).

Hitler ordered the Nazis in about 1936 to secure occult artefacts of great power, such as the Ark of the Covenant, the Holy Grail and Silver Nemesis's bow, which had been stolen from Windsor Castle in 1788. The bow eventually fell into the hands of De Flores, along with a formula that enabled him to calculate the time and location of the statue's return to Earth (7K).

In 1938, the Silver Nemesis approached Earth, heralding the approach of the Second World War (7K). Another unsuccessful attempt was made to open the barrow known as Devil's End. It led to what became known as the Cambridge University fiasco (JJJ).

A German V-1 was snatched through time, c1941, by the Master who used the power of the Kronos crystal to stop the Third Doctor, Jo Grant and Mike Yates in 1973 (OOO).

In a lonely village on the coast of Northumbria, c1943, the Seventh Doctor and Ace fought Fenric, who had finally succeeded in his scheme to get released from the flask in which he had been imprisoned. In spite of the help of his vampiric Haemovores, however, and the unwitting collaboration of his human pawns (nicknamed 'wolves'), Fenric again lost the battle (7M).

The Seventh Doctor and Mel, c1959, rescued the young Chimeron queen Delta from her nemesis, Gavrok, and his evil galactic mercenaries, the Bannermen, in a Welsh holiday village (7F). (Both Delta and Gavrok came from the future, and were travellers in time and space.)

While escaping from the Daleks, c1960, the First Doctor briefly landed in the midst of a cricket game at the Oval (V).

In 1955, the Doctor visited St Cedd's college in Cambridge. In 1956 Chris Parsons was born. In 1958 the Doctor again visited St Cedd's and in 1960 took an honourary degree there. He returned in 1964 (5M).

THE PRESENT

The 1960s

In 1963, the First Doctor and his granddaughter Susan met Ian Chesterton and Barbara Wright in the junkyard at 76 Totter's Lane. The two school teachers discovered the TARDIS and inadvertently precipitated its departure for 100,000 BC (A).

That sudden departure prevented the Doctor from recovering the Hand of Omega, which he had left behind. Eventually, in his seventh incarnation, he and Ace returned for it, but had to fight both Daleks and Imperial Daleks from the future to secure it (7H).

That same year, possibly precipitating the above events as well as the assassination of President Kennedy, the Silver Nemesis circled near Earth (7K).

In 1964, the First Doctor and his companions, Susan, Ian and Barbara, found themselves miniaturized to insect size, but still defeated Forester, an evil industrialist whose lethal pesticide DN6 threatened all life on Earth (J).

In 1965, fleeing Daleks from the future, the First Doctor, Ian, Barbara and Vicki made a quick landing at the top of the Empire State Building in New York. Soon afterwards, Ian and Barbara returned to London in the Dalek time machine (R).

On Christmas Day of that same year, the First Doctor and his companions, again trying to escape the Daleks, made a brief stop at a Liverpool police station. A week later, the time travellers made a short appearance in Trafalgar Square during the New Year festivities (V).

In 1966, the First Doctor and Steven Taylor paused briefly in London to pick up a new companion, Dodo Chaplet, on Wimbledon Common (W).

Later that year, the First Doctor, Ben Jackson, Polly and Dodo defeated the evil computer WOTAN and its War Machines, which threatened to take over London. At the end of this adventure, Dodo decided to stay in London, while Ben and Polly left with the Doctor (BB).

The Second Doctor, now accompanied by Jamie, brought

Ben and Polly back to England (Gatwick Airport) the very same day they had left, but much later in the time travellers' own timeline. There, they fought the alien Chameleons. Afterwards, Ben and Polly chose to remain behind (KK).

Immediately following the previous adventure, the Second Doctor and Jamie were lured back to 1866 by Professor Waterfield's time machine. There, they met Victoria Waterfield and thwarted an attempt by Daleks from the future to infect mankind with the Dalek factor (LL).

In 1969, the Second Doctor, Jamie and Victoria renewed their acquaintance with a much older Professor Travers, and fought the Great Intelligence and its robot Yeti in the London Underground. There, the Doctor met Lethbridge-Stewart, then a colonel, for the first time (QQ). (The Yeti invasion was, with the possible exceptions of the Daleks' brief attack of 1963 and the Chameleons' secret assault of 1966, the first credible instance of an alien enemy attempting to invade or destroy Earth. This convinced the powers that be of the necessity for an international, United-Nations-backed entity to deal with such global threats. It led to the formation of several multinational organizations such as UNIT and the World Ecology Bureau. Thus began a process of international cooperation, which resulted in the unification of Earth by the beginning of the 21st century.)

Soon afterwards, the Second Doctor, Jamie, Ben Jackson and Polly helped stop a mad scientist, Professor Zaroff, from using the unwitting help of Atlantean survivors to destroy Earth (GG).

Then, the Second Doctor, Jamie and Victoria defeated a sentient weed that threatened a North Sea gas refinery. Victoria chose to remain with the Harris family (RR).

(It was probably after Victoria's departure, and before the Second Doctor's initial meeting with Zoe, that the Doctor and Jamie went on two unrecorded adventures, the memory of which were erased from their minds by the Time Lords. In the first adventure, the two time travellers fought the Cybermen on Planet 14. The Cybermen were, at the time, preparing to invade Earth, a fact that the Doctor and Jamie did not discover until the following year (VV). In the second adventure, the Time Lords' Celestial Intervention Agency, which had secretly been monitoring, and possibly even influencing, the Doctor's travels for many years, asked the two time travellers to investigate unauthorized time travel experiments on Space Station J7. This brought the Second Doctor and Jamie in contact with the Doctor's sixth incarnation and his companion Peri. Together they fought the Androgum Chessene and the Sontarans in Spain during 1985 (6W).)

The 1970s

In 1970, the Second Doctor, Jamie and Zoe, assisted by the newly formed UNIT, defeated the Cybermen's plan to invade the Earth, using the resources of Tobias Vaughn's multinational corporation, International Electromatics. Using a device implanted in I.E.'s pocket radios, the Cybermen succeeded in paralyzing Earth's population. The Doctor, however, foiled their scheme and the Cybermen's first invasion fleet was destroyed (VV). (The Cybermen's second invasion fleet was destroyed by the Silver Nemesis in 1988. The Cybermen mentioned above were 'space' Cybermen, an offshoot branch of the original Mondasians, who returned only in 1986. Presumably, the first moon landing occurred on the Earth-Who at the same time as it did on our world, 1969, but it probably happened under more international auspices. In any event, the failed Cybermen invasion accelerated the process of international cooperation in space exploration. By 1971, manned space probes were dispatched to Mars (CCC). By 1977, mankind had sent a manned spaceship to Jupiter (4J). All this led to the formation of the International Space Command organization by the late 1970s or early 1980s (DD).)

In 1971, after being tried by the Time Lords, and summarily forced to regenerate, the Third Doctor was exiled to Earth, his knowledge of time travel erased from his memory. He became UNIT's scientific adviser, and with Liz Shaw's help, defeated the first invasion of the Nestenes and their deadly plastic creatures, the Autons (AAA).

Soon afterwards, the Third Doctor and Liz helped UNIT deal with the Silurians, who left their caves following accidental electrical discharges caused by an atomic reactor. The Doctor was saddened to see the noble creatures re-entombed by Brigadier Lethbridge-Stewart (BBB).

Next, the Third Doctor and Liz prevented General Carrington from destroying the so-called Ambassadors of Death, in reality a trio of peaceful aliens (CCC). (This adventure occurred at the time of the launch of Earth's first manned space probes to Mars which, by then, had long been evacuated by the Ice Warriors.)

Later, the Third Doctor and Liz stopped Professor Stahlman from completing his insane Inferno project, which would have doomed the Earth (DDD).

(During the course of this adventure, the Doctor travelled to an alternative Earth where England was ruled by a fascist dictatorship. That Earth was destroyed by the forces unleashed by Inferno.)

Soon afterwards, Liz Shaw left UNIT to return to Cambridge and pursue her scientific studies.

In 1972, the Third Doctor, now assisted by Jo Grant, helped UNIT thwart a second Nestene/Auton invasion, this time triggered by his old enemy, the renegade Time Lord known as the Master, who had just arrived on Earth (EEE).

Then, the Third Doctor, Jo and UNIT defeated the Master's attempts to use an evil Mind Parasite to sabotage the first World Peace Conference (FFF). (The conference reflected the growing process of international cooperation mentioned above. The Chinese, however, did not fully participate until the next decade.)

Soon afterwards, the alien parasite Axos was brought to Earth by the Master. Promising to usher in a new Golden Age, Axos planned to absorb all living energy on Earth. Ultimately, the Third Doctor was forced to team up with the Master to imprison the evil entity in a time loop (GGG). (The threat of Axos undoubtedly reinforced international cooperation, especially with the Soviet Bloc. One can hypothesize that the series of events known as perestroika took place in the 1970s and not the 1990s on Earth-Who.)

After a brief interlude with the Brigadier before being dispatched to 2472 by the Time Lords' Celestial Intervention Agency (HHH), the Third Doctor and Jo were confronted with the awesome threat of Azal. The last Daemon had been summoned by the Master, who wished to inherit Azal's vast powers. Azal, however, was unable to comprehend Jo's attempt to sacrifice her life to save the Doctor's, and the Daemon perished in the ensuing conflagration. The Master was captured by UNIT (JJJ).

1973 opened with the Third Doctor, Jo and UNIT defeating an attempt to assassinate a famous diplomat, Sir Reginald Styles. It turned out that guerillas from an alternative future where the Daleks had conquered Earth after the Third World War blamed him for their enslavement. They thought that by travelling back to the past and killing him, they would prevent that future from happening. In fact they achieved the opposite: Styles' murder was the starting point of the war. The Doctor's intervention saved Styles' life and Earth's future (KKK). (By 1973, peace efforts were concentrated on getting the Chinese to join the now-growing world community.)

Next, the Third Doctor and Jo fought the Sea Devils, aquatic cousins of the Silurians, whom the Master planned to use first to help him break out of prison and then to conquer the world. The Master failed in his world domination scheme, but managed to escape (LLL).

Soon afterwards, the Third Doctor, Jo and UNIT thwarted another of the Master's nefarious plots. This time posing as Professor Thascales, the renegade Time Lord planned to release the powerful Kronovore known as Kronos from the Atlantean crystal that held it prisoner. Eventually, the Doctor and Jo followed the Master back to the time of Atlantis. They could not, however, prevent Kronos's release and the ensuing destruction of the fabled island kingdom (OOO).

In 1974, the Time Lords gathered the first three incarnations of the Doctor to defeat the menace of Omega who, from within a black hole, threatened the entire universe. After Omega's defeat, the Doctor was pardoned by the Time Lords, who restored his knowledge of time travel (RRR).

Then, in an unrecorded adventure, the Third Doctor and Jo, who were probably looking for Metebelis 3, arrived on the planet Karfel. While there, the Doctor reported the scientist who later became the Borad to the Inner Sanctum for his unethical experiments.

Next, the Third Doctor and UNIT fought the evil computer BOSS, who had taken over the multinational Global Chemicals and its pollution-created green death. During this adventure, Jo fell in love with ecologist Professor Clifford Jones and quit UNIT to marry him (TTT).

In 1975, the Third Doctor met journalist Sarah Jane Smith. Together they investigated the disappearances of several scientists who had been kidnapped and taken back to 1190 by Linx, a stranded Sontaran commander (UUU).

Upon returning to 1975, the Third Doctor, Sarah and UNIT fought a dinosaur invasion engineered by Sir Charles Grover as a decoy for his Operation Golden Age, with which he hoped to reverse time and wipe out all of Earth's history (WWW).

Later, the Third Doctor, Sarah and UNIT defeated an invasion of giant, mutated spiders from the failed Earth space colony of Metebelis 3 in the future. At the end of this adventure, his body ravaged by a deadly dose of radiation, the Doctor regenerated with the help of fellow Time Lord K'Anpo (ZZZ).

Almost immediately, in an unrecorded adventure, the newly regenerated Fourth Doctor travelled to a nameless planet in the future. There, he met a group of humans whose ship had crashed. The Doctor tried to fix their experimental artificial intelligence, a system called Xoanon, but because of his own mental condition at the time, he instead gave it a split personality. The Doctor then returned to Earth at the very same time he had left it, having forgotten most of what had happened (4Q).

Next, along with Sarah, UNIT medical officer Surgeon-Lieutenant Harry Sullivan and the Brigadier, the Fourth Doctor defeated a plot by an organization called the Scientific Reform Society to take over the world, using Professor Kettlewell's giant, experimental robot (4A).

In 1976, the Fourth Doctor, Sarah and Harry returned from their journeys through time and space to help UNIT fight the shape-changing Zygons who had emerged from Loch Ness and were using their Skarasen monster to try to conquer the Earth (4F). (During the course of this story, we learn that Britain's Prime Minister was a woman, which leads us to assume that on Earth-Who, Mrs Margaret Thatcher became Britain's Prime Minister eleven years before she did in our world.)

After the Zygons' defeat, Harry chose to stay behind with

UNIT, but Sarah pursued her travels with the Fourth Doctor, who briefly took her back to an alternative present (or a potential timeline) where Earth had been destroyed by Sutekh (4G).

In 1977, the Fourth Doctor and Sarah again teamed up with Harry and UNIT, this time to thwart the alien Kraals' android invasion (4J). (This was soon after mankind launched its first manned rocket to Jupiter.)

Soon afterwards, the Fourth Doctor and Sarah helped the World Ecology Bureau and UNIT destroy a Krynoid, a hostile, alien, vegetable lifeform whose pods had been recovered in the Antarctic and which had been allowed to grow to full size by the insane millionaire Harrison Chase (4L).

Next, the Fourth Doctor fought Eldrad the Kastrian, whose fossilized hand had been buried during the Jurassic Period and which was accidentally found by Sarah. To protect Earth from Eldrad's powers, the Doctor took the alien back to his home-world, which by then had become a barren, lifeless world. Then, after receiving a summons to Gallifrey, the Fourth Doctor had no choice but to take Sarah back to her own time (4N).

It was at about the same time that Brigadier Lethbridge-Stewart retired from UNIT and took a job as a teacher at Brendan School, leaving the UK branch of UNIT in the capable hands of Colonel Crichton. RSM Benton also left, eventually to take over a car dealership (6F).

Later that year, Tegan Jovanka and Nyssa of Traken, two of the Fifth Doctor's companions, met the retired Brigadier at Brendan School. Together they fought Mawdryn in 1983. The Brigadier, however, emerged from the encounter with his future self suffering from selective amnesia (6F).

In 1978, the Fourth Doctor, Leela and K9 defeated the Fendahl, which had been brought back to unholy life by Dr Fendelman's experiments. The Doctor eventually jettisoned the Fendahl skull near a supernova (4X).

In 1979, during their search for the components of the Key to Time, the Fourth Doctor, Romana and a second version of K9 prevented the pirate planet Zanak from rematerializing around Earth and crushing the planet (5B).

Next, they rematerialized near an English stone circle, where they met Professor Rumford and the mysterious Vivien Fay, who turned out to be the alien criminal Cessair of Diplos. The Fourth Doctor, Romana and K9 defeated Cessair and her Stones of Blood (in reality, the alien Ogri) and outsmarted the Megara justice machines (5C).

In 1979, in Paris, the Fourth Doctor and a regenerated Romana met Scaroth's twelfth splinter, Count Scarlioni, who had been selling Mona Lisas to finance Professor Kerensky's time travel experiments. The two Time Lords failed to stop the Jagaroth from going back in time but they did stop him from preventing the destruction of his ship and, as a result, ensured the creation of life on Earth (5H).

Later that year, in an adventure of which there are only partial records, the Fourth Doctor and Romana fought Skagra in Cambridge (5M).

The 1980s

In 1980, an Earthman was kidnapped by the alien Gaztaks who served the shape-changing Meglos of Zolfa-Thura. Meglos impersonated the Fourth Doctor in an attempt to steal the Tigellan Dodecahedron, but was eventually defeated by the two Time Lords and K9 (5Q).

In 1981, the Master returned, having stolen the body of Tremas of Traken. He then engaged the Fourth Doctor in a battle of TARDISes near Heathrow, during which the evil Time Lord murdered Tegan Jovanka's Aunt Vanessa. Before taking off for Logopolis, the Fourth Doctor was mysteriously warned of his impending regeneration (5V).

Next after unwittingly causing the destruction of Logopolis, the Master attempted to use the Pharos Project radio-telescope to blackmail the entire universe. With the help of Adric, Tegan and Nyssa of Traken (Tremas's daughter), the Fourth Doctor was able to stop the Master. During the battle, the Doctor fell from the radio-telescope's tower and regenerated once again (5V).

The newly regenerated Fifth Doctor was then taken by Nyssa and Tegan (Adric had been kidnapped by the Master) to Castrovalva, where he confronted and defeated the evil Time Lord (5Z).

Meanwhile, Sarah Jane Smith, and a third version of K9 sent to her by the Doctor, fought a coven of witches in Moreton Harwood (K9).

In 1982, the Fifth Doctor, Nyssa and Tegan solved the mystery of the disappearance of a Concorde aeroplane. The craft had been hijacked back to the Jurassic Period by the Master who, disguised as Kalid, was trying to gain control of the alien Xeraphin. At the end of this adventure, Tegan accidentally left the TARDIS crew (6C).

In 1983, Omega tried to take over the Fifth Doctor's body. Tegan returned and rejoined the TARDIS crew in Amsterdam, where the Doctor finally confronted and defeated Omega (6E).

Next, after a landing on a mysterious spaceship in orbit around the Earth, the Fifth Doctor became separated from Tegan and Nyssa. The Time Lord beamed down to the Brendan School where he met the mysterious Turlough and the retired Brigadier Lethbridge-Stewart, who had forgotten their adventures. There, they confronted the alien Mawdryn, who had stolen the Time Lords' Metamorphic Symbiosis Regenerator, and was cursed to live in a state of perpetual regeneration (6F).

Meanwhile, Nyssa and Tegan had been transported to the Brendan School of 1977 where they too met the Brigadier. Eventually, the explosion generated by the encounter between the two Brigadiers (from 1977 and 1983) proved sufficient to end Mawdryn's suffering and restore the modern-day Brigadier's memory (6F).

Later that year, Sarah Jane Smith was kidnapped by Borusa to take part in the Game of Rassilon. She teamed up with the Third Doctor and, together with the Doctor's other four incarnations and various companions, helped thwart the megalomaniacal Time Lord's plans for immortality (6K).

Meanwhile, having recovered his full memory, the Brigadier renewed his contacts with UNIT. Borusa snatched him and the Second Doctor (who had transgressed the Laws of Time to visit his old friend) the day of a UNIT reunion. Together with the Doctor's other four incarnations and various companions, the Brigadier helped defeat Borusa (6K). Soon after that, he married Doris. That year, Ace burned down Gabriel Chase (7O).

In 1984, the Fifth Doctor, Tegan and Turlough defeated the

Malus in the village of Little Hodcombe (6M). In Princeton that year, a scientist discovered strange matter (7D).

Then, the Fifth Doctor and his companions were caught in a time corridor set up by Daleks from the future. The corridor took the time travellers to the London docks, where they fought a bloody battle against the Daleks. Sick of the violence, Tegan decided to leave the TARDIS crew for good. One of the Daleks' mercenaries, Lytton, was stranded on Earth (6P).

Soon afterwards, the Fifth Doctor and Turlough met Peri Brown. They then travelled to the planet Sarn, where they fought the Master. At the end of this adventure, Turlough met his brother, Malkon, and chose to return to his homeworld of Trion (6Q).

In 1985, following the Cryons' secret plan, Lytton made contact with Cybermen from the future who were trying to save Mondas (from the fate in store for it the following year) by crashing Halley's comet into Earth. Their plans were eventually thwarted by the Sixth Doctor and Peri (6T).

Next, in Spain, the Sixth Doctor and Peri teamed up with the Second Doctor and Jamie McCrimmon to stop the Sontarans and the Androgum Chessene from acquiring the secret of the Rassilon Imprimature (6W).

In 1986, the First Doctor, Ben Jackson and Polly rematerialized near an International Space Command Antarctic tracking station. Soon, space scanners showed that Earth's twin planet, Mondas, had returned. The Doctor and his companions thwarted a second Cybermen invasion, this time by the Mondasian Cybermen. In the resulting conflict, Mondas was destroyed (DD).

In 1987, owing to the machinations of Fenric, a teenage British girl nicknamed Ace was taken away from her home in Perivale and transported through time and space to Ice World, a galactic trading post on Svartos (7G, 7M).

On 23 November 1988, the Silver Nemesis returned to Earth and landed near Windsor Castle. The Seventh Doctor and Ace fought a number of enemies who each tried to claim the deadly artifact for their own: Lady Peinforte, who had travelled forward in time from 1638 with the statue's arrow, a group of Neo-Nazis led by De Flores, who had obtained the statue's bow, and finally the Cybermen's second invasion fleet (from their 1970 invasion). The Doctor eventually won, and the Silver Nemesis destroyed the Cybermen (7K).

In 1989, the Seventh Doctor took Ace back to Perivale and, together, they solved the mysterious disappearances of several local youths who had been captured by the Cheetah People. The Doctor also defeated the Master, who had fallen victim to the curse of the Cheetah People (7P).

The 1990s and Beyond

In 1992, the Seventh Doctor and Ace teamed up with retired Brigadier Lethbridge-Stewart and met Brigadier Bambera of UNIT. Together, they fought the sorcery of a Morgaine from an alternative Earth. The prize was Excalibur, which had been buried beneath a lake at Cadbury by a future incarnation of the Doctor (7N). (This story is another proof that the Doctor's adventures take place on an Earth very similar but not quite identical to our world, because there is no lake at Cadbury on our planet.)

In 1996, fleeing the Daleks, the First Doctor, Ian Chesterton, Barbara Wright and Vicki paid a brief visit to a Horror Pavilion featuring robotic versions of Dracula and the Frankenstein Monster, at Ghana World's Fair (R).

Sometime during the late 1990s, the Urbankans returned to Earth for a fifth time. The Fifth Doctor, Tegan, Nyssa and Adric prevented their leader, Monarch, from poisoning all humans (5W).

THE FUTURE

Earth and the Exploration of the Solar System

As the 21st century began, countries increasingly grouped themselves into blocs which became known as zones (PP), while the management of the planet was entrusted more and more to international organizations and councils.

This was not achieved without a number of local conflicts, during which tactical nuclear devices were used. The young and brilliant Mexican scientist Salamander conceived a plan to sequester some 'survivors' in a vast underground shelter in Australia, making them believe that the Earth's surface had turned into a radioactive wasteland (PP).

Meanwhile, on the surface, global international cooperation had been achieved. Priority was given to solving a number of ecological problems, such as the availability of adequate food supplies, an issue made more acute by population growth. The development of planetary weather control was one of the tools being researched to that end.

In the early days of the new century, 2010–2020, a Moon Base managed by international personnel was finally built, along with a number of orbiting space stations, known as Wheels in Space. This was done primarily with an eye towards helping the above-mentioned ecological effort on Earth, but it also fostered further exploration of the rest of the solar system – and beyond.

In addition to the use of robot probes, several interstellar ships were launched. Travelling at sub-light speed, they were crewed by volunteers placed in hibernation. At least one of these ships made it to its final destination, forming the colony later known as Vulcan (EE). (The Vulcan colonists kept their original dating system, hence for them it was still 2020, even though the Earth calendar indicated it was much later.)

The Cybermen returned c2020 and with the help of their Cybermats they attacked Space Station W3, plotting to use it to conquer Earth (SS). By then, mankind had explored the asteroid belt, after dismissing Mars as a world incapable of sustaining life. The various aborted alien invasions of the late 20th century were no more than historical events. Humanity was relatively unprepared to face a new series of hostile alien attacks.

Fortunately, the Cybermen's plans were defeated by the intervention of the Second Doctor and Jamie, and that of the young and brilliant scientist Zoe Heriot, who joined the TARDIS crew (SS).

In 2030, food sufficiency was achieved on Earth, thanks to Salamander's Suncatcher satellite. But the megalomaniacal villain tried to use it to create violent earthquakes that would have killed off Earth's population. He then would have repopulated the planet with his own survivors. His efforts were thwarted by the Second Doctor, Jamie and Victoria Waterfield (PP).

By 2050, weather control was perfected with the use of the Gravitron device, housed on the Moon Base. Mankind's space exploration had now spread out to encompass the entire solar system.

In 2070, the Cybermen returned, invading the Moon Base and plotting to use the Gravitron to destroy Earth. They were defeated by the Second Doctor, Ben Jackson, Polly and Jamie (HH).

Next, several events caused mankind to turn its back on space travel. First, there was the Cybermen's attack, and the disasters it created on Earth. Second, there were a series of serious setbacks in space exploration: accidents with high death tolls, possibly connected with the research and development of faster-than-light engines. Third, and possibly of greater relevance, was the fact that mankind was about to go through a phase when great enthusiasm for exploration and expansion was followed by a desire for retrenching and cocooning. Although the solar system was virtually in their grasp, many on Earth began to wonder if it had been worth it, and campaigned to stop further wasteful exploration. Such changes of attitude would occur several times in the future.

The nail in the coffin of space travel, however, was the development of T-Mat (XX) – instantaneous travel between two relay stations.

Coordinated from the Moon Base, T-Mat not only took care of most of Earth-based travel, but also of journeys between Earth and its network of space stations.

With the advent of T-Mat, mankind stopped using manned spaceships. All travel within the solar system was entrusted to T-Mat and space exploration was all but abandoned. Meanwhile, on Earth, relations between the zones had deteriorated, perhaps as a result of this claustrophobic retrenchment.

In 2084, the Fifth Doctor, Tegan and Turlough prevented the Silurians and the Sea Devils from starting a war between the blocs (6L). In 2068 AD, Galactic Salvage and Insurance had been formed in London. It was driven into bankruptcy by T-Mat and went into liquidation in 2096 AD (5K).

Opposition to T-Mat had already begun to appear, but the final straw was when c2090, the Martians returned to the solar system. They invaded the Moon Base and tried to use the so-called Seeds of Death in an attempt to alter Earth's atmosphere and take over the planet. Their plans were foiled by the Second Doctor, Jamie and Zoe (XX). (The Martians had by then resettled on another planet – New Mars – but had become politically divided into two clans: one favoured a return to the solar system and a conquest of Earth; the other, continued peaceful existence. The conquest party won, which led to the attempted invasion. After their defeat, the peace party took over, and the Martians did not attack Earth again.)

The Martians' aborted invasion provided mankind the boost it needed to rediscover manned space travel and enter a new phase of expansion. On Earth, a true world government was established, in the form of a presidency. A new push outward was initiated.

The First Break Out

As the 21st century ended and the 22nd century began, mankind discovered the first, still rudimentary faster-than-light (warp) propulsion. A second wave of colonization ships, this time, using warp drives, was launched. As a result, Earth started to colonize its neighbouring solar systems and to have its first encounters with alien races on other worlds.

Some of these early ships, however, never reached their

intended destinations. Or if they did, they were never heard from again. These became known as the Lost Ships. One such ship was the exploration vessel *Hydrax*, whose captain was Miles Sharkey. En route to Beta Two, the *Hydrax* found itself diverted into E-space, possibly drawn there by the Great Vampire. Its three officers built a decaying civilization of servants, preparing for the Great One's eventual rising. A thousand years later, their plans were shattered by the Fourth Doctor, Romana and Adric (5P).

Another ship that was lost during the early days of the 22nd century crashlanded on the blue planet, Metebelis 3. The Earth spiders it unwittingly carried mutated under the influence of native crystals, and ended up ruling the human colonists for 430 years, until they were destroyed through the intervention of the Third Doctor and Sarah Jane Smith (ZZZ).

Between 2100 and 2150, mankind spread through its local galactic arm, settling new worlds, establishing new colonies, and meeting its first alien threats.

Contact was re-established with the Vulcan colony, which had awakened from suspended animation and thrived. Their calendar was off by a century (EE).

Another Earth colony was secretly taken over by the crab-like Macra, which forced the humans to toil to extract a gas the aliens needed for their survival. They were exposed and defeated by the Second Doctor, Jamie, Ben Jackson and Polly (JJ).

In 2116, the Fourth Doctor, Romana and K9 accidentally found themselves aboard the ships *Empress* and *Hecate*, which had both rematerialized in orbit around the planet Azure at the same time. They were able to unmask the villainous Tryst, who used the alien Mandrels and a primitive version of the Scope to traffic in the deadly drug vraxoin (5K).

The First Dalek War
Mankind's slow but steady space expansion inevitably attracted the hostile attentions of other galactic powers. One such power was the Daleks. By then, the Daleks had already conquered their space sector and driven their ancient foes, the Thals, off their homeworld of Skaro. The Daleks were generally

feared throughout known space for their aggression and ruth-lessness.

By 2160, the Daleks had launched a secret plan to invade Earth. First, they spread virulent plagues through a swarm of meteorites. As a result of the ensuing diseases, the solar system was put under quarantine by the other human-colonized worlds, leaving the Daleks the free hand they sought (K).

The Daleks struck in 2164, invading an almost depopulated Earth. Any attempt at space intervention by the other human worlds was firmly dealt with by the Daleks' space fleet, which blockaded the planet. Obviously, other friendly races proved unwilling or unable to help. This became known as the First Dalek War (K).

Among the colonists who participated in the First Dalek War – and, sadly, never returned – were the adult inhabitants of Paradise Towers, an award-winning residential complex which, once abandoned, reverted to savagery. Threatened by the return of its insane architect, Paradise Towers was saved by the opportune visit of the Seventh Doctor and Mel (7E).

Meanwhile, the Daleks believed that, once Earth was gone, the other human-dominated worlds would be easily picked off, one by one. This would have been so, if it had not been for the Doctor.

In 2167, the First Doctor, Susan, Ian Chesterton and Barbara Wright helped Earth-based rebels to defeat the Daleks, who had ultimately planned to turn Earth into a mobile planet by draining its core and replacing it with giant star drives. Susan chose to remain on Earth with freedom fighter David Campbell (K). (The Third Doctor once visited an alternative future where mankind suffered a nuclear war in the late 20th century, and where the Dalek invasion was totally successful (KKK).)

In about 2187, Susan was kidnapped by Borusa to take part in the Game of Rassilon. She teamed up with the First Doctor and, together with the Doctor's other four incarnations and various companions, helped thwart the megalomaniacal Time Lord's plan for immortality (6K).

The Dalek invasion had shown Earth and its colonies that there was force only in strength and unity. Mankind could count on only its own resources. That lesson was not forgotten, and

Earth took its first steps towards developing into a major galactic power.

The First Cyber Wars

As the 23rd century began, Earth (the term now included its colonies and allied worlds) came into direct conflict with another deadly galactic foe, one that had already attacked at least four times in the past: the Cybermen.

During the First Cyber Wars, man and his allies ultimately defeated the Cybermen by discovering that gold, which existed in abundance on the planet Voga, was fatal to their enemies. Driven from their world(s), the Cybermen had no choice but to flee. Before they did so, they made an attempt to destroy Voga, but were only partly successful. A fragment survived and began to drift towards the solar system (4D).

Soon afterwards, the Cybermen conquered the planet Telos and its native Cryons, and built 'tombs' in an attempt to heal and preserve their species for future assaults (MM, 6T).

Meanwhile, c2220 (c2020 by Vulcan calendar), a few Daleks who had crashed on Vulcan after the First Dalek War were brought back to life and attempted to take over the colony. They were defeated by the Second Doctor, Ben Jackson and Polly (EE).

After the Cyber Wars, Earth pursued its expansionist policies in its local galactic quadrant, meeting alien races, establishing new colonies and developing business opportunities. Slowly but surely, Earth became a space power to be reckoned with.

In 2250, the Argolins and the reptilian Foamasi fought a war during which most of Argolis was wiped out. The surviving Argolins created the Leisure Hive. In 2290 the Fourth Doctor and Romana visited the Leisure Hive and resolved the conflict between the Argolins and Foamasi.

It was also during that time that Earth's multi-planetary corporations began to thrive, and often displayed a ruthlessness in the pursuit of their business objectives that made them formidable foes.

But Earth's corporations also had adversaries to equal them, such as the cunning and rapacious Mentors of Thoros Beta. It was during the late part of the 23rd century that the Sixth Doctor and Peri defeated the Mentor Sil's attempts to corner the market of zyton 7, on behalf of the Galatron Corporation, by exploiting the inhabitants of the planet Varos, the unfortunate descendants of a colony for the criminally insane (6V).

During the 24th century, possibly as a reaction to Earth's growing authoritarianism, or that of its corporations, several colonies grew increasingly independent, isolated, and some might say, idiosyncratic.

One such example was the colony of Terra Alpha, where residents were literally forced to be happy under pain of death. The Seventh Doctor and Ace put a stop to ruler Helen A's misguided regime (7L).

Earth's strong arm of the law was the Intergalactic Taskforce, which c2310 helped the newly regenerated Sixth Doctor and Peri avert the threat of Mestor, tyrant of Jocunda (6S).

The rest of the 24th century, as had happened before during mankind's cyclical history, was spent in retrenchment and regrouping.

In 2479, the Sixth Doctor and Peri confronted Sil on his homeworld. Peri almost died through a series of events created by the Time Lords to prevent the Thoros Betans from acquiring the secret of Dr Crozier's mind transfer technique. Peri lived, and eventually married King Yrcanos of Thoros Alpha. The Sixth Doctor was taken to a huge space station to face a tribunal of Time Lords (7B).

The Second Dalek War

As the 25th century began, Earth started a new period of expansion.

It was probably during this time that Earth and its colonies came into contact with the Draconians, rulers of another, powerful, but peaceful, galactic empire (QQQ).

The Daleks, who had watched mankind from afar since their initial defeat, decided the time was right to launch a second offensive. Again, they may have decided to use a familiar weapon: a virus, which became a space plague. An antidote was found – parrinium – and ultimately located on the planet Exxilon. But it was only because of the intervention of the Third Doctor and Sarah Jane Smith that Earth's Marine Space Corps was able to defeat the Daleks and secure a supply of parrinium (XXX).

Once the Daleks' role in the space plague became known, several galactic races – possibly stirred up by the exiled Thals – united to attack and punish the Daleks. Thus was born the Alliance, which included Earth and the Draconian Empire. The war that ensued became known as the Second Dalek War.

During it, the Daleks were driven from Skaro, which was reconquered by the Thals. The Daleks were forced to relocate to another world which, out of pride, they christened Skaro (although it will be referred to here as New Skaro).

One of the Second Dalek War's side effects was that a number of planets, stricken by the Dalek plagues, became vehemently xenophobic. One such world was Inter Minor (PPP).

Towards the late part of the 25th century, it was business as usual for Earth. Several times, the Doctor found himself in conflict with various corporations.

In 2472, the Third Doctor and Jo Grant helped colonists fight the devious plans of the Interplanetary Mining Corporation, in addition to preventing the Master from using the Doomsday Machine (HHH).

About the same time, the Fifth Doctor, Turlough, Tegan Jovanka and Nyssa of Traken fought the inhumane policies of Terminus Incorporated and helped prevent a second Big Bang. Nyssa chose to stay and help the victims of Lazar disease, possibly an offshoot of the Dalek plagues (6G).

Of little importance in galactic terms was the First Doctor, Ian Chesterton and Barbara Wright's first encounter with Vicki on the planet Dido (which the Doctor had visited before) in 2493. The time travellers rescued the young girl from the villainous Bennett.

Towards the tail end of the 25th century, the Fourth Doctor, Sarah Jane Smith and Harry Sullivan thwarted the efforts of a small band of isolated Cybermen, remnants of the First Cyber Wars, who were trying to destroy the remains of Voga, which had drifted near Space Beacon Nerva in Earth's solar system (4D).

The Second Cyber Wars

The 26th century began with the insane Logician Klieg's attempt to resurrect the dreaded Cybermen, whose tombs had been located on Telos, although his plans were foiled by the Second Doctor, Jamie and Victoria Waterfield (MM). (It is likely that either once the tombs were opened, they continued to reactivate Cybermen, who then emerged in force, or other Cyber Forces drifting in space may have appeared to complete the job the humans had begun. In any event, the Cybermen, who had had time to regroup and reform, re-emerged as a serious galactic threat.)

In 2526, made aware of this new Cyber menace, the same Alliance that had defeated the Daleks agreed to meet on Earth in a galactic congress to decide what steps to take.

The Cybermen then attempted to destroy the congress by causing a space freighter to crash on the planet, but their scheme was thwarted by the Fifth Doctor and his companions. The young Alzarian Adric sacrificed himself, dying on board the freighter, which he had sent back through time to 65 million BC (6B).

A second series of Cyber Wars ensued. Having found Voga, mankind was in possession of a vast supply of gold. The result was yet another defeat for the Cybermen.

Just before the Alliance's forces made a final attack on Telos, the Cybermen's stronghold, the Cybermen used a captured time-vessel to launch a final, desperate attack. They tried to not only save themselves, but alter the course of history. This time, they planned to cause Halley's comet to crash into Earth in 1985. They were defeated by the Sixth Doctor and the courageous Cryons, who had secretly survived and contacted Commander Lytton, stranded in Earth's past (6T).

About the same time, c2530, the human colonists of Metebelis 3 were finally able to free themselves of the domination of the mutated giant spiders, owing to the Third Doctor's self-sacrifice (ZZZ).

The Third Dalek War

Soon after the end of the Second Cyber Wars, c2540, the Daleks, who had been driven from Skaro but were still at large, returned. They decided that their best tactic would be to create a split between the two most powerful members of the Alliance: Earth and the Draconian Empire.

They engaged the services of the Master to foment a war between Earth and Draconia, even offering him the use of their Ogron slaves. But the Master's schemes were ultimately exposed and defeated by the efforts of the Third Doctor and Jo Grant (QQQ).

Next, the Third Doctor and Jo, with the help of a Thal commando unit that had been monitoring the Daleks' moves, successfully froze an entire Dalek army which had been stored on Spiridon and was poised to attack the Alliance. They also prevented the Daleks from gaining the Spiridons' secret of invisibility (SSS).

Eventually, the Thals notified the Alliance of the Daleks' activities, and the Alliance struck back. This became known as the Third Dalek War.

Soon afterwards, Inter Minor cautiously reopened itself to galactic trade. The Third Doctor and Jo stopped there briefly, and resolved a crisis caused by galactic showman Vorg's use of an illegal Scope (PPP).

The End of the Alliance and the Dalek–Movellan War
It was during the late part of the 26th century that the galactic Alliance began to fall apart. Its resources depleted by the Dalek and Cyber Wars, the Draconian Empire had begun the long period of stagnation that would eventually lead to its 'long night', the Draconians no longer being powerful players in galactic affairs.

The Morok and Manussan Empires disappeared about the same time. The Morok Empire simply crumbled as its components revolted or broke away. The First Doctor, Ian, Barbara and Vicki were the witnesses of such a revolution in the Space Museum on planet Xeros (Q). The Manussan Empire was a victim of its own unleashed evil, as embodied in the Mara (6D).

Meanwhile, mankind had spread ever further through the galaxy, escaping the control of Earth. Deciding to open a new galactic arm, the robotic mechanoids (R) were launched in order to prepare new planets for colonization. However, Earth itself (or, more accurately, the political entity now known as the Solar System) entered another period of retrenchment and almost forgot about the Mechanoids.

During that time, the Fourth Doctor and Romana stopped on the alien world of Ribos, which was under the protection of the Alliance, in their quest for the Key to Time, and helped thwart the Graff Vynda-K's warlike plans (5A).

The Daleks took advantage of the Alliance's slow disintegration to launch an attack on Skaro. They succeeded in exterminating most of the Thals, but the planet itself was turned into a bombed-out ruin of no further use to them (or so they thought).

Towards the end of the 26th century, however, the Daleks encountered a new enemy – the robotic race of the Movellans – which they could not crush. Caught between the still powerful Alliance and the undefeated Movellans, the Daleks felt truly trapped. New ways had to be found if they were to save their species.

So, as the 27th century began, the Daleks, still deadlocked against the Movellans, returned to the original Skaro to recover their long-buried creator, Davros. But their efforts were thwarted by the Fourth Doctor and a newly regenerated Romana. Davros was taken to Earth, where he was tried and sentenced to life in suspended animation (5J).

Early in the century, Steven Taylor accidentally landed on a planet colonized by the Mechanoids, and became their prisoner. Two years later, he met the First Doctor, Ian Chesterton, Barbara Wright and Vicki, who were fleeing Daleks from the future. The Daleks and the Mechanoids exterminated each other, and the travellers escaped. Ian and Barbara returned to 1965 in the Dalek time machine. When the Doctor and Vicki left, they unknowingly took Steven with them (R).

Eventually, deprived of Davros's help, the Daleks lost their war against the Movellans, which turned the tables on them by using a virus to devastate their enemies. While striving to defeat the Movellans, the Daleks had made the most important discovery of their history: the secret of time travel. It was a rudimentary form of time travel, however, involving the use of time corridors. (Although the Time Lords did not openly move to prevent the Daleks from acquiring time travel capabilities, certain facts suggest that they did not remain idle. It is possible that the seemingly never-ending war of the Doctor against the Daleks – which would, one day, result in the annihilation of the Dalek race (LL) – was caused by the Celestial Intervention Agency's manipulations. It is also possible that it was at this point that the CIA sent the Fourth Doctor back to Skaro to prevent the genesis of the Daleks (4E). It is interesting to note that the Daleks themselves had identified the Time Lords as among their enemies, because they planned to use replicas to assassinate the High Council of Gallifrey (6P).)

Ninety years after Davros's trial, towards the end of the 27th century, the Daleks hired galactic mercenary Lytton to free Davros from the space penitentiary where he was kept. They also used their time corridor to trap the Fifth Doctor and plotted to use him in a devious scheme to strike back at the Time Lords. With the help of Tegan and Turlough, the Fifth Doctor outwitted the Daleks and Davros. The latter barely escaped the penitentiary's destruction with his life (6P).

Davros found refuge on the world of Nekros and infiltrated the mortuary known as Tranquil Repose. There, he used human bodies to build his own army of Imperial Daleks, who would obey only him. His efforts were thwarted by the Sixth Doctor and Peri. Betrayed by an employee from Tranquil Repose, Davros was taken back to New Skaro by the Daleks, who now considered him a traitor to their cause (6Z). (Davros somehow managed to escape the fate the Daleks had in store for him, and continued the production of Imperial Daleks. Later, he either returned to the original Skaro, or took over New Skaro – the records are unclear.)

The Empire

Meanwhile, as the 28th century began, Earth entered a new expansion phase. Stepping into the void left by the disintegration of the Alliance, it christened itself the Empire and embarked upon a new, imperialistic course.

The Empire ruled the galaxy until the end of the 30th century, mercilessly crushing and exploiting alien races to serve its own needs.

The First Doctor, Susan, Ian Chesterton and Barbara Wright

helped protect the shy, telepathic Sensorites from becoming one more victim of the Empire in about 2750 (G).

Another species preserved from the Empire's encroachments was the Kinda (also plagued by the evil Manussan spirit entity, the Mara), saved by the Fifth Doctor's intervention (5Y).

Other alien species were not so lucky. Among those exploited by the Empire were the insect-like Wirrn (4C), and the Mogarians (7C). The Empire was possibly responsible for the annihilation of the Movellans, which had won a Pyrrhic victory against the Daleks.

It was during the Empire that the Second Doctor, Jamie and Zoe fought the notorious space pirate Caven (YY).

A last battle took place between the Daleks and Davros's own Imperial Daleks in about 2960. The two camps used their time corridor technology to travel to 1963 Earth and tried to seize the Hand of Omega. As a result of the Seventh Doctor's intervention, both Dalek races were utterly devastated and Skaro (unless it was New Skaro) was destroyed. Davros, who had already taken to calling himself the Emperor Dalek, escaped (7H).

About 2986, the Sixth Doctor and Mel fought the Vervoids on board the space liner *Hyperion* en route from Mogar to Earth. This incident was used by the Valeyard during the Doctor's second trial (7C).

The so-called Solos Crisis, which occurred towards the end of the 30th century, was one of the catalysts of the fall of the Empire. The Third Doctor and Jo Grant were dispatched by the Time Lords to help the Solonian Mutants to reach their true, superhuman form (NNN).

The Solonians then became the unacknowledged models in a series of revolutions and guerilla actions that severely damaged the Empire. It is possible that the Time Lords were secretly afraid of Imperial Earth's growing power and ruthlessness, and used both the Doctor and the Solonians to trigger its downfall.

Another factor behind the fall of the Empire was trouble on Earth itself. That trouble was caused by an unprecedented string of solar flares. Some Imperial scientists theorized that the flares, which at the time were estimated to last 10,000 years, would cause permanent damage to the human genoplasm.

In the greatest secrecy, Space Beacon Nerva was converted into a Space Ark named *Terra Nova* where 'pure' specimens of humanity were stored. All records of the Terra Nova Ark were then carefully hidden, and its existence became almost a legend. The Ark's passengers remained in suspended animation for the next 10,000 years (4C).

The strain on the Empire's resources, however, proved to be the breaking point and the Emperor was finally deposed. The Empire had fallen.

The Federation

As the 31st century began, the Empire had dissolved. On Earth, surprisingly, the solar flares had abated. They had not damaged the human genoplasm, but had had one unexpected consequence: a new Ice Age now threatened the Earth.

The advent of the ice was fought off with the help of ionizers. It was during that time of transition that the Second Doctor, Jamie and Victoria helped defeat a spaceship crew of Martian Ice Warriors which had been discovered frozen in a glacier (OO).

Meanwhile, in space, the once-mighty Empire evolved into a loose combine of human and alien races, which the new democratic Earth was invited to join, but where it was to be no more than a single member.

Manussa was now part of a local Federation. There, the Fifth Doctor, Nyssa and Tegan finally defeated the Mara sometime during the 31st century (6D).

By the 32nd century, all these regional alliances had evolved into a new entity, which called itself the Federation. The Federation included not only humans from Earth and other human civilizations which had developed elsewhere, but also aliens such as Draconians, Alpha Centauri, Arcturians, the 'new' Martians and so on.

The Fourth Doctor and Romana, c3200, found themselves in E-Space and, with Adric's help, discovered the transformed officers of the lost ship *Hydrax* and killed the Great Vampire (5P).

It was sometime between the 32nd and 38th centuries that the Daleks re-emerged. By then, they had not only restored

Skaro (or New Skaro?) to its former glory, but they had also refined their time travel technology. Using the rare element taranium, they were now able to build a crude, prototype time machine.

One of their first enterprises was to send an execution squad to pursue the First Doctor, Vicki, Ian Chesterton and Barbara Wright through time and space. The Dalek squad was eventually destroyed by the Mechanoids, and their prototype time machine put to good use by Ian and Barbara (R).

First in about 3700, and again in 3750, the Third Doctor helped the planet Peladon. The first time, he helped it gain admission to the Federation with the Martians' help, against the designs of Arcturus (MMM). The second time, he helped protect Peladon's trisilicate mines from the machinations of the traitor Eckersley, an agent of the hostile Galaxy 5 (YYY).

In 3922, the first successful cloning experiments took place.

Towards the 40th century, Earth (also called the Solar System) gained more influence within the Federation. Also, other galaxies were increasingly resentful and envious of the Federation. The time had come for the Daleks to make their move.

The Fourth Dalek War

At the onset of the 41st century, the Daleks allied themselves with various other galaxies (including Galaxy 5), and plotted to attack the solar system, which they perceived - possibly blinded by their centuries-old feud with mankind - as the Federation's lynchpin. This became known as the Fourth Dalek War.

The Dalek invasion plans were first discovered on planet Kembel by Space Security agent Marc Cory, who was murdered by the Daleks (T/A).

Soon afterwards, the First Doctor, Steven Taylor and Katarina arrived on Kembel, and discovered a tape left by Cory. With the help of another Space Security agent, Bret Vyon, they decided to warn Earth of the impending Dalek attack, and of the treachery of Mavic Chen, the Guardian of the Solar System. Chen had given the Daleks the replacement taranium they needed to activate their supreme weapon: the Time Destructor.

The time travellers stole the Daleks' taranium core, and fled Kembel. In the course of their escape, Katarina sacrificed herself to save her companions. Bret Vyon was killed by his sister, Sara Kingdom, who later found out the truth and helped the Doctor. When the Time Destructor was finally activated, it was on Kembel, which put a stop to the Dalek invasion. Unfortunately, its deadly effects also killed Sara Kingdom (V).

Presumably, the Federation retaliated and the Daleks were again driven back to Skaro, their power and influence severely curtailed.

A century or so later, however, the Daleks managed to obtain some more taranium, and decided again to use their time travelling capabilities to attack Earth. By then, they were ruled by an Emperor Dalek, who could very well have been Davros, after possibly subjecting himself to further mutations.

Resorting again to their favourite weapon, the biological one, the Daleks planned to infect humanity with the Dalek factor. Having detected Professor Waterfield's early time travel experiments, the Daleks travelled to 1866 Earth. The Emperor's efforts were thwarted by the Second Doctor, Jamie and Victoria Waterfield. Instead of infecting mankind, it was the Daleks themselves who became contaminated with the human factor. A 'civil war', in which the Dalek race perished, erupted on Skaro (LL).

The End of the Federation

The period from the 41st to 50th centuries was marked by several notable developments. First, on Earth, following the upheaval caused by Mavic Chen's betrayal, several important political changes occurred, each causing severe rifts with the Federation and within the Solar System Administration.

Earth eventually turned its back on the Federation, which it blamed for its problems, and entered into a new period of isolationism.

In the galaxy, the Federation continued to thrive, except that it had now acquired a harder, more authoritarian – some might even say militaristic – style. The discovery of spectrox, a life-extending drug, had a profound impact on all the components of the galactic society.

On Androzani Minor, the Fifth Doctor and Peri became involved in a conflict between Sharaz Jek, Morgus – the corrupt chairman of the Sirius Conglomerate – and Federation troops led by General Chellak. Poisoned by raw spectrox, the Fifth Doctor sacrificed himself to save Peri's life, then regenerated (6R).

Over the course of the next five hundred years, with Terran influence diminished, and its growing reputation for military interventions of the type mentioned above, the Federation began to disintegrate into new empires, new federations and so on.

The Development of Artificial Intelligences

Meanwhile, on Earth, as the 50th century approached, scientists at New Heidelberg developed the first artificial intelligences (AIs). (By then, early attempts at creating sentient computers, such as WOTAN or BOSS, had been either dismissed or forgotten.)

Professor Marius created the K-series of AIs, culminating with the K9 mobile AI (4T). Other experimental AIs included sentient computers, such as Xoanon (4Q), which were installed aboard survey ships.

It was during this period that the Fourth Doctor and Leela helped Professor Marius and K9 defeat a space swarm, which had taken over the Titan Base (4T).

Within the next hundred years, AIs were well on their way to becoming widely used in several parts of the galaxy, in spite of the latent robophobia inherent in humans. One famous case took place on a sand miner where the Fourth Doctor and Leela stopped the mad Taren Capel from turning AI robots into instruments of death (4R).

AIs were later refined into androids of great sophistication by the neo-medieval Tarans. The planet Tara was visited by the Fourth Doctor and Romana during their quest for the Key to Time (5D).

On Earth, however, robophobia was more intense, and the presence of AIs was not welcome. It arrived at the end of a long list of problems plaguing the planet, including increased xenophobia, depletion of natural resources, growing pollution and so on.

As a result of the above, during the 51st century, a neo-Luddite revolution occurred and the Supreme Alliance, a league of ruthless dictators, took control of the Earth.

The Supreme Alliance was finally overthrown almost a hundred years later, at the Battle of Reykjavik, in which the Doctor claimed to have taken part. After the battle, the Supreme Alliance's Minister of Justice, the evil Magnus Greel, and his Peking Homunculus, fled to the 19th century in a newly developed time cabinet, christened the Zigma Experiment (4S).

The Second (or Great) Break Out and the Sunmakers

By the 52nd century, Earth was not only a war-torn, emptied husk, but it was also becoming increasingly polluted, to the point of being virtually uninhabitable.

The alien Usurians offered to move the human population to Mars, as long as they would work for their company.

Some humans chose to go along with the Usurians' offer. Others decided to leave Earth en masse – a movement that became known as the Second (or Great) Break Out (4T).

One of the ships which left at that time crashed on a nameless planet. In an unrecorded adventure, the Fourth Doctor, fresh from his regeneration, tried to fix their experimental AI, Xoanon, but instead gave it a split personality. As a result, Xoanon caused the survey team and the ship's technicians to evolve into two different tribes, who went to war with each other (4Q).

Elsewhere in the galaxy, Earth's lesson had not gone unnoticed. The Sons of Earth, who did not want to see other worlds become as polluted as Earth, made their appearance. On Delta Magna's third moon, the Fourth Doctor and Romana, during their quest for the Key to Time, were caught up in a conflict between the native Swampies and human colonists, themselves in conflict with the Sons of Earth (5E).

Several centuries later, the Fourth Doctor returned to Leela's world, and helped repair the damage he had caused to Xoanon's personality (4Q).

Meanwhile, Earth was placed in ecological quarantine. Those who had elected to stay in the solar system lived under Usurian control on Mars. Several centuries later, they were moved to

Pluto, around which six artificial suns had been built. The Solarians lived a heavily taxed life, toiling ceaselessly for a Usurian-dominated company. This was finally ended through the intervention of the Fourth Doctor, Leela and K9, who helped the Plutonians to rebel. By then, Earth had returned to normal and mankind was able to return to its homeworld (4W).

The duration of this period of Earth's history, known as that of the Sunmakers, is hard to determine with accuracy, but it is likely that mankind reclaimed Earth about AD 10,000, almost five thousand years after it had abandoned it.

During those five thousand years, a strange, new lifeform arose on polluted Earth: that of the vampiric Haemovores. One of them, the Ancient One, was brought by Fenric to 1943 to help him defeat the Seventh Doctor, but turned against the evil entity and helped destroy it (7M).

As the planet's ecological balance was restored, the Haemovores became extinct and Earth was ready to be reclaimed by humanity.

The Morbius Crisis and the Ravolox Interlude

By 10,000, the galactic civilization had become a cluster civilization encompassing several galaxies, including Earth's Milky Way, Galaxy Four (T), Galaxy Five and Andromeda. At that time, many species began to engage in cautious attempts to obtain or duplicate the Time Lords' secrets of time travel and bodily regeneration.

Before this era, the Time Lords had often taken drastic steps to prevent their secrets from falling into alien hands. Back in the galactic equivalent of 20th century Earth, they had sent the Second Doctor and Jamie to investigate unauthorized experiments on Space Station J7 of the Third Zone (6W) and had even fought the Sontarans to protect the secrets of time travel (6W, 4Z). Later, the Time Lords had outlawed the Scopes, which involved rudimentary time travel (PPP), and probably made successful attempts to stop the Cybermen from acquiring such secrets (6T).

The Time Lords, however, had been unable to prevent the determined Daleks from developing time travel. Nevertheless, to many galactic observers the fact that the Daleks had eventually become extinct, mostly because of the intervention of a Time Lord – the Doctor – often manipulated by the Gallifreyan Celestial Intervention Agency, was incentive enough not to pry into the Time Lords' affairs.

By 10,000, two factors prompted many races to cautiously change this policy: one, the mistaken belief that the Time Lords had not seemingly intervened in another race's affairs since the Daleks' extinction almost five thousand years ago; and two, what became known as the Morbius Crisis.

A member of the High Council of Gallifrey, Morbius had sought to lead the Time Lords on a path of conquest. Rejected by his peers, he had then left Gallifrey and raised an army of followers, promising them time travel and immortality, using the Elixir of Life produced by the Sisterhood of Karn's Sacred Flame. Eventually, Morbius and his army were defeated by the Time Lords on Karn. The Renegade Time Lord was placed in a disposal chamber and his body was vaporized (4K).

Several years later, the Celestial Intervention Agency found out that the Brain of Morbius had been secretly preserved by one of his followers, Dr Solon. They sent the Fourth Doctor and Sarah Jane Smith to Karn, where they not only destroyed Morbius, but also restored the Sisterhood's dying flame (4K).

Meanwhile, the Morbius Crisis had spurred other races to look cautiously into the Time Lords' secrets. Spies from Andromeda successfully infiltrated the Gallifreyan Matrix, choosing Earth as their base of operations. When they discovered the Andromedans' plan, the Time Lords struck back. The actions they took against Andromeda itself are unknown, but they moved Earth out of the solar system and rechristened it Ravolox. This action, which seems to have occurred c14,000, resulted in considerable death and destruction, but was blamed on a freak cosmic phenomenon (7A).

The Ravolox stratagem was eventually uncovered by the Sixth Doctor during his trial, soon after he and Peri visited Ravolox. Indeed, it is permissible to think that the Doctor was put on trial because the corrupt High Council of Gallifrey was afraid that he would eventually uncover and expose the Ravolox deception (7A–7C).

After their callous scheme had been revealed, it is unclear whether the Time Lords moved Earth back to its original location, or simply allowed it to be rediscovered. In any event, the destruction caused by the planetary move was still being explained away as a fireball or solar flares.

This was presumably the time when the Seventh Doctor met Ace and, together with Mel, fought Kane, the master of Ice World on planet Svartos. Mel eventually left to travel with Sabalom Glitz, whom the Doctor had previously met on Ravolox (7G).

Ultimately, it seems that the Time Lords were unsuccessful in their attempts to prevent other races from discovering time travel, since by the time the Seventh Doctor and Mel met the young Chimeron Queen, Delta, and her enemies, the Bannermen, time travel appeared to have become widely accessible throughout the known universe. By then, Earth and its past seemed a quaint, backwater curiosity, a Shangri-La for alien tourists (7F).

The Rediscovery of Earth

The rediscovery of Earth probably took place between 15,000 and 20,000. This was when the passengers of the Space Ark *Terra Nova*, who had been placed in secret suspended animation by the Empire, c3000, awoke. They were meant to sleep for only 10,000 years, but overslept by several thousand years. When they awoke, they found that Nerva had been infiltrated by the vengeful Wirrn, a race once crushed by the Empire. It was only the intervention of the Fourth Doctor, Sarah Jane Smith and Harry Sullivan, and the sacrifice of the Ark's leader, Noah, which enabled the Ark to survive (4C).

Spacemen from Earth's colonies had begun to return to Earth. Like the passengers of the Ark, they assumed it to be lifeless because of the solar flares or the fireball. (Unlike the Nerva people, however, they believed these flares to have happened c14,000, that is, when the Time Lords had moved the planet and not during the 30th to 31st centuries.)

The Fourth Doctor, Sarah and Harry helped the colonists thwart an attempt by the Sontarans to take over this space sector

(4B). Earth was now safe again for resettlement by the human race.

At some undetermined date after the resettlement, the Seventh Doctor and Ace defeated the Gods of Ragnarok at the Psychic Circus on Segonax (7J).

The Far Future

Only fragmentary records exist of the future Earth history after 20,000.

In about 37,166, the Fourth Doctor and Sarah Jane Smith rescued the crew of a Morestran spaceship from an antimatter creature on Zeta Minor, a planet on the edge of the known universe (4H).

Even further in the future, Earth's sun was the victim of a cosmic collision that forced the Solarians to undertake another Great Break Out. The Fifth Doctor, Tegan and Turlough helped a group of indomitable survivors defeat the alien Tractators on the planet Frontios (6N).

Ten million years in the future, in what was then known as the 57th Segment of Time, Earth's sun went nova (X). By then, mankind had spread throughout the universe, and probably evolved into many different forms. Its relationship with the planet of its birth was unknown.

The Solarians and the alien Monoids, and all life on Earth (in a miniaturized form) embarked on a seven-hundred-year journey to the planet Refusis. Eventually, the First Doctor, Dodo and Steven Taylor helped men and Monoids peacefully to resettle on Refusis (X).

2: *WHO'S WHO IN* WHO

This chapter is divided into four alphabetically arranged sections: the Actors, the Creative Team (producers, script editors, directors and writers), a selective listing of Key Technical Personnel (music, visual effects, costume, set design and so on), and the authors of the *Doctor Who* novelizations.

A careful reader may find certain (small) discrepancies between these listings and *Doctor Who – The Programme Guide*. These may be either the result of corrections made after the earlier volume went to press (in which case, check the Errata section for full details), or simply because of a few instances when the BBC credits are not always complete or accurate. In the latter case, and after a review of the facts, calls have been made on individual judgment, with which fans should feel free to disagree.

THE ACTORS

ACTOR	STORY (production code)	ACTOR	STORY (production code)
Abbott, John	4V	Alexander, Paul	UU
Abineri, John	RR, CCC, XXX, 5E	Alexander, Terence	6X
		Alkin, John	6Q
Acheson, John	4L	Allaby, Michael	E
Adams, Dallas	6Q	Allan, Dominic	VV
Adams, Terry	ZZ	Allef, Tony	5Q
Adams, Tom	6L	Allen, Dean	5P
Adams, Tony	TTT	Allen, Ronald	TT, CCC
Adrian, Max	U	Alless, Tony	4G
Ainley, Anthony	5T-5Z, 6C, 6J, 6K, 6Q, 6R, 6X, 7C, 7P	Allison, Bart	M
		Allister, David	5N, 7C
		Anderson, Bob	PP
Ainley, John	6T	Anderson, David	F, P, S
Alderson, John	Z	Anderson, Keith	H
Aldous, Robert	K	Andrews, Barry	5K
Aldred, Sophie	7G-7P	Angelo, Callen	DD
Aldridge, David	GGG	Anholt, Christien	7M
Alexander, Geraldine	6V	Anil, Paul	GG
		Annis, Tony	6J

78

ACTOR	STORY (production code)	ACTOR	STORY (production code)
Anthony, Philip	V	Baker, John	HHH, 5X
Anton, Marek	7N, 7M	Baker, John Adam	6P
Appleby, Bob	5L, 7C	Baker, Lucy	6F
Appleby, James	KK, 4M	Baker, Tom	4A-5V, 6K
Archard, Bernard	EE, 4G	Baldock, Peter	4Q
Arden, Suzi	6B	Bale, Terry	H, MMM
Aris, Ben	WWW	Ballantine, George	6D
Arlen, David	NNN	Bangerter, Michael	6Q
Arliss, Ralph	ZZZ	Banks, David	6B, 6K, 6T, 7K
Armitage, Graham	JJ	Baraker, Gabor	D, P
Armstrong, Gareth	4M	Barber, Neville	OOO, K9
Armstrong, Iain	5F	Barker, Ken	6Z
Armstrong, Ray	CCC	Barker, Tim	7L
Arnatt, John	4Z	Barkworth, Peter	OO
Arnold, Sydney	FF	Barlow, Tim	5J
Arthur, Edward	4X	Barnes, Howard	5Q
Arthur, Max	6Q	Barnes, Richard	5K
Ashby, Robert	6Y	Baron, David	NN
Ashcroft, Chloe	6P	Baron, Lynda	6H
Ashford, David	7J	Barr, Patrick	HH
Ashley, Graham	GG	Barrard, John	H
Ashley, Keith	4E, 4F, 4L	Barrass, Paul	7K
Ashley, Lyn	T	Barratt, Reginald	J
Ashley, Richard	6N	Barrett, Ray	L
Ashton, Barry	HH, OOO, QQQ	Barrington, Albert	V
Ashton, David	6Y	Barrington, Michael	4L
Ashworth, Dicken	6Y	Barron, Keith	6H
Aspland, Robin	7F	Barron, Ray	4L
Asquith, Conrad	4S	Barrs, Johnny	FFF
Asquith, John	6L	Barry, Anna	KKK
Atherton, Richard	FFF	Barry, Brendan	BBB
Atkyns, Norman	HHH, LLL	Barry, Christopher	JJJ
Atterbury, John	UU, ZZ	Barry, Morris	5G
Attwell, Michael	OO, 6T	Barton, Paul	BBB
Avon, Roger	P, V	Barton, Will	7P
Bache, David	6B	Baskcomb, John	EEE
Bacon, Norman	5R, 7H	Bassenger, Mark	6K
Badcoe, Brian	WWW	Bate, James	6Q
Badger, Peter	K	Bateman, Geoffrey	5K
Bailey, Edmund	AAA	Bates, Leslie	D, W
Bailey, John	G, LL, 5L	Bateson, Timothy	5A
Bailie, David	4R	Bathurst, Peter	EE, GGG
Baker, Colin	6E, 6R-7C	Baxter, Lois	5D
Baker, George	5R		

ACTOR	STORY (production code)	ACTOR	STORY (production code)
Baxter, Trevor	4S	Bisset, Donald	FF
Bay, John	P	Blackman, Honor	7C
Bayldon, Geoffrey	5G	Blackwell Baker, Mark	4R
Bayler, Terence	X, ZZ		
Bayly, Johnson	TT	Blackwood, Adam	7A
Beacham, Rod	QQ	Blaine, Bob	EEE
Beale, Richard	X, Z, JJ, TTT	Blair, Isla	6J
Beardmore, John	6N	Blake, Arthur	N
Beatles, The	R	Blake, Stuart	5P, 6K, 6L
Beatty, Robert	DD	Bland, June	6B, 7N
Beck, Glenn	DD	Blatch, Helen	4P, 6S
Beckett, James	6T	Bleasdale, John	4R
Beckley, Tony	4L	Blessed, Brian	7B
Bedford, Melvyn	4H, 4G	Bligh, Jack	CC
Beevers, Geoffrey	CCC, 5T	Block, Giles	TT
Bell, Colin	LLL, WWW	Block, Timothy	6A
Bell, Joanne	7M	Blomley, Paul	FFF
Bell, RJ	6G	Bloomfield, Philip	5T
Bell, Rachel	7L	Blowers, Sean	7G
Bellingham, Lynda	7A–7C	Boddey, Martin	LLL
Benda, Kenneth	GGG	Bond, Philip	B
Benjamin, Christopher	DDD, 4S	Booth, Jolyon	N
		Booth, Tom	F
Bennett, Clive	5B	Bork, Tomek	7M
Bennett, Hywel	R	Borman, Miranda	7G
Bennett, John	WWW, 4S	Borza, Peppi	7C
Bennett, Vivienne	R	Bough, Jane	5H
Bennion, Alan	XX, MMM, YYY	Boulay, Andre	F
		Bowden, Betty	AAA
Benson, Peter	6G	Bowen, Christopher	7N
Berger, Sarah	6T		
Berry, Ron	7H	Bowen, Dennis	QQQ
Bettany, Thane	5P	Bowen, William	6N
Bevan, Stewart	TTT	Bower, Ingrid	OOO
Beverton, Hugh	7C	Bowerman, Lisa	7P
Bewes, Rodney	6P	Bowman, Tom	FF
Bickford-Smith, Imogen	4Y	Boxer, Andrew	6E
		Boyd, Danny	7K
Bidmead, Kathleen	7H, 7P	Boyd, Roy	4N
Bidmead, Stephanie	T	Boyd-Brent, John	BB
		Boyle, Marc	GGG, OOO
Bilton, Michael	W, 4G, 4P	Braben, Mike	6L, 6P, 6T
Birdsall, Jocelyn	N	Bradley, Norman	6B, 6K
Birrel, Peter	QQQ	Braham, Beryl	Y
Bishop, Sue	4K	Branch, Thomas	7B

80

ACTOR	STORY (production code)	ACTOR	STORY (production code)
Brandon, John	DD	Burn, Jonathan	7L
Branigan, Roy	BBB	Burnell, Nick	4G
Brayshaw, Deborah	KKK	Burnham, Edward	VV, 4A
Brayshaw, Edward	H, ZZ	Burridge, Bill	GG, RR
Breaks, Jasmine	7H	Burroughs, Peter	6J
Bree, James	ZZ, 5R, 7C	Burt, Andrew	6G
Brennon, Julie	7E	Bush, Maurice	KKK
Brent, Roy	5A	Butler, Alan	4S
Breslin, John	AAA	Butterworth, Peter	S, V
Bresslaw, Bernard	OO	Byfield, Judith	6C
Briant, Michael E	4D	Byrne, Toby	5J, 6P, 6Z
Brierley, David	5G–5M	Caddick, Edward	AA
Brierley, Roger	V, 7A	Cady, Gary	6X
Briers, Richard	7E	Caesar, John	M, X, JJ, LLL, WWW
Brimble, Vincent	6L		
Bron, Eleanor	5H, 6Z	Caffrey, Sean	4V
Brook, Russell	7F	Cain, Simon	PP, BBB
Brook, Terence	4H	Cairncross, James	H, WW
Brooks, Harry	DD	Cairnes, Elliott	PP
Brown, Christopher	6H	Calcutt, Stephen	5F, 5R
Brown, Faith	6T	Calder, Derek	HH
Brown, Gilly	4K	Calderisi, David	FFF
Brown, June	UUU	Caldinez, Sonny	LL, OO, XX, MMM, YYY
Brown, Terence	WW		
Browne, Michael Gordon	5Q, 6B	Calf, Anthony	5X
		Callaghan, Ray	4Z
Browning, Chris	B	Callender, Bruce	5Q
Browning, Maurice	V	Calvin, Tony	5R
Bruce, Angela	7N	Cameron, Earl	DD
Bruce, Barbara	FF	Campbell, George	6N
Bruce, Brenda	7E	Campion, Gerald	5M
Brunswick, Steve	UUU	Cannon, David	UU
Bryans, John	5G	Cannon, John	4N, 5F, 6H
Bryant, Nicola	6Q–7B	Cant, Brian	V, TT
Bryant, Sandra	BB, JJ	Caplan, Jonathan	6Q
Brydon, Michael	5Q	Carey, Denis	5M, 5T, 6Y
Bryson, George	WWW	Carin, Victor	Z
Bulbeck, David	5N	Carlton, Tony	7K
Bulloch, Jeremy	Q, UUU	Carney, John J	UUU
Burden, Hugh	AAA	Carr, Andrew	KKK
Burgess, Adrienne	4W	Carrick, Antony	4M
Burgess, Christopher	PP, EEE, ZZZ	Carrigan, Ralph	X, JJ, UU, VV
		Carroll, Mark	7L
Burgess, Jean	TTT	Carroll, Susanna	T
Burgoyne, Victoria	5M	Carson, John	6D

ACTOR	STORY (production code)	ACTOR	STORY (production code)
Carson, Paul	D	Churchill, John	BBB
Carter, Dave	BBB, DDD, EEE, FFF, OOO, WWW, 4J	Churchman, Ysanne	MMM, YYY, ZZZ
		Clamp, John	4M
Carter, Patrick	R	Claridge, Norman	W
Carter, Wilfrid	KKK	Clark, Les	EEE, FFF
Cartland, Robert	T, T/A	Clarke, Trisha	6T
Carvic, Heron	E	Clayton, James	CCC
Casdagli, Penny	5J	Cleary, Denis	H
Cashfield, Katie	B	Cleese, John	5H
Cashman, Michael	6C	Cleeve, David	5Q
Cassandra	5J	Clegg, Karen	7D
Cater, John	BB	Clements, Anne	6B
Caunter, Tony	P, HHH, 6H	Clifford, Clare	6B
Cavell, Dallas	H, V, FF, CCC, 5Z	Clifford, John	HH
		Clunes, Martin	6D
Cawdron, Robert	CCC	Coady, Simon	7E
Cazes, Clive	W	Cochrane, Martin	6R
Cecil, Hugh	W	Cochrane, Michael	6A, 7Q
Cellier, Peter	6C	Coe, Richard	R
Chadbon, Tom	5H, 7A	Colbourne, Maurice	6P, 6T
Chagrin, Nicholas	6V	Colby, Anthony	P
Challis, John	4L	Cole, David	Z, 5Q
Chambers, Barbara	KKK	Cole, Graham	5R, 6B, 6K
Chandler, David	6Y	Coleman, Alec	DD
Chandler, Jeremy	4E	Coleman, Noel	ZZ
Chapman, Sean	K9	Coleridge, Sylvia	4L
Charles, Alan	4Q	Coll, Christopher	XX, NNN
Charles, Oscar	4G	Collier, Ian	OOO, 6E
Charlton, Alethea	A, S	Collin, John	5N
Charlton, Howard	H	Collings, David	4D, 4R, 6F
Charlton, James	5H, 5X	Collins, Forbes	6V
Chazen, Arnold	HH		
Chering, Chris	7K	Collins, John D	6E
Cheshire, Geoffrey	S, V, VV	Collins, Laura	7F
Childs, Peter	6X	Collins, Noel	7N
Ching, Hi	5Q	Collins, Pauline	KK
Chinnery, Dennis	R, 4E, 6S	Colliver, Edward	BB
Chitty, Erik	W, 4P	Colville, Geoffrey	LL
Christou, Christopher	4Z	Comer, Norman	6L
		Condon, Clive	7F
Chuntz, Alan	RRR, TTT, 4L, 5P	Condren, Tim	KKK
		Connery, Jason	6V
Churchett, Stephen	6T	Conrad, Andrew	6S

ACTOR	STORY (production code)	ACTOR	STORY (production code)
Conrad, Les	EEE, FFF	Creasey, Terence	5Q
Conrad, Mark	7M	Crest, Philip	D
Conrad, Paul	6S	Crewe, Derek	4W
Conroy, Jean	K	Crisp, Alan	4K
Conway, Carl	BB, CCC	Croft, Jon	JJJ
Cook, Peter Noel	CCC	Cross, George	BB
Cooke, Howard	7E	Cross, Gerald	5C
Cooklin, Shirley	MM	Cross, John	TT
Coombes, James	5M, 6L	Croucher, Brian	4R
Cooper, George A	CC	Crowden, Graham	5L
Cooper, Mark	4R	Crowley, JeanAnne	6Y
Cooper, Trevor	6Z	Cull, Graham	6V
Cope, Kenneth	5S	Cullen, Ellen	DD
Copeland, James	WW	Cullen, Ian	F
Copley, Peter	4G	Culliford, James	QQQ
Corbett, Matthew	JJJ	Cullingford, Brian	RR
Cormack, George	OOO, ZZZ	Cullum-Jones,	BB
Cornelius, Billy	P, Q	Desmond	
Cornes, Lee	5Y	Cumming, Alastair	6E
Cornwell, Judy	7E	Cunningham, Ian	BBB
Corri, Adrienne	5N	Cunningham, Jack	H
Cort, Martin	E, XX	Curran, Nell	4T
Cossette, Lorne	G	Curry, Nicholas	6P
Coulouris, George	E	Curtis, Alan	BB
Coulter, Edmund	X	Curtis, Gerald	B
Courtney, Nicholas	V, Q, VV, AAA–KKK, OOO, RRR, TTT–WWW, ZZZ, 4A, 4F, 6F, 6K, 7N	Cusack, Catherine	7E
		Cuthbertson, Iain	5A
		Czajkowski, Peter	7M
		Daglish, Neil	6E
		Dahlsen, Peter	6C
		Daker, David	UUU, 5K
Cowne, Judy	5C	Dalling, Laidlaw	H
Cox, Arthur	TT	Dalton, Keith	OOO
Cox, Clifford	AAA	Danielle, Suzanne	5J
Craig, Michael	7C	Daniely, Lisa	YY
Craig-Raymond, Vaune	4S	Danot, Eric	4Z
		Danvers Walker, Aubrey	TT
Crane, Jonathan	B		
Crane, Michael	YYY	Danvers, Wendy	MMM
Crane, Simon	6P	Darnley, Brian	6F
Craven, Timothy	QQQ, WWW, 4A	Darrow, Paul	BBB, 6Y
		Dartnell, Stephen	E, G
Crawshaw, Frank	J	Davenport, Claire	D
Craze, Michael	BB-KK	Davenport, Roger	6P
Craze, Peter	Q, ZZ, 5K	David, Jonathan	6T

ACTOR	STORY (production code)	ACTOR	STORY (production code)
Davidson, Lawrence	QQQ	Dent, Reg	FF
		Dentith, Edward	VV
Davies, Ann	K	Denton, Roy	W
Davies, Bernard	ZZ	Denyer, Philip	5G
Davies, Griffith	LL	Dewild, Michael	4N
Davies, Harry	V	Diamond, Peter	M, Q, FF, OO
Davies, Rachel	5P	Diffring, Anton	7K
Davies, Richard	7F	Dillon, John	AA
Davies, Stacy	VV, 5P	Ditta, Douglas	R
Davies, Windsor	LL	Ditton, Cordelia	6X
Davis, Eddie	BB	Dixon, Peggy	4M
Davis, Leon	7C	Dixon, Shirley	5M
Davis, Michael	K	Dobtcheff, Vernon	ZZ
Davison, Peter	5V-6R	Dodd, Ken	7F
Davy, Pamela Ann	EE	Dodimead, David	DD
Dawson, John	4P	Dodson, Eric	5X
Dawson, Robin	BB, KK	Donald, Alex	GG
De La Torre, Raf	E	Donovan, Anthony	YY
De Marney, Terence	CC	Dorward, Helen	AAA
		Douglas, Angela	7N
De Polnay, Gregory	4R	Douglas, Colin	PP, 4V
		Douglas, Donald	4B
De Rouen, Reed	Z	Douglas, Tony	GG
De Souza, Edward	T/A	Dowdall, Jim	6N
De Vries, Hans	MM	Downie, Andre	FF
De Winter, Roslyn	N, R	Doye, John	BB
De Wolff, Francis	E, U	Drinkel, Keith	6C
Deacon, Eric	6Y	Du Pre, Barry	KK
Deadman, Derek	4Z	Duce, Sharon	7Q
Dean, Dougie	E	Ducrow, Peter	RR
Deare, Morgan	7F	Duggan, Tommy	FFF
Dearth, John	TTT, ZZZ	Dunham, Christopher	DD
Delahunt, Vez	B		
Delamain, Aimee	6W	Dunlop, Lesley	6N, 7L
Delaney, Decima	5C	Dunn, Sheila	V, VV, DDD
Delaney, Jim	FFF	Dwyer, Leslie	PPP
Delgado, Kismet	ZZZ	Dyall, Valentine	5F, 6F-6H
Delgado, Roger	EEE-JJJ, LLL, OOO, QQQ	Dyce, Hamilton	AAA
		Dyer, Alys	5N
Delieu, John	4N	Dyer, Peter Hamilton	7H
Delmar, Vi	5B		
Denham, Christopher	AA	Dysart, William	FF, CCC
		Eagles, Leon	4Q
Denham, Maurice	6S	Earl, Clifford	V, VV
Dennis, Johnny	7F	Earle, Freddie	5S

ACTOR	STORY (production code)	ACTOR	STORY (production code)
Easton, Richard	6C	Faulkner, Sally	VV
Eaton, Kate	7P	Fawcett, Nicholas	6W
Eccles, Donald	OOO	Fay, Colin	4K
Eden, Mark	D	Fay, Sheila	UUU
Edwards, Dennis	M, 4Z	Fayerman, Stephanie	7G
Edwards, Jack	4M	Felgate, Ric	BB, XX, CCC
Edwards, Nicholas	DD	Fell, Stuart	MMM, PPP, YYY, ZZZ, 4C, 4J, 4K, 4M, 4S, 4Z, 5A, 5P
Edwards, Rob	4Q, 4R		
Elkin, Clifford	QQQ		
Elles, Mike	4Q		
Elliott, David	4X		
Elliott, Eric	X		
Elliott, Ian	EEE, 4L	Fenn, Edwin	W
Ellis, Brian	4B, 4M	Ferris, Fred	J
Ellis, James	7N	Fiander, Lewis	5K
Ellis, Janet	5L	Fielder, Harry	4L, 4Q, 5F, 5M, 5Q
Elwyn, Michael	FF		
Ely, Michael	FFF	Fielding, Janet	5V-6P, 6R
Emerson, Steve	JJ	Finch, Bernard	5B
Emmanuel, Heather	4J	Finch, Charles	VV
		Findley, Jim	6P
Engel, Susan	5C	Fisk, Martin	5N
Enshawe, Jane	JJ	Fitzgerald, Walter	TT
Etherington, Cynthia	W	Fleming, Catherine	N
		Fletcher, Mark	6B
Eton, Graeme	YYY	Flint, John	P, 6C
Evans, Edward	4X	Float, Ray	6K
Evans, John	7H	Flood, Gerald	6J, 6Q, 6R
Evans, Mostyn	TTT, XXX	Flood, Kevin	5H
Evans, Murray	VV	Flynn, Eric	SS
Evans, Nicholas		Flynn, Stephen	6Z
Evans, Nick	K	Foote, Freddie	SS
Evans, Peter	RRR	Forbes, Andrew	5R
Evans, Roy	V, TTT, YYY	Forbes-Robertson, Peter	EE, HHH, LLL
Evans, Tenniel	PPP		
Fairbairn, Ian	JJ, VV, DDD, 4L	Ford, Carole Ann	A-K, 6K
		Ford, Patrick	7J
Faith, Gordon	PP	Forgione, Carl	ZZZ, 7Q
Fanning, Rio	4V	Forrest, Brett	4Q
Farrell, Royston	GGG	Forster, Brian	ZZ
Farries, Christopher	6L	Forsyth, Brigit	LL
		Foster, Dudley	YY
Faulkner, Max	CCC, YYY, ZZZ, 4E, 4J, 4Z	Fothergill, Miles	4R
		Fowler, Harry	7H
		Fox, Eden	GGG

ACTOR	STORY (production code)	ACTOR	STORY (production code)
Fox, Julian	XXX	Gaunt, William	6Z
Frances, Myra	5G	Gauntlett, Richard	7D
Francis, Derek	M	Gee, Donald	YY, YYY
Francis, Eric	G	George, Frank	X
Franklin, Richard	EEE-GGG, JJJ, KKK, OOO, TTT, WWW, ZZZ, 6K	Georgeson, Tom	4E, 5V
		Geraint, Martyn	7F
		Gerrard, Alan	TT
		Gibbs, Adrian	5R, 5V
Franklyn-Robbins, John	4E	Gibson, Felicity	TT
		Gifford, Wendy	OO
Fraser, Bill	5Q, K9	Gilbert, Derrick	SS
Fraser, Gilly	KK	Gilbert, Henry	MMM
Fraser, John	5V	Gilbert, Kenneth	4L
Fraser, Peter	K	Gilbert, Marcus	7N
Fraser, Ronald	7L	Gilbert, Oliver	KKK
Frederick, Geoffrey	AA	Giles, George	MMM
Fredericks, Scott	KKK, 4X	Gill, John	RR
Freedman, Ryan	7L	Gill, Sheila	6F
French, Leslie	7K	Gillan, Gilbert	6K
Freud, Esther	6T	Gillett, John	6N
Friend, Martin	4J	Gilmore, Peter	6N
Frieze, Anthony	4Q	Gipps-Kent, Simon	5L
Frost, Ian	X, QQQ	Gittins, Jeremy	5S
Fullarton, Alistair	4M	Glaze, Peter	G
Furst, Joseph	GG	Gledhill, Karen	7H
Fusek, Vera	QQQ	Gleeson, Colette	5Q
Futcher, Hugh	LLL	Gleeson, John	4E, 4L
Fyfer, Valerie	5X	Glenister, Robert	6R
Gable, Christopher	6R	Glenny, Kevin	B
Gabriel, Nancy	FF	Glover, Brian	6T
Galloway, Jack	6M	Glover, Julian	P, 5H
Gamble, Rollo	JJJ	Goacher, Denis	JJ
Gannon, Chris	4S	Goddard, Liza	6G
Garbutt, James	4E	Godfrey, Michael	CC
Gardner, Anthony	JJ	Godfrey, Patrick	AA, FFF
Gardner, Jimmy	D, 4Y	Godfrey, Roy	BB
Gardner, Lynn	7G	Goldblatt, Harold	QQQ
Garfield, David	ZZ, 4Q	Goldie, Michael	K, SS
Garlick, Stephen	6F	Gomez, Carmen	6W
Garth, David	FF, EEE	Good, Maurice	Z
Garvin, John	RR	Goode, Laurie	NNN, 5Q
Gates-Fleming, Peter	5Q, 6B	Gooderson, David	5J
		Goodman, Keith	HH
Gatliff, Frank	YYY	Goodman, Robert	5K
		Goodman, Tim	AA

ACTOR	STORY (production code)	ACTOR	STORY (production code)
Goodman, Walter	4A	Gribble, Dorothy-Rose	M
Gordino, Patricia	GGG	Gridneff, Yuri	5A
Gordon, Arne	N, R	Griffin, David	LLL
Gordon, Colin	KK	Griffiths, Sara	7F
Gordon, Hannah	FF	Grist, Paul	GGG
Gordon, Martin	FFF	Groen, Guy	6E
Goring, Marius	LL	Grover, Ray	MM
Gorman, Pat	VV, ZZ, BBB, DDD, EEE, HHH, LLL, WWW, ZZZ, 4E, 4D, 4M, 4T, 5F, 6T	Grumbar, Murphy	Q, R, LL, KKK, MMM, RRR, QQQ, SSS, XXX
		(also see Murphy, Peter)	
Gosling, Bill	NNN	Guard, Christopher	7J
Gostelow, Gordon	YY	Guard, Dominic	6G
Gough, Michael	Y, 6E	Guest, Keith	5R
Gough, Ronald	4F, 4L	Guest, Michael	S, V
Gower, Martin	6Y	Gupta, Sneh	6P
Graham, Anita	7F	Hagar, Karol	QQQ
Graham, David	B, K, R, T/A, V, Z, 5H	Hagon, Garrick	NNN
		Haig, David	5N
Graham, David J	NNN	Haines, John	DD
Grahame, Leonard	V	Hale, Gareth	7P
Grainger, Gawn	6X	Hale, Georgina	7L
Grant, Robert	WW	Hall, Cheryl	PPP
Grant, Sheila	TT, HHH	Hall, Frederick	6M
Grantham, Les	6P	Hall, James	H, V
Gray, Billy	5K	Hall, William	V
Gray, Dolores	7K	Hallam, John	7Q
Gray, Elspet	6E	Hallett, John	5M
Green, Seymour	4L, 6S	Hallett, Neil	6Y
Greene, Peter	HH	Halliday, Peter	VV, BBB, CCC, PPP, 5H, 7H
Greene, Sarah	6T		
Greenhalgh, Paul	X		
Greenstreet, Mark	7D	Halstead, John	X
Greenwood, John	UU	Hamill, John	5A
		Hammam, Nadia	5W
Greer, Pamela	V	Hammond, Marcus	B
Gregg, John	4C	Hammond, Roger	R, 6F
Gregory, Nigel	K9	Hampton, Richard	5X
Greig, Joe	G	Hampton, Sandra	P
Grellis, Brian	4D, 4T, 6D	Hancock, Prentis	AAA, SSS, 4H, 5A
Grenville, Cynthia	4K		
Grey, David	NN	Hancock, Sheila	7L
Greyn, Clinton	5P, 6W	Handy, Ray	TTT

ACTOR	STORY (production code)	ACTOR	STORY (production code)
Handy, Tony	GG	Henderson, Don	7F
Hanley, Aaron	7M	Henfrey, Janet	7M
Hardy, Mark	6B, 6K, 7K	Henney, Del	6P
Hargrave, Robin	4N	Henry, Norman	AA
Hargreaves, Janet	7J	Henry, Richard	7B
Harley, Michael	4Z	Henry, Walter	DDD, 5H
Harries, Davyd	5F	Herrick, Roy	H, 4Q, 4T
Harrington, Laurence	FFF, QQQ	Herrington, John	V, HHH
		Hewlett, Arthur	5P, 7C
Harrison, Ann	Y	Hewlett, Donald	GGG
Harrison, David	7H	Heymann, Roy	HHH, XXX
Harrison, Joy	XXX	Hibbard, Brian	7F
Harrison, Ruth	B	Hickey, Margaret	PP
Hartley, Norman	S, VV	Hicks, John	TT, GGG
Hartnell, William	A-DD, RRR	High, Bernard G	QQ, 4F
Harvey, John	BB, JJ	Highmore, Edward	6Q
Harvey, Keith	6R	Hill, Adrienne	U-V
Harvey, Malcolm	6E	Hill, Daniel	5M
Harvey, Max	6E	Hill, Jacqueline	A-R, 5Q
Harwood, Tony	MM, NN, OO, XX, ZZ, CCC	Hill, Lesley	B
		Hill, Peter	KKK
Haswell, James	CCC	Hillier, Paul	7C
Hawkes, Ridgewell	6S	Hillyard, Eric	JJJ
Hawkins, Michael	QQQ	Hines, Frazer	FF-ZZ, 6K, 6W
Hawkins, Peter	B, K, Q, R, T/A, V, DD, EE, HH, LL, MM, SS		
		Hines, Ian	UU
		Hinsliff, Geoffrey	4X, 5K
		Hobbs, Nick	EEE, FFF, GGG, MMM, YYY, 4C
Hawksley, Brian	6A		
Hawthorne, Denys	7C		
Hawtrey, Nicholas	EE		
Hayes, Hugh	6C	Hobson, Meriel	K
Hayman, Damaris	JJJ	Hodiak, Keith	6K
Haywood, Alan	U	Hogan, John	MM, NN
Headington Quarry Men, The	JJJ	Hogg, Ian	7Q
		Holder, Roy	6R
		Holland, John	5Q
Healey, Mary	7L	Holland, Tony	AA
Heap, Alan	7J	Holley, Bernard	MM, GGG
Heard, Daphne	4X	Hollingsworth, Dean	6Y, 7J
Heath, Mark	HH		
Heesom, Stephanie	X	Hollis, John	NNN
Heggie, Caron	6A	Holloway, Ann	6B
Heiner, Thomasine	BBB	Holloway, Julian	7P
Helsby, Eileen	X	Holmes, Chris	6D
		Holmes, Jerry	SS

ACTOR	STORY (production code)	ACTOR	STORY (production code)
Holmes, Peter	GGG	Jack, Stephen	EEE
Holt, Derek	6D	Jackson, Barry	M, T, T/A, 5F
Hooper, Lewis	5Q	Jackson, Inigo	X
Hopkin, Carole	4W	Jackson, James	5R
Hornery, Bob	5L	Jackson, Michael J	6J
Horrigan, Billy	FFF, TTT	Jackson, Nancie	BBB
Horsfall, Bernard	UU, ZZ, SSS, 4P	Jacobs, Anthony	Z
		Jacobs, Brian	4C
Horton, Timothy	UU	Jacombs, Roger	QQ
Houston, Glyn	4N, 6M	Jaeger, Frederick	AA, 4H, 4T
How, Jane	SSS	James, Alan	E
Howard, Ben	TTT	James, David	V
Howard, Sam	7C	James, Emrys	5P
Howe, Catherine	GG	James, Godfrey	4Y
Howell, Peter	NNN	James, Keith	DDD
Hubay, Stephen	ZZ	James, Polly	6M
Huby, Nina	JJ	James, Rick	NNN
Hughes, Colin	L	James, Robert	EE, 4M
Hughes, Geoffrey	7C	James, Sarah	6X
Hughes, Nerys	5Y	Jameson, Louise	4Q-4Z
Hulley, Annie	7L	Jarvis, Frank	BB, 4Y, 5E
Humphreys, Nigel	6L	Jarvis, Martin	N, WWW, 6V
Hunt, Caroline	H, QQQ	Jason, Neville	5D
Hunt, Derek	6A	Jayne, Keith	6M
Hunt, Gareth	ZZZ	Jayston, Michael	7A-7C
Hunter, Robert	H	Jeavons, Colin	GG, K9
Hunter, Russell	4R	Jeffrey, Peter	JJ, 5D
Huntley, Martyn	G, K, Z	Jeffries, Michael	6P, 6T
Hurndall, Richard	6K	Jenkins, Clare	AA, SS, ZZ
Hurndell, William	Z	Jenkins, Tony	FFF
Hurst, Christopher	5V	Jenn, Stephen	5K
Hutchinson, Bill	ZZ	Jennings, Ernest	M
Hutton, Marcus	7M	Jerome, Roger	JJ
Ikeda, O	D	Jerricho, Paul	6E, 6K
Ilkley, William	6X	Jessup, Reginald	W, 4Z
Ingham, Barrie	U	Jewell, Robert	B, K, N, R, T/A, V, EE, JJ, LL, ZZ
Inman, Dione	6S		
Innocent, Harold	7L		
Ireson, Richard	UU, WW	Jezek, Robert	7N
Isaac, Jeffrey	V	John, Caroline	AAA-DDD, 6K
Ismay, Steven	LLL, NNN, XXX, 6B		
		John, David	7P
		John, Leee	6H
Ives, Kenneth	TT	John, Margaret	RR
Ives-Cameron, Elaine	5C	John, Souska	5Z

ACTOR	STORY (production code)	ACTOR	STORY (production code)
Johns, Alan	MM	Kelly, Steve	5R, 6L
Johns, Andrew	4E	Kelly, Tom	4Q, 4W, 4Z
Johns, Milton	PP, 4J, 4Z	Kelsey, Edward	M, EE, 5G
Johns, Nigel	BBB	Kemp, Gypsie	KKK
Johns, Stratford	5W	Kempner, Brenda	7Q
Johnson, Nigel	6X	Kendall, Cavan	U
Johnson, Noel	GG, WWW	Kendall, Kenneth	BB
Johnson, Rosemary	J	Kennedy, Richie	7H
Johnson, Sidney	NNN	Kennelly, Juba	W
Jones, Dudley	DD	Kenny, Joann	7M
Jones, Ellis	AAA	Kenton, William	6K
Jones, Emrys	UU	Kerley, Richard	MM, NN
Jones, Emyr Morris	6K	Kerr, Bill	PP
		Keyes, Karol	JJ
Jones, Glyn	4B	Khalil, Ahmed	6A
Jones, Haydn	EEE, FFF	Khursandi, Hedi	6N
Jones, Mark	4L	Kilgarriff, Michael	MM, QQQ, 4A, 6T
Jones, Melville	OOO, 4D		
Jones, Myrddin	6K	Kincaid, David	5S
Jones, Norman	NN, BBB, 4M	Kinder, David	7F
Jones, Roger	OO	King, Jeremy	QQ
Joseph, Carley	7F	King, Martin	EE
Josephs, Elroy	CC	King, Richard	VV
Joss, Barbara	N	King, Steve	GGG
Joyce, David	KKK	Kinghorn, Barbara	6R
Joyce, John	JJJ	Klauber, Gertan	M, JJ
Judd, Alan	K	Kneller, Clive	6H
Judge, Pat	6P	Knight, Esmond	YY
Jury, Chris	7J	Knight, Ray	4H, 5Q, 5V, 6Q
Justice, Barry	W		
Justice, Brian	LLL, TTT	Knight, Sheila	DD
Kane, John	ZZZ	Knott, John	DD
Kane, Richard	EE	Konyils, Chris	P
Kane, Stephen	5Q	Korff, David	5K, 5N
Kavanagh, Christine	6Y	Kum, Kristopher	FFF
		Kurakin, Adam	5B
Kay, Bernard	K, P, KK, HHH	Kwouk, Burt	5W
		La Bassiere, Robert	WW
Kaye, Jimmy	T		
Kaye, Stubby	7F	Lack, Simon	FFF, 5D
Keating, Michael	4W	Ladkin, Michael	KK
Keegan, Robert	5A	Laing, John	5Q
Keller, Derek	7H	Laird, Jenny	ZZZ
Kells, Janie	4K	Laird, Peter	SS
Kelly, David Blake	R, CC	Laird, Trevor	7B

ACTOR	STORY (production code)	ACTOR	STORY (production code)
Lake, Alan	4Y	Leigh-Hunt, Ronald	XX, 4D
Lambden, Tony	M	Lemkow, Tutte	D, P, U
Lambert, Annie	5W	Lennie, Angus	OO, 4F
Lambert, Nigel	5N	Lenska, Rula	6P
Lamont, Duncan	XXX	Leopold, Malcolm	V
Landen, Dinsdale	7M	Lester, Rick	KKK, QQQ
Lane, Andrew	5N	Levene, John	QQ, VV, ZZ, CCC-GGG, JJJ, KKK, OOO, RRR, TTT, WWW, ZZZ, 4A, 4F, 4J
Lane, Jackie	W-BB		
Lane, Maureen	JJ		
Lane, Mike Lee	4H		
Lang, Howard	A		
Lang, Tony	RRR		
Langford, Bonnie	7C-7F		
Langley, Martin	UU		
Langtry, Peter	4R	Levent, Hus	6X
Lankesheer, Robert	P	Lever, Reg	Y
Latham, Philip	6K	Lewis, Rhoda	5P
Laurimore, Jon	4M	Lill, Denis	4X, 6M
Lavender, Ray	6D	Lim, Pik-Sen	FFF
Lavers, Paul	5D	Lindberg, Jakob	6J
Law, John	H	Lindon, Delia	Y
Lawes, Symond	7K	Lindsay, Kevin	UUU, ZZZ, 4B
Lawrence, Barney	5R, 6B, 6C, 6D	Lindsay, William	5P
Lawrence, Ken	H	Line, John	HHH
Lawrence, Peter	D	Linstead, Alec	JJJ, 4A, 6Z
Lawrence, Trevor	WWW	Lister, Penny	4S
Layton, George	YY	Liston, Ian	5F
Le Touzel, Sylvestra	UU	Little, George	P
		Livesey, John	ZZ
Le White, Jack	V	Llewellyn, Raymond	NN
Leader, Michael	5X		
Leake, Barbara	EEE	Lloyd, Hugh	7F
Leaman, Graham	JJ, RR, XX, HHH, RRR	Lloyd, Judith	4S
		Lloyd, Rosalind	5B
Leclere, Pat	KK	Locke, Philip	5W
Lee, George	AAA, OOO	Lockwood, Preston	6D
Lee, John	B	Lodge, Andrew	AA
Lee, Penelope	6Z	Lodge, Terence	JJ, PPP, ZZZ
Lee, Ronald	HH, MM	Loft, Barbara	UU
Leech, Richard	4W	Logan, Crawford	5Q
Leeson, John	4T-5F, 5N-5S, K9, 6K, 7H	London, Debbie Lee	GGG
		Lonnen, Ray	QQQ
Legree, Simon	OOO	Lonsdale, Jennifer	5K
Lehmann, Beatrix	5C	Lord, John	QQ, CCC

ACTOR	STORY (production code)	ACTOR	STORY (production code)
Lord, Tony	4D	Mantle, Peter	4E
Lucas, Mike	CC	Maranne, Andre	HH
Lucas, Victor	4Q	Marcell, Joseph	7H
Lucas, William	6N	March, David G	GGG
Luckham, Cyril	5A, 6H	Marcus, James	WWW, 4Y
Luckham, Robert	EE	Markham, Petra	P
Lucy, Thomas	6T	Marks, Chris	5Q
Ludlow, Kathryn	7J	Marley, Patrick	H
Lund, Hugh	N, 4J	Marlowe, Fernanda	FFF, GGG
Luxton, Jon	U	Marlowe, William	FFF, 4D
Lye, Reg	PP	Marriott, Sylvia	5Q
Lynch, Alfred	7M	Marsden, Robert	R
Lynch, Michael	ZZ, 4E	Marsh, Jean	P, V, 7N
Lynch-Blosse, Bridget	6Z	Marshall-Fisher, Ian	6K, 6T
Lynn, James	U	Marshe, Sheena	Z
Lynton, Maggie	6T	Martell, Gillian	K9
Lyons, Bill	PP	Marter, Ian	PPP, 4A-4F, 4J
MacDonnell, Chris	7G		
Machin, Steven	V	Martin, Bernard	CCC
Macintosh, Alex	KKK	Martin, Derek	4X
Mack, Jimmy	GG	Martin, Hugh	4F, 6V
Mack, Johnnie	6K	Martin, Jessica	7J
Mackay, Angus	4P, 6F	Martin, John Scott	N, R, T/A, V,
Mackay, Fulton	BBB		EE, LL, HHH,
Mackenzie, Ian	7G		KKK, NNN,
Mackintosh, Steven	6Y		RRR, QQQ,
			SSS, TTT,
Macready, Roy	4W		XXX, 4A, 4E,
Maddern, Victor	RR		4K, 4T, 6K,
Madoc, Philip	WW, ZZ, 4K, 5E		6P, 6Z, 7H
		Martin, Marina	T
Maguire, Leonard	5R	Martin, Michelle	7P
Maguire, Oliver	5A	Martin, Trevor	ZZ
Mahoney, Louis	QQQ, 4H	Mason, Alan	BBB
Malcolm, Michael	6N	Mason, Eric	FFF, LLL
Malikyan, Kevork	SS	Mason, Stanley	HHH, JJJ
Malin, Bill	7K	Masterman, David	4L
Mallard, Grahame	5E	Masters, Christopher	4C
Manley, Jerry	7C		
Manning, Katy	EEE-TTT	Mather, Dibbs	PP
Mansell, Ronald	TT	Mathews, Richard	6K
Manser, Kevin	B, K, N, R, T/A, V, EE	Matthews, Bill	BBB, FFF
		Matthews, Christopher	DD
Manship, Deborah	7J		

92

ACTOR	STORY (production code)	ACTOR	STORY (production code)
Matthews, MJ	V	McStay, Michael	4L
Matthews, Martin	5D	Meadows, Leslie	7F, 7G
Maxim, John	R	Meilen, Bill	V
Maxwell, James	4Y	Melbourne, David	KKK
May, Jack	YY	Melford, Jack	U
Maybank, Leon	HH, KKK	Melia, Michael	5X
Mayes, Richard	RR	Mellor, James	SS, NNN
Maynard, Patricia	4A	Menzies, Frank	KKK
Mayne, Belinda	7F	Meredith, Stephen	6K
Mayock, Peter	4G, 4P	Merrison, Clive	MM, 7E
McAlister, David	5C	Merton, Zienia	D
McArdle, Nicholas	5C	Mervyn, William	BB
McCarthy, Denis	HH	Messaline, Peter	KKK
McCarthy, Henry	AAA	Michael, Ralph	5B
McCarthy, Neil	FFF, 5E	Middleton, Guy	FF
McClaren, Ian	7F	Miles, Peter	BBB, WWW, 4E
McClure, James	6H		
McColl, Billy	7A	Miles-Thomas, Nigel	7G
McConnochie, Rhys	PP		
McCormack, Colin	4W	Miller, Brian	6D, 6P, 7H
McCoy, Sylvester	7D–7P	Miller, Martin	D
McCracken, Jenny	PPP	Miller, Michael	S
McCulloch, Ian	6L	Mills, Adrian	5Y
McCulloch, Keff	7F	Mills, Bob	6D
McDermott, Brian	6C	Mills, Eric	FF
McEwan, Tony	ZZ, 4H	Mills, Frank	EEE
McFarlane, Jean	KKK	Mills, Madeleine	WW
McGeagh, Stanley	HHH, LLL	Mills, Royce	6P, 6Z, 7H
McGough, Jessica	7F	Milne, Gareth	6A
McGough, Philip	6P	Milner, Patrick	JJJ
McGowan, Stan	4Z	Milner, Roger	5Y
McGrath, Jay	6W	Milward, Charles	6K
McGuire, Jack	6V	Minnice, Roger	GGG
McGuire, Lloyd	4Q	Minster, Hilary	SSS, 4E
McGuirk, William	PP	Mitchell, Allan	AAA
McKail, David	4S	Mitchell, Bill	QQQ
McKenna, TP	7J	Mitchell, Norman	V
McKenzie, Diane	P	Mitchell, Scott	7K
McKenzie, Mitzi	TTT	Mitchley, Richard	7F
McKillop, Don	JJJ	Molineaux, Cheryl	CCC
McLinden, Dursley	7H	Molloy, Terry	6P, 6T, 6Z, 7H
McManus, Jim	4T	Monast, Fernando	6W
McNally, Kevin	6S	Monk, Conrad	V
McNeff, Richard	K	Monro, Joanna	ZZZ
		Montague, Roy	5N

93

ACTOR	STORY (production code)	ACTOR	STORY (production code)
Moore, Kenton	4C	Murray, James	5C
Moore, Wanda	OOO	Murtagh, Raymond	6N
Morell, Andre	W	Murzynowski, Jan	5K
Moreno, Juan	CCC	Muscat, Angelo	T
Morgan, Charles	NN, 4Z	Musetti, Valentino	P
Morgan, Richardson	QQ, 4C	Myers, Justin	7F
		Myers, Stuart	GGG
Morley, Donald	H	Nagy, Stephen	5Q
Morley, Steve	6B	Nakara, Ranjit	5Q
Morris, Clinton	GGG	Napier-Brown, Michael	ZZ
Morris, Geoffrey	ZZZ		
Morris, Jim	6A	Naylor, Richard	6K
Morris, Johnathon	6D	Neal, David	6R
Morris, Mary	5Y	Neame, Christopher	5M
Morris, Maureen	ZZZ		
Morris, Wolfe	NN	Neil, Martin	6L
Morton, Clive	LLL	Neill, Jay	4M, 4T, 4Y
Morton, Hugh	XX	Nesbitt, Derren	D
Mosley, Bryan	V	Nettheim, David	PP
Moss, Antonia	HHH	Nettleton, John	7Q
Moss, Bill	K	Neve, Philip	7L
Mothle, Ernest	7K	Newall, Arthur	G
Mount, Peggy	7J	Newark, Derek	A, DDD
Mowbray, Gabrielle	4K	Newby, Ricky	KKK, NNN, RRR
Muir, James	5C, 5K, 5M, 5N, 5Q, 6A		
		Newell, Patrick	4J
Mulholland, Declan	LLL, 5D	Newman, John	BBB
		Newman, Kate	X
Mullins, Bartlett	G	Newth, Jonathan	4Y
Muncaster, Martin	6G	Nichol, David	4Q
Mundell, Michael	4Z	Nicol, Madalena	KK
Mungarvan, Mike	NNN, 5C, 5J, 6P, 7C	Noble, Barry	HH
		Nolan, Brian	LLL
Munro, Tim	5G, 6G	Norgate, Clifford	5L, 5N
Munroe, Carmen	PP	Norman, Elizabeth	4T
Munroe, Ian	5C	Normington, John	6R, 7L
Murcott, Derek	OOO	Northover, Miles	WW
Murphy, Aidan	OOO	Nott, Roger	6S
Murphy, Gerard	7K	Novak, Raymond	P
Murphy, Glen	7A	O'Brien, Maureen	L-U
Murphy, June	RR, LLL	O'Connell, Joseph	QQ
Murphy, Peter	B, K	O'Connell, Maurice	6N
(also see Grumbar, Murphy)			
		O'Connell, Patrick	K
Murray, Barbara	6A	O'Leary, Tom	EEE

94

ACTOR	STORY (production code)	ACTOR	STORY (production code)
O'Mara, Kate	6X, 7D	Peake, Michael	M
O'Neil, Colette	6D	Pearce, Jacqueline	6W
Oates, Chubby	ZZZ	Pearce, Roy	KK, ZZ,
Ogwen, John	6Z		NNN, 4X
Oliver, Roland	5T	Peck, Brian	YY
Oliver, Sean	7P	Pedro, Illarrio Bisi	5W
Organ, Stuart	7G	Peel, Edward	7G
Orme, Richard	RRR	Pegge, Edmund	4T
Orrell, Brian	6T, 7K	Pelmear, Donald	UUU
Osborn, Amy	7F	Pemberton, Charles	MM, ZZ
Osborne, Michael	5L	Pemberton, Victor	HH
Osoba, Tony	5J, 7G	Pendrell, Nicolette	TT
Ould, Dave	6L, 7K	Penhaligon, Susan	OOO
Ould, John	7K	Pennell, Nicholas	HHH
Owen, Christopher	5Q	Perrie, William	6L, 7C
Owen, Glyn	5E	Perry, Morris	HHH
Owens, John	JJJ	Pertwee, Jon	AAA–ZZZ, 6K
Oxenford, Daphne	7G	Peters, Annette	5K
Oxley, Stephen	K9	Peters, Luan	QQQ
Pace, Norman	7P	Peters, Steve	XX, YY, CCC
Packer, Tina	QQ	Petersen, Maggie	5K
Padbury, Wendy	SS–ZZ, 6K	Phibbs, Giles	G
Padden, Bernard	5R	Phillips, Eden	5K
Padmore, Chris	6J	Phillips, Edward	HH
Page, June	5R	Phillips, Paul	JJ
Paine, Vanessa	6A	Phillips, Robin	E
Pajo, Louise	XX	Philpin, Harriet	4E
Palfrey, Yolande	7C	Pickering, Donald	E, KK, 7D
Palmer, Denys	RRR	Pickering, Vincent	5S
Palmer, Geoffrey	BBB, NNN	Pickess, Charles	EEE
Palmer, Gregg	DD, ZZ	Pickup, Ronald	H
Palmer, Valentine	KKK	Pidgeon, Frances	4N
Paris, Judith	4N	Pigott-Smith, Tim	GGG, 4M
Parsons, Alibe	7B	Pilleau, Margaret	5C
Parsons, Nicholas	7M	Pinder, Michael	ZZZ
Pastell, George	MM	Pine, Courtney	7K
Pastell, Jean	V	Pinnell, Ron	HH
Patrick, Kay	M, AA	Pirie, Christine	UU
Pattenden, Sian	6F	Pitt, Gordon	UUU
Patison, Roy	QQQ, 4N	Pitt, Ingrid	OOO, 6L
Paul, Anthony	T	Pitt, Jack	N, R, V
Paul, Brigit	KK	Plant, Darren	OOO
Payne, Laurence	Z, 5N, 6W	Plaskitt, Nigel	5A
Peach, Mary	PP	Plytas, Steve	DD
Peacock, Daniel	7J	Pokol, Steve	B

ACTOR	STORY (production code)	ACTOR	STORY (production code)
Polan, Linda	K9	Rawle, Jeff	6N
Pollitt, Clyde	ZZ, RRR	Ray, Philip	XX
Pollitt, Derek	QQ, BBB, 5M	Raymond, Al	R
Pollon, Christine	4Y	Raynham, Tim	6W
Pooley, Olaf	DDD	Read, Martyn	7K
Pope, David John	7L	Reddington, Ian	7J
Pope, Roger	6T	Redgrave, Dave	5G
Potter, Martin	6G	Rees, Hubert	RR, ZZ, 4L
Poupee, Pepi	T	Rees, John	QQQ
Powell, Gregory	OOO	Rees, Llewellyn	4P
Pratt, Peter	4P	Reeves, Richard	4E
Pravda, George	PP, NNN, 4P	Reford, Fred	6D
Preece, Tim	SSS	Reid, Adrian	7K
Prendergast, Liam	5T	Reid, Anne	7M
Price, Brendan	4Q	Reid, Beryl	6B
Price, Stanley	QQQ	Reid, Gordon	WWW
Prince, Sarah	5Y	Reid, Michael	4M
Prior, Patricia	RRR	Reid, Sheila	6V
Pritchard, Reg	P, V	Reynolds, Christopher	UU
Proctor, Ewan	BB		
Proudfoot, Brian	M	Reynolds, David	UU
Prowse, Dave	OOO	Reynolds, Harriet	5N
Pulford, Sue	UU	Reynolds, Linda	JJ
Pulman, Cory	7M	Reynolds, Mary	7K
Purcell, David	4N	Reynolds, Tommy	T, EEE
Purcell, Roy	FFF, RRR	Rich, Ronald	S, T/A
Purchase, Bruce	5B	Richards, Aubrey	MM
Purves, Peter	R, R-AA	Richardson, Gordon	BBB
Pyott, Keith	F		
Quarmby, John	K9	Richardson, James	6Y
Quick, Maurice	4P	Riches, Alan	6K
Quinn, Patricia	7G	Richfield, Edwin	LLL, 6S
Race, Maureen	FFF	Ridge, Veronica	4K
Rae, Danny	JJ	Ridler, Anne	SS
Rae, Dorota	7N	Rigby, Graham	K
Raistrick, George	KKK	Rigg, Carl	5E
Ramanee, Sakuntala	7P	Righty, Geoff	GGG
		Rimkus, Stevan	7M
Ranchev, Jeremy	4R	Rimmer, Shane	Z
Randall, Walter	F, P, V, VV, DDD, ZZZ	Ringham, John	F, CC, HHH
		Ritchie, Libby	4N
Rathborne, Michael	BB	Robbie, Christopher	UU, 4D
Rattray, Iain	5P	Robbins, Michael	5X
Raven, John	AA	Roberts, Ivor	4E

ACTOR	STORY (production code)	ACTOR	STORY (production code)
Roberts, Peter	5K	Sadler, Dee	7J
Robertson, Andrew	5B	Sadler, Paul	7J
Robertson, Annette	W	Sadler, Philip	7J
Robertson, Robert	CCC	Salem, Pamela	4Q, 4R, 7H
Robinson, Rex	RRR, YYY, 4N	Sallis, Peter	OO
		Salmins, Ralph	7F
Rodgers, Ilona	G	Salter, Ivor	Q, U, 6A
Rodigan, David	7A	Sammarco, Gian	7J
Roe, Douglas	GGG	Sanders, Damon	NNN
Roeves, Maurice	6R	Sanders, Peter	Q
Roger, Clive	GGG	Sansby, Lionel	5K, 5M
Rogers, Malcolm	R, V	Santo, Joe	NNN
Rogers, Tania	4R	Sarony, Paul	V
Rolfe, John	BB, HH, TTT	Saul, Christopher	6M
Rollason, Jon	QQ	Saul, Nitza	6L
Romane, George	W	Savident, John	5X
Rose, Clifford	5S	Savile, David	ZZ, GGG, 6K
Ross, Alec	LL	Saxon, James	6W
Ross, Joanna	CCC	Sayle, Alexei	6Z
Ross, Mark	V	Saynor, Charles	FFF
Rossini, Ricco	7J	Saynor, Ian	5F
Rossini, Jeanette	B	Scammell, Roy	CCC, DDD
Roubicek, George	MM	Schell, Catherine	5H
Rouse, Simon	5Y	Schlesinger, Katharine	7Q
Rowbottom, Jo	LL	Schofield, Katharine	E
Rowe, Alan	HH, UUU, 4V, 5R	Schofield, Leslie	ZZ, 4Q
Rowland, Rex	LLL	Schrecker, Frederick	QQ
Rowlands, Anthony	4T	Schwartz, Stefan	7N
Rowlands, David	4W	Scoggo, Tony	7C
Roy, Deep	4S	Scott, Clive	FFF
Roy, Peter	FFF, 4N, 5V	Scott, Jonina	4W
Ruddock, Pamela	5K	Scott, Peter Robert	6Y
Ruskin, Sheila	5T	Scott, Robin	HH
Russell, Peter	S	Scott, Steven	EE
Russell, Robert	EE, 4F	Scott, Tim	7F, 7L
Russell, William	A–R	Scully, Terry	XX
Rutherford, Peter	4B	Seager, Richard	4R
Ryan, Christopher	7B	Sears, Ian	K9
Ryan, Hilary	4Z	Seaton, Derek	4P
Ryan, Philip	UU, DDD	Seed, Paul	5A
Ryecart, Patrick	7B	Seeger, Kenneth	MM
Sabin, Alec	6B	Segal, John	7D
Sachs, Leonard	W, 6E		

ACTOR	STORY (production code)	ACTOR	STORY (production code)
Segal, Zohra	P	Simpson, Graham	4X
Seiler, Neil	LLL, XXX	Sims, Bert	QQ
Selby, Tony	7A, 7C, 7G	Sims, Joan	7A
Selway, George	KK	Siner, Guy	4E
Selway, Kevin	4G	Singer, Campbell	Y
Selwyn, Maurice	WW	Skelton, Roy	X, DD, LL,
Sesta, Hilary	6D		OO, SS, WW,
Setna, Renu	4N		HHH, SSS,
Seton, Frank	LLL		TTT, 4E, 4J,
Sewell, George	7H		4N, 5J, 6K,
Shaban, Nabil	6V, 7B		6Z, 7H
Shaps, Cyril	MM, CCC,	Skilbeck, Alison	6N
	ZZZ, 5D	Skinner, Keith	6V
Sharma, Madhav	QQQ	Skipper, Susan	5F
Sharp, Richard D	7L	Sladen, Elisabeth	UUU-4N, K9,
Shaw, Bronson	WW		6K
Shaw, Richard	Q, QQQ, 4Y	Slater, Derrick	XX
Shaw, Simon	5Q	Slater, Simon	7C
Shaw, Tessa	AAA	Slavid, John	W, BB
Sheard, Michael	X, FFF, 4G,	Sleigh, William	6P
	4T, 5Z, 7H	Smart, Patsy	4S
Shearer, William	T	Smart, Steve	GGG
Sheldon, Douglas	V	Smee, Derek	AAA
Shelley, Barbara	6Q	Smith, Andrew	6R
Shelley, Paul	5W	Smith, Barrie	6D
Shelton, Shane	DD	Smith, Eric	B
Sheridan, Astra	7E	Smith, Ernest	W
Sheridan, Dinah	6K	Smith, Gai	4Z
Sheridan, Tom	L	Smith, Gary	TT
Sherrier, Julian	V	Smith, Iain	AAA
Sherringham, Robin	5L	Smith, Neville	H
		Smith, Nicholas	K
Sherwin, Jane	ZZ	Smith, Oliver	6S
Sherwood, Jonathan	NNN	Smith, Roderick	4T
		Smith, Stephen	6R
Sibbald, Tony	4F	Snell, James	JJJ
Sibley, David	5B	Soans, Robin	5T
Sidaway, Robert	AA, VV	Solon, Ewen	AA, 4H
Silva, Adele	7P	Sommer, Eddie	NNN, 5Q
Silvera, Carmen	Y, WWW	Sorrel, Viviane	P
Simeon, David	DDD, JJJ	Sotiris, Byron	6H
Simmonds, Carolyn Mary	6B	Spaull, Colin	6Z
		Speed, Stephen	6N
Simons, Neville	CCC	Spencer, Gladys	4C
Simons, William	4W	Spencer, Roy	X, RR

ACTOR	STORY (production code)	ACTOR	STORY (production code)
Spenser, David	NN	Summerton, Michael	B
Spice, Michael	4K, 4S	Sumpter, Donald	SS, LLL
Spight, Hugh	7H	Suthern, Derek	4N, 5K, 5M, 5V
Spradbury, John	VV		
Spriggs, Elizabeth	7E	Sutton, Sarah	5T-6G, 6R
Squire, Robin	JJJ, 5V	Sutton, Simon	6Q
Squire, William	5F	Swift, Clive	6Z
St Clair, Gordon	MMM	Swift, Harry	BBB
St John Hacker, Trevor	5L	Swinscoe, Steve	7L
Staines, Andrew	PP, EEE, PPP, ZZZ	Sydney, Derek	M
		Symonds, Peter	4F
Stampe, Will	W	Syms, Sylvia	7Q
Stamper, Henry	PP	Tablian, Vik	4G
Stanbury, Jacqueline	UUU	Tai, Ling	7N
		Talbot, Alan	6X
Stanley, Norman	EEE	Talbot, Ian	BBB, 5N
Stanton, Barry	6S	Tallents, John	6K
Stanton, Peter	ZZ	Tamm, Mary	5A-5F
Staples, Ian	6R	Tang, Basil	D, FFF
Stark, Douglas	4H	Tann, Paul	FFF
Starr, Tony	SSS, 5J, 6P, 6Z, 7H	Tarff, Bob	6V
		Tarran, Jack	W
Steele, Richard	ZZ, BBB, 6X	Taylor, Colin	6R
Stenson, Peter	E	Taylor, Gerald	B, K, N, R, T/A, V, BB, EE, GG, LL, JJJ, YYY
Stephens, PG	GG		
Stephens, Peter	Y, GG		
Sterne, Gordon	CCC		
Stevens, Mike	EEE	Taylor, Malcolm	OO
Stewart, Jeffrey	5Y	Taylor, Martin	NNN, WWW
Stewart, Roy	MM, EEE	Taylor, Shirin	5C, 7G
Stewart, Salvin	Q	Teale, Owen	6V
Stirling, Pamela	5H	Telfer, David	5G
Stock, Nigel	6C	Tendeter, Stacey	4Y
Stoney, Kevin	V, VV, 4D	Terris, Malcolm	TT, 5L
Stothard, Gordon	QQ, SS, FFF	Then, Tony	4S
Straker, Mark	6B	Thomas, Colin	4Q
Straker, Peter	5J	Thomas, Henley	E
Stratton, John	6W	Thomas, Margot	M
Strickson, Mark	6F-6Q, 6R	Thomas, Nina	YYY
Stride, Sebastian	5K	Thomas, Peter	AA
Strong, David	5M	Thomas, Talfryn	AAA, TTT
Stuart, John	L	Thomas, William	7H
Summer, David	5X	Thompson Hill, Nick	NNN
Summerford, Barry	4N, 5A		

ACTOR	STORY (production code)	ACTOR	STORY (production code)
Thompson, Eric	W	Turner, Linsey	6P
Thompson, Ian	N, R	Turner, Michael	SS
Thompson, Peter	VV, DDD	Tyler, Reg	K
Thorne, Stephen	JJJ, RRR, QQQ, 4N	Tyllson, Ken	G, R, LL
Thornett, Kenneth	V	Underdown, Edward	5Q
Thornhill, James	VV	Valla, David	ZZ
Thornton, Peter	VV	Van Der Burgh, Margot	F, 5T
Tickner, Royston	V, LLL	Van Dissel, Peter	5X
Tierney, Malcolm	7C	Vaughan, Brian	LLL
Tillinger, John	W	Ventham, Wanda	KK, 4X, 7D
Tilvern, Alan	J	Verini, Desmond	KKK
Tipton, Norman	4Y	Verner, Anthony	E
Tirard, Ann	M, 5A	Verney, Adam	PP
Todd, Geoffrey	KKK	Villiers, Christopher	6J
Todd, Richard	5Y	Voss, Philip	D, TT
Tomany, Paul	7N	Vowles, Robert	5S
Tomasin, Jenny	6Z	Wade, Barry	FFF
Tontoh, Frank	7K	Wade, Charles	D
Toone, Geoffrey	MMM	Wain, Gerry	UU
Topham, Paula	V	Wale, Stephen	6T
Tordoff, John	HHH	Wales, Gordon	E
Torres, Mike	NNN	Walker, Fiona	E, 7K
Tourell, Andrew	6A	Walker, Gloria	GGG
Tovey, George	4G	Walker, Lillias	4F
Towb, Harry	XX, EEE	Walker, Michael	GGG, OOO
Town, Cy	RRR, QQQ, SSS, XXX, 4E, 5J, 6P, 6Z, 7H, 7L, 7M	Walker, Peter	H
		Walker, Rudolph	ZZ
		Walker, Timothy	7A
Townsend, Primi	5B	Wall, Tony	H
Tranchell, Christopher	W, KK, 4Z	Waller, Kenneth	4T
Treves, Frederick	5Q	Wallis, Alec	LLL, 4D
Trickett, Raymond	7M	Walmsley, Peter	6F
Trolley, Leonard	KK	Walsh, Terry	EEE, LLL, NNN, OOO, TTT, WWW, XXX, YYY, ZZZ, 4B, 5E, 5G
Troughton, David	ZZ, MMM		
Troughton, Patrick	EE-ZZ, RRR, 6K, 6W		
Troy, Alan	6V		
Tucker, Alan	SSS		
Tuddenham, Peter	4C, 4M, 7D	Walshe, Peter	4B, 4M
Tudor Owen, Sion	7A	Walters, Hugh	R, 4P, 6Z
Tull, Patrick	WW	Walters, Jules	6L
Tuohy, Dermot	EEE	Walters, Matthew	FFF

ACTOR	STORY (production code)	ACTOR	STORY (production code)
Ward, Barbara	7C	Westwell, Raymond	FFF
Ward, Lalla	5F–5S, 6K	Wetherell, Virginia	B
Ward, Tara	6L	Wheatley, Alan	B
Ward, Tracy Louise	6Y	Whincup, Mark	6K
Ware, Derek	P, R, V, CC, DDD, GGG	Whitaker, Peter	KK, XX
		Whitby, Martyn	6X
Waring, Derek	5Z	White, Alan	DD
Waring, George	OO	White, Frances	U
Warman, Colin	QQ	White, Kevin	6X
Warnecke, Gordon	7B	Whitehead, Reg	DD, HH, MM, NN
Warwick, David	5B		
Warwick, Edmund	E, R	Whiteman, Dolore	5V
Warwick, James	6B	Whitestone, Geoff	5Q
Waterhouse, Matthew	5R–6B, 6R	Whitfield, Gess	7C
		Whitsun-Jones, Paul	CC, NNN
Waters, Harry	5S		
Watling, Deborah	LL–RR, SS	Whittaker, Stephen	QQ
Watling, Jack	NN, QQ	Whittingham, Christopher	6B
Watson, Gary	LL		
Watson, Kenneth	SS	Whylie, Dwight	BB
Watson, Malcolm	TT	Wickham, Jeffry	H
Watson, Moray	6A	Wickham, Steve	6S
Watson, Ralph	QQ, YYY, 4V	Wightman, Bruce	P, V, 4F
Watson, Stephen	5R	Wild, Nigel	7H
Watson, Tom	GG	Wilde, Bill	QQQ
Way, Eileen	A, 5G	Wilde, David	6A
Wayne, Jeff	5X, 6B	Wilkin, Jeremy	4D
Weaver, Rachael	6G	Wilkinson, Nick	5A
Webb, Antony	AAA	Williams, Francis	FFF
Webb, David	HHH	Williams, Irela	6T
Webb, Esmond	ZZ	Williams, Lloyd	6K
Webb, Jacki	7D	Williams, Ramsay	QQQ
Webb, Laurie	RRR	Williams, Simon	7H
Webster, Mitzi	HHH	Williams, Wendy	4C
Weedon, Martin	7C	Willis, Jerome	TTT
Weekes, Leslie	FFF	Willis, Richard	5R
Weisener, Bill	UU	Willis, Sonnie	HH
Welch, Peter	FF, 4J	Wills, Anneke	BB–KK
Wells, Alan	HH	Wills, John	HH
Wells, Bruce	DD, KKK	Wilsher, Barry	KK
Wentworth, Robin	JJJ	Wilson, Freddie	TT, ZZ
West, Neil	5X	Wilson, Hamish	UU
Weston, David	W, 5S	Wilson, John	6S
Weston, Graham	ZZ, 4H	Wilson, Jodie	7F

ACTOR	STORY (production code)	ACTOR	STORY (production code)
Wilson, Neil	AAA	Wylie, Frank	5Z
Wilson, Tracey	7F	Wyngarde, Peter	6Q
Wilton, Terence	WWW	Wynne, Gilbert	WW
Wimbush, Mary	K9	Wyse, John	OOO
Winding, Victor	KK	Yardley, Stephen	4E, 6V
Windrush, Buddy	V	Yarrow, Arnold	XXX
Windsor, Frank	6J, 7Q	Yenal, Metin	7K
Wing, Anna	5Y	Yip, David	5J
Winston, Jimmy	KKK	Young, David	5A
Winterton, Andre	6C	Young, Jeremy	A, T/A
Winward, Tommy	6C	Young, Joan	W
Wisher, Michael	CCC, EEE, PPP, QQQ, SSS, XXX, 4E, 4D, 4H	Young, Joseph	7E
		Yunus, Tariq	4R
		Yuresha, Annabel	7E
		Zaran, Nik	YY
Witherick, Jeff	LLL		
Witty, John	XX		
Wolf, Michael	HH		
Wolfe, Chris	6L		
Wolfe, Frederick	6K		
Wolff, Kathy	4M		
Wong, Vincent	4S		
Wood, Drew	4E		
Wood, Haydn	4H		
Woodfield, Terence	V, X		
Woodnutt, John	AAA, QQQ, 4F, 5T		
Woodnutt, Roma	GG		
Woods, Aubrey	KKK		
Woods, Lee	6K		
Woods, Reg	5M		
Woodvine, John	5F		
Woolf, Gabriel	4G		
Woolf, Henry	4W		
Woolfe, Maya	6E		
Woolgar, Jack	QQ		
Woollett, Annette	4V		
Worth, Helen	HHH		
Wray, Christopher	JJJ, LLL		
Wright, Brian	X		
Wright, Lincoln	RRR		
Wright, Terry	JJ, UU		
Wright, Tommy	5G		
Wu, John	4S		

THE CREATIVE TEAM

Abbreviations
Exec Prod – Executive Producer; *Prod* – Producer; *A Prod* –
Associate Producer; *Sc Ed* – Script Editor (Story Editor during
the first five seasons); *Dir* – Director; *Writ* – Writer.

NAME	ROLE ON PROGRAMME
Aaronovitch, Ben	*Writ* 7H, 7N
Adams, Douglas	*Sc Ed* 5J–5M
with Williams, Graham as	
Agnew, David	*Writ* 5H
Agnew, David	
pen-name of Williams, Graham	
and Read, Anthony	*Writ* 4Z
pen-name of Williams, Graham	
and Adams, Douglas	*Writ* 5H
Ashby, Norman	
pen-name of Haisman,	
Mervyn and Lincoln, Henry	*Writ* TT
Bailey, Christopher	*Writ* 5Y, 6D
Baker, Bob	*Writ* 5K
with Martin, Dave	*Writ* GGG, NNN, RRR, 4B, 4N, 4T, 4Y, 5F
Baker, Pip and Jane	*Writ* 6X, 7D
with Holmes, Robert	*Writ* 7C
Barry, Christopher	*Dir* L, M, AA, EE, JJJ, NNN, 4A, 4K, 5G
with Martin, Richard	*Dir* B
Barry, Morris	*Dir* HH, MM, TT
Bennett, Rodney	*Dir* 4C, 4B, 4M
Bernard, Paul	*Dir* KKK, OOO, QQQ
Bickford, Lovett	*Dir* 5N
Bidmead, Christopher H	*Sc Ed* 5N–5V
	Writ 5V, 5Z, 6N
Black, Ian Stuart	*Writ* AA, JJ
with Pedler, Kit and Dunlap, Pat	*Writ* BB
Black, John	*Dir* 5T, K9, 5W
Blake, Darrol	*Dir* 5C
Blake, Gerald	*Dir* NN, 4Z
Bland, Robin	
pen-name of Dicks, Terrance	
with Holmes, Robert	*Writ* 4K
Boucher, Chris	*Writ* 4Q, 4R, 4X

NAME	ROLE ON PROGRAMME
Briant, Michael E	*Dir* HHH, LLL, TTT, XXX, 4D, 4R
Briggs, Ian	*Writ* 7G, 7M
Bromly, Alan	*Dir* UUU, 5K
Bryant, Peter	*A Prod* KK
	Prod MM, QQ-YY
	Sc Ed NN-PP
with Davis, Gerry	*Sc Ed* LL
Byrne, Johnny	*Writ* 5T, 6E, 6L
Camfield, Douglas	*Dir* P, S, V, QQ, VV, 4F, 4L
with Pinfield, Mervyn	*Dir* J
with Letts, Barry	*Dir* DDD
Cartmel, Andrew	*Sc Ed* 7D-7P
Clarke, Kevin	*Writ* 7K
Clegg, Barbara	*Writ* 6H
Clough, Chris	*Dir* 7C, 7F, 7G, 7L, 7K
Coburn, Anthony	
with Webber, CE	*Writ* A
Combe, Timothy	*Dir* BBB, FFF
Cotton, Donald	*Writ* U, Z
Cox, Frank	
with Martin, Richard	*Dir* C
with Pinfield, Mervyn	*Dir* G
Crockett, John	*Dir* F
with Hussein, Waris	*Dir* D
Cumming, Fiona	*Dir* 5Z, 6D, 6H, 6Q
Curry, Graeme	*Writ* 7L
David, Hugh	*Dir* FF, RR
Davies, John	*Dir* JJ
Davis, Gerry	*Sc Ed* W-KK
with Bryant, Peter	*Sc Ed* LL
with Pedler, Kit and Dunlap, Pat	*Writ* DD
with Jones, Elwyn	*Writ* FF
with Pedler, Kit	*Writ* HH, MM
with Holmes, Robert	*Writ* 4D
De Vere Cole, Tristan	*Dir* SS
Dicks, Terrance	*Sc Ed* VV-XX, ZZ-ZZZ
	Writ 4A, 4V, 5P, 6K
with Hulke, Malcolm	*Writ* ZZ
with Holmes, Robert as Bland, Robin	*Writ* 4K
Dudley, Terence	*Dir* 5Q
	Writ K9, 5W, 6A, 6J
Dunlap, Pat with Black, Ian Stuart and Pedler, Kit	*Writ* BB
with Pedler, Kit and Davis, Gerry	*Writ* DD
Ellis, David with Hulke, Malcolm	*Writ* KK
Emms, William	*Writ* T

NAME	ROLE ON PROGRAMME
Erickson, Paul with Scott, Lesley	*Writ* X
Ferguson, Michael	*Dir* BB, XX, CCC, GGG
Fisher, David	*Writ* 5C, 5D, 5G, 5N
Flanagan, John with McCulloch, Andrew	*Writ* 5Q
Gallagher, Steve	*Writ* 5S, 6G
Goodwin, Derrick	*Dir* 4T
Gorrie, John	*Dir* E
Griefer, Lewis with Holmes, Robert as Harris, Stephen	*Writ* 4G
Grieve, Ken	*Dir* 5J
Grimwade, Peter	*Dir* 5R, 5V, 5Y, 6B
	Writ 6C, 6F, 6Q
Haisman, Mervyn with Lincoln, Henry	*Writ* NN, QQ
with Lincoln, Henry as Ashby, Norman	Writ TT
Harper, Graeme	*Dir* 6R, 6Z
Harris, Stephen	
pen-name of Holmes, Robert and Griefer, Lewis	*Writ* 4G
Hart, Michael	*Dir* YY
Hayes, Michael	*Dir* 5D, 5F, 5H
Hayles, Brian	*Writ* Y, CC, OO, XX, MMM, YYY
Hellings, Sarah	*Dir* 6X
Hinchcliffe, Philip	*Prod* 4C-4S
Hirsch, Henric	*Dir* H
Holmes, Robert	*Sc Ed* 4A-4W
	Writ WW, YY, AAA, EEE, PPP, UUU, 4C, 4P, 4S, 4W, 5A, 5E, 6R, 6W, 7A
with Davis, Gerry	*Writ* 4D
with Griefer, Lewis as Harris, Stephen	*Writ* 4G
with Dicks, Terrance as Bland, Robin	*Writ* 4K
with Baker, Pip and Jane	*Writ* 7C
Houghton, Don	*Writ* DDD, FFF
Hulke, Malcolm	*Writ* BBB, HHH, LLL, QQQ, WWW
with Ellis, David	*Writ* KK
with Dicks, Terrance	*Writ* ZZ
Hussein, Waris	*Dir* A
with Crockett, John	*Dir* D
Imison, Michael	*Dir* X
Jones, Elwyn with Davis, Gerry	Writ FF

NAME	ROLE ON PROGRAMME
Jones, Glyn	*Writ* Q
Jones, Ron	*Dir* 6A, 6C, 6E, 6N, 6V, 7B
Joyce, Paul	*Dir* 5S
Kerrigan, Michael	*Dir* 7N
Kohll, Malcolm	*Writ* 7F
Lambert, Verity	*Prod* A–T/A
Leeston-Smith, Michael	*Dir* U
Leopold, Guy	
pen-name of Letts, Barry and	
Sloman, Robert	*Writ* JJJ
Letts, Barry	*Exec Prod* 5N–5V
	Prod BBB–4A
	Dir PP, EEE, PPP, ZZZ, 4J
with Camfield, Douglas	*Dir* DDD
with Sloman, Robert as Leopold,	
Guy	*Writ* JJJ
Lincoln, Henry with Haisman,	
Mervyn	*Writ* NN, QQ
with Haisman, Mervyn as Ashby,	
Norman	*Writ* TT
Ling, Peter with Sherwin, Derrick	*Writ* UU
Lloyd, Innes	*Prod* Y–LL, NN–PP
Lucarotti, John	*Writ* D, F
with Tosh, Donald	*Writ* W
Mallett, Nicholas	*Dir* 7A, 7E, 7M
Maloney, David	*Dir* UU, WW, ZZ, QQQ (small portion), SSS, 4E, 4H, 4P, 4S
Marks, Louis	*Writ* J, KKK, 4H, 4M
Martin, Dave with Baker, Bob	*Writ* GGG, NNN, RRR, 4B, 4N, 4T, 4Y, 5F
Martin, Philip	*Writ* 6V, 7B
Martin, Richard	*Dir* K, N, R
with Barry, Christopher	*Dir* B
with Cox, Frank	*Dir* C
Martinus, Derek	*Dir* T, T/A, DD, LL, OO, AAA
Mayne, Lennie	*Dir* MMM, RRR, YYY, 4N
McBain, Kenny	*Dir* 5L
McCoy, Glen	*Writ* 6Y
McCulloch, Andrew with	
Flanagan, John	*Writ* 5Q
Mill, Gerry	*Dir* KK
Moffatt, Peter	*Dir* 5P, 5X, 6F, 6K, 6S, 6W
Moore, Paula with Saward, Eric	*Writ* 6T
Morgan, Andrew	*Dir* 7D, 7H
Morris, Michael Owen	*Dir* 6M
Munro, Rona	*Writ* 7P
Nathan-Turner, John	*Prod* K9, 5N–7P

NAME	ROLE ON PROGRAMME
Nation, Terry	*Writ* B, E, K, R, T/A, SSS, XXX, 4E, 4J, 5J
with Spooner, Dennis	*Writ* V
Newman, Peter R	*Writ* G
Newman, Sydney with Wilson, Donald	*Co-creator*
Orme, Geoffrey	*Writ* GG
Pedler, Kit with Black, Ian Stuart and Dunlap, Pat	*Writ* BB
with Dunlap, Pat and Davis, Gerry	*Writ* DD
with Davis, Gerry	*Writ* HH, MM
with Whitaker, David	*Writ* SS
with Sherwin, Derrick	*Writ* VV
Pemberton, Victor	*Sc Ed* MM
	Writ RR
Pinfield, Mervyn	*A Prod* A-M
	Dir Q
with Cox, Frank	*Dir* G
with Camfield, Douglas	*Dir* J
Platt, Marc	*Writ* 7Q
Pringle, Eric	*Writ* 6M
Read, Anthony	*Sc Ed* 4Y-5F
	Writ 5L
with Williams, Graham as Agnew, David	*Writ* 4Z
Ridge, Mary	*Dir* 6G
Roberts, Pennant	*Dir* 4Q, 4W, 5B, 5M, 6L, 6Y
Robinson, Matthew	*Dir* 6P, 6T
Root, Antony	*Sc Ed* 5W, 5X, 6B
with Saward, Eric	*Sc Ed* K9
Russell, Paddy	*Dir* W, WWW, 4G, 4V
Saward, Eric	*Sc Ed* 5Z, 5Y, 6A, 6C, 6E-7B
	Writ 5X, 6B, 6P, 6Z
with Root, Antony	*Sc Ed* K9
with Moore, Paula	*Writ* 6T
Scott, Lesley with Erickson, Paul	*Writ* X
Sellars, Bill	*Dir* Y
Sherwin, Derrick	*Prod* ZZ-AAA
	Sc Ed QQ-UU, YY
with Ling, Peter	*Writ* UU
with Pedler, Kit	*Writ* VV
Sloman, Robert	*Writ* OOO, TTT, ZZZ
with Letts, Barry as Leopold, Guy	*Writ* JJJ
Smith, Andrew	*Writ* 5R
Smith, Julia	*Dir* CC, GG
Spenton-Foster, George	*Dir* 4X, 5A

NAME	ROLE ON PROGRAMME
Spooner, Dennis	*Sc Ed* L-R
	Writ H, M, S
with Nation, Terry	*Writ* V
Steven, Anthony	*Writ* 6S
Stewart, Norman	*Dir* 4Y, 5E
Stewart, Robert Banks	*Writ* 4F, 4L
Strutton, Bill	*Writ* N
Tosh, Donald	*Sc Ed* S-W
with Lucarotti, John	*Writ* W (small portion)
Tucker, Rex	*Dir* Z
Virgo, Tony	*Dir* 6J
Wareing, Alan	*Dir* 7J, 7Q, 7P
Webber, CE with Coburn, Anthony	*Writ* A
Whitaker, David	*Sc Ed* A-K
	Writ C, L, P, EE, LL, PP, CCC
with Pedler, Kit	*Writ* SS
Wiles, John	*Prod* U-X
Williams, Graham	*Prod* 4V-5M
with Read, Anthony as Agnew, David	*Writ* 4Z
with Adams, Douglas as Agnew, David	*Writ* 5H
Wilson, Donald with Newman, Sydney	*Co-creator*
Wyatt, Stephen	*Writ* 7E, 7J

KEY TECHNICAL PERSONNEL

Abbreviations
SetD - Set Design; *VisFX* - Visual Effects; *CosD* - Costume Design; *Mus* - Incidental Music.

NAME	ROLE ON PROGRAMME
Acheson, James	*CosD* NNN, RRR, PPP, UUU, 4A, 4F, 4M
with Ellacott, Joan	*CosD* 4P
Allen, Paul	*SetD* XX, AAA, 4V
Anderson, John	*SetD* 6P, 7A
Arnold, Ann	*CosD* K9
Asbridge, John	*SetD* 7F, 7G, 7L, 7K
Auger, Tony	*VisFX* 6A
Ayres, Mark	*Mus* 7J, 7Q, 7M
Baron, Lynda	*Singer* Z
Bartlett, Bobi	*CosD* VV, WW, XX, FFF
Barton, David	*VisFX* 6X
Baugh, Martin	*CosD* NN, OO, PP, QQ, RR, SS, TT
with Wheel, Susan	*CosD* UU
Bear, Jeremy	*SetD* NNN
with Murray-Leach, Roger	*SetD* 4L
Bennett, Richard Rodney	*Mus* F
Bezkorowajny, Dave	*VisFX* 7N
Bloomfield, John	*CosD* 4Q, 4S
Blyton, Carey	*Mus* BBB, XXX, 4D
Botterill, Charles	*Mus* S
Bowman, Steve	*VisFX* 6B, 7J
Brace, John	*VisFX* 5R, 6Z
with Kelt, Mike	*VisFX* 6K
Brachacki, Peter	*SetD* A1
Brahan, Perry	*VisFX* 7L, 7K
Brisdon, Stuart	*VisFX* 6F, 6S, 7H
with Francis, Jim	*VisFX* 6R
Brown, Graham	*VisFX* 7M
Buckingham, David	*SetD* 6N
Budden, Janet	*SetD* 5R, 5Z
Bullen, Nicholas	*CosD* YY, ZZ
Burdle, Michael	*CosD* HHH, 5F
Burgon, Geoffrey	*Mus* 4F, 4L
Burrough, Tony	*SetD* 5T, 5W, 6A, 6L, 6W
Burrowes, John	*SetD* TTT
Cann, Roger	*SetD* 5K, 5S

NAME	ROLE ON PROGRAMME
Cary, Tristram	*Mus* B, D, L, V, X, Z, EE, NNN
Chagrin, Francis	*Mus* K
Chapman, Spencer	*SetD* K, Q
Cheetham, Keith	*SetD* UUU
Cheveley, Roger	*SetD* ZZ
Clarke, Malcolm	*Mus* LLL, 6B, 6H, 6P, 6S, 6T, 7C (1)
Clayton, Gloria	*SetD* MMM, YYY
Coles, Dick	*SetD* 4Y, 6G
Collin, Dinah	*CosD* 6B, 6H, 6X
Collins, Martin	*SetD* 7E, 7H, 7N
Conway, Richard	*VisFX* 4L, 4R, 4Y
with Mapson, Colin and Oates, Ron	*VisFX* TTT
with Mapson, Colin	*VisFX* 4Z
Cove, Bob	*SetD* 6Y
Croft, Richard	*CosD* 7F, 7G, 7L, 7K
Culley, Clifford	*VisFX* SSS, WWW, 4A
Curzon, Nigel	*SetD* 4F
Cusick, Raymond	*SetD* B1–5, 7, C, E, G, J, L, M, V1–2, 5–7, 11
with Wood, John	*SetD* R
with Hunt, Richard	*SetD* T/A
Dare, Daphne	*CosD* B, C, D, E, G, H, J, L, M, N, P, R, S, T, T/A, V, W, X, Y, Z, AA, BB, CC, JJ
with Pearce, Tony	*CosD* F, K, U
with Mansfield-Clarke, Pauline	*CosD* Q
with Woods, Mary	*CosD* HH
with Reid, Sandra	*CosD* KK
Davies, Jeremy	*SetD* B6, OO, DDD
Day, Peter	*VisFX* CCC, JJJ, LLL, YYY, 4E
with Harris, Michael John	*VisFX* MM
with Hutton, Len	*VisFX* RR, 4P
with Logan, Peter	*VisFX* 4W
Dicks-Mireaux, Odile	*CosD* 5Z, 5X
Dodd, Derek	*SetD* EE, SS
Drewett, Steven	*VisFX* 5Q, 6W
Ebbutt, Rosalind	*CosD* 6A, 7J
Edwards, Mickey	*VisFX* 5W
Ellacott, Joan with Acheson, John	*CosD* 4P
Fletcher, Maggie	*CosD* LLL
Ford, Roger	*SetD* JJJ
Francis, Jim with Horton, John and Lucas, Steve	*VisFX* 5F
with Brisdon, Stuart	*VisFX* 6R

NAME	ROLE ON PROGRAMME
Friedlander, John with Oxley, Tony	*VisFX* 4C, 4B
Gibbs, Jonathan	*Mus* 6L, 6V, 6X
with Howell, Peter	*Mus* 6J
Giles, Don	*SetD* 5E
Gleeson, Tim	*SetD* HHH, OOO
Glynn, Dominic	*Mus* 7A, 7C (2), 7G, 7L, 7P
Godfrey, Pat	*CosD* 6S, 6Z
Gosnold, Barbara	*SetD* 4Z
Green, Colin	*SetD* XXX, 6H
Grossner, Ulrich with Oates, Ron	*VisFX* NN
Handley, Prue	*CosD* 4D
Harding, Tony	*VisFX* 5E, 5P, 6J, 6M
with Scoones, Ian	*VisFX* 4T
Hardinge, Anne	*CosD* 6V
Harper, Don	*Mus* VV
Harris, Michael John	*VisFX* LL, ZZ, EEE, 4S
with Day, Peter	*VisFX* MM
with Pegrum, Peter	*VisFX* OOO
with Hutton, Len	*VisFX* RRR
Harrison, Shaunna	*CosD* 7C
Hartley, Richard	*Mus* 7B
Havard, Dave	*VisFX* 4H, 5A, 5M, 6N
Hawkins, Joyce	*CosD* 4V
Hearne, John	*CosD* 7B
Heneghan, Mauree	*CosD* A
Hercules, Evan	*SetD* UU
Horton, John	*VisFX* AAA, GGG, NNN, PPP, 4F, 4K, 5V
with Lucas, Steve and Francis, Jim	*VisFX* 5F
Howe-Davies, Andrew	*SetD* 7B
Howell, Peter	*Mus* 5N, 5Q, 5S, K9, 5Y, 6D, 6K, 6M, 6Q, 6W
with Gibbs, Jonathan	*Mus* 6J
Hudson, June	*CosD* 5A, 5J, 5G, 5L, 5N, 5Q, 5S, 5V
Hughes, Alun	*CosD* 6Y
Hughes, Raymond	*CosD* 4T
Hunt, Richard	*SetD* T, CC, VV
with Cusick, Raymond	*SetD* T/A
Hurst, John	*SetD* SSS, 6R
Husband, Mary	*CosD* KKK
Hutton, Len	*VisFX* DDD, 4J, 5D
with Day, Peter	*VisFX* RR, 4P
with Harris, Michael John	*VisFX* RRR
Irvine, Mat	*VisFX* 4Q, 5C, 5G, 5S, K9, 6L

111

NAME	ROLE ON PROGRAMME
James, Doreen	*CosD* 5D, 5H
James, Malcolm	*VisFX* 7Q, 7P
Jarvis, Rupert	*CosD* 4Y, 5C, 5K
as Roxburghe-Jarvis, Rupert	*CosD* 5M
Jeanes, Charles	*VisFX* 6V
Johnson, Martin	*SetD* MM
Jones, Nigel	*SetD* K9
Jones, Raymond	*Mus* M, AA
Jones, Rhys with Wilkie, Bernard	*VisFX* QQQ
Kay, Norman	*Mus* A, E, G
Kelly, Dee	*CosD* 4Z
Kelt, Mike	*VisFX* 6H, 7A
with Brace, John	*VisFX* 6K
Kidd, Barbara	*CosD* QQQ, TTT, WWW, YYY, 4A, 4C, 4B, 4E, 4G, 5Y
Kindred, Peter	*SetD* DD, RR
Kine, Jack with Wilkie, Bernard	*VisFX* UU
King, Bill	*VisFX* SS, UU, VV, WW, XX
Kingsland, Paddy	*Mus* 5R, 5P, 5V, 5Z, 5X, 6F, 6N
Kirkland, Geoff	*SetD* FF, KK
Kljuco, Cynthia	*SetD* QQQ
Laing, Roderick	*SetD* H
Lane, Barbara	*CosD* GGG, JJJ, MMM, OOO, 4J, 4L, 4N
Laskey, David	*SetD* 7J, 7M
Lavers, Colin	*CosD* 5E, 5W, 6J, 6K
Lawson, Christopher	*VisFX* 6E, 6Q, 6T
Lazell, Andrew	*VisFX* 5N, 6D
Ledsham, Ken	*SetD* 5A, 5J, 6J
Limb, Roger	*Mus* 5T, 5W, 6A, 6C, 6E, 6G, 6R, 6Z
Liminton, Roger	*SetD* RRR, PPP
Lindley, Philip	*SetD* 4J, 5Q
Lloyd-Jones, Bernard	*SetD* 6B
Logan, Peter	*VisFX* 5J, 5T, 5Y, 6C, 6Q
with Day, Peter	*VisFX* 4W
London, Raymond	*SetD* BB, WW, FFF
Lucas, Steve with Horton, John and Francis, Jim	*VisFX* 5F
Mansfield-Clarke, Pauline with Dare, Daphne	*CosD* Q
Mapson, Colin	*VisFX* 4N, 4X, 5B, 5K, 7D
with Conway, Richard and Oates, Ron	*VisFX* TTT
with Conway, Richard	*VisFX* 4Z
McCulloch, Keff	*Mus* 7D, 7E, 7F, 7H, 7K, 7N
McDonald, Simon	*VisFX* 5Z

NAME	ROLE ON PROGRAMME
McManan-Smith, Richard	*SetD* 5F, 5H, 6C
McVean, Andy	*VisFX* 7F, 7G
Meredith, Victor	*SetD* 5M
Middleton, Malcolm	*SetD* NN
Molloy, Kevin	*VisFX* 6Y, 7C
Morris, Richard	*SetD* WWW
Murray-Leach, Roger	*SetD* 4C, 4B, 4D, 4H, 4P, 4S
with Bear, Jeremy	*SetD* 4L
Myers, Stanley	*Mus* H
Myerscough-Jones, David	*SetD* QQ, CCC, KKK
Newbery, Barry	*SetD* A2-4, D, F, P, S, V3-4, 8-10, 12, X, Z, TT, BBB, 4K, 4M, 4T, 6M
Nieradzik, Anushia	*CosD* 6N, 6T, 7N
Oates, Ron	*VisFX* QQ, TT
with Grossner, Ulrich	*VisFX* NN
with Wilkie, Bernard	*VisFX* OO
with Conway, Richard and Mapson, Colin	*VisFX* TTT
Oxley, Tony with Friedlander, John	*VisFX* 4C, 4B
Parker, Liz	*Mus* 6Y
Peacock, John	*CosD* 6Q
Pearce, Tony with Dare, Daphne	*CosD* F, K, U
Pegrum, Peter	*VisFX* 4V, 5L, 6G
with Harris, Michael John	*VisFX* OOO
Pemsel, Christopher	*SetD* PP
Pepperdine, Judy	*CosD* 6L
Pethig, Hazel	*CosD* SSS
Powell, Geoff	*SetD* 7D
Pratt, Marjorie	*SetD* 6E, 6T
Pusey, Jon	*SetD* 5B
Rawlins, Christine	*CosD* AAA, BBB, CCC, DDD, 4W
Rawnsley, Ian	*SetD* 4A
Reid, Sandra	*CosD* DD, EE, FF, HH, LL
with Robinson, Juanita	*CosD* GG
with Dare, Daphne	*CosD* KK
with Wallace, Dorothea	*CosD* MM
Ridley, Anna	*SetD* 4X
Roberts, Amy	*CosD* 4X, 5R, 5P, 5T, 6C, 6F
Robinson, Jack	*SetD* GG
Robinson, Juanita with Reid, Sandra	*CosD* GG
Robson, Dee	*CosD* 6E, 6G
Rose, Andrew	*CosD* 4H, 6R, 7C
Rowland-Warne, L	*CosD* XXX, ZZZ, 4K, 5B
Roxburghe-Jarvis, Rupert	See Jarvis, Rupert
Ruddy, Austin	*SetD* 4Q
Ruscoe, Christine	*SetD* 4G, 4N, 5P

NAME	ROLE ON PROGRAMME
Scoones, Ian	*VisFX* MMM, 4G, 4M, 5H
with Jones, Rhys and Wilkie, Bernard	*VisFX* QQQ
with Harding, Tony	*VisFX* 4T
Scott, Stephen	*SetD* 6F
Searle, Humphrey	*Mus* U
Selwyn, Rochelle	*SetD* ZZZ
Sharp, Kenneth	*SetD* JJ, GGG, 4R
Shaw, Colin	*SetD* HH
Simpson, Dudley	*Mus* J, P, R, Y, GG, JJ, LL, OO, RR, XX, YY, ZZ, AAA, CCC, EEE, FFF, GGG, HHH, JJJ, KKK, MMM, OOO, RRR, PPP, QQQ, SSS, TTT, UUU, WWW, YYY, ZZZ, 4A, 4C, 4B, 4E, 4H, 4G, 4J, 4K, 4M, 4N, 4P, 4Q, 4R, 4S, 4V, 4T, 4X, 4W, 4Y, 4Z, 5A, 5B, 5C, 5D, 5E, 5F, 5J, 5H, 5G, 5K, 5L, 5M
Snoaden, Tony	*SetD* LLL, 4W, 6V
Somerville, Nick	*SetD* 7Q, 7P
Southern, Jackie	*CosD* 6M
Spalding, Alan	*SetD* 6Z
Spoczynski, Jan	*SetD* 6D
Spode, David	*SetD* 4E
Starkey, Ken	*SetD* 5X
Story, Graeme	*SetD* 5L, 5S
Stout, John	*SetD* 5C
Tayler, Simon	*VisFX* 7E
Tharby, Janet	*CosD* 6P, 7E
Thompson, Chris	*SetD* LL
Thornton, Malcolm	*SetD* 5V, 5Y, 6K, 6Q
Trerise, Paul	*SetD* 6X
Trevor, Michael	*SetD* 7C(2)
Trew, Ken	*CosD* EEE, 6D, 7A, 7D, 7H, 7Q, 7M, 7P
Walker, Dinah	*SetD* 7C(1)
Walker, Stuart	*SetD* AA
Wallace, Dorothea with Reid, Sandra	*CosD* MM
Waller, Elizabeth	*CosD* 4R
Ward, Jim	*VisFX* BBB, FFF, KKK, UUU, XXX, 4D
Warrender, Valerie	*SetD* 5D, 5G, 6S
Watson, Ian	*SetD* YY, EEE
Wheel, Susan with Baugh, Martin	*CosD* UU
Wilkie, Bernard	*VisFX* HHH, ZZZ
with Oates, Ron	*VisFX* OO

114

NAME	ROLE ON PROGRAMME
with Kine, Jack	*VisFX* UU
with Jones, Rhys and Scoones, Ian	
	VisFX QQQ
Wood, John	*SetD* N, U, Y
	VisFX YY
with Cusick, Raymond	*SetD* R
Woods, Mary with Dare, Daphne	*CosD* HH
Wragg, Peter	*VisFX* 5X, 6P, 7B
Wright, Jan	*CosD* 6W
Yardley-Jones, Tom	*SetD* 5N
Young, Michael	*SetD* W

THE NOVELIZATION WRITERS

The following writers are those who have written novelizations of televised TV stories only.

WRITER	STORY (production code)
Aaronovitch, Ben	7H
Baker, Pip and Jane	6X, 7C (2), 7D
Bidmead, Christopher H	5V, 5Z, 6N
Bingeman, Alison with Davis, Gerry	Y
Black, Ian Stuart	AA, BB, JJ
Briggs, Ian	7G, 7M
Clarke, Kevin	7K
Clegg, Barbara	6H
Cotton, Donald	M, U, Z
Curry, Graeme	7L
Davis, Gerry	DD, FF, HH, MM
with Bingeman, Allison	Y
Dicks, Terrance	A, J, K, CC, KK, NN, QQ, SS, WW, XX, YY, AAA, CCC, DDD, EEE, FFF, GGG, KKK, NNN, OOO, RRR, PPP, SSS, UUU, XXX, YYY, ZZZ, 4A (including junior edition), 4E, 4D, 4F, 4H, 4G, 4J, 4K (including junior edition), 4N, 4P, 4Q, 4R, 4S, 4V, 4T, 4X, 4W, 4Y, 4Z, 5C, 5D, 5E, 5F, 5J, 5K, 5L, 5Q, 5P, 5T, 5W, 5Y, 6E, 6D, 6K, 6L, 6R, 7A
Dudley, Terence	K9, 6A, 6J
Emms, William	T
Erickson, Paul	X
Fisher, David	5G, 5N
Gallagher, Steve	See Lydecker, John
Grimwade, Peter	6C, 6F, 6Q
Hayles, Brian	OO, MMM
Hinchcliffe, Philip	E, 4L, 4M
Holmes, Robert	6W
Hulke, Malcolm	ZZ, BBB, HHH, LLL, QQQ, TTT, WWW
Jones, Glyn	Q
Kohll, Malcolm	7F
Letts, Barry	JJJ
Ling, Peter	UU

WRITER	STORY (production code)
Lucarotti, John	D, F, W
Lydecker, John	
pen-name of Steve Gallagher	5S, 6G
Marter, Ian	H, L, PP, TT, VV, 4C, 4B, 5A, 6B
Martin, Philip	6V, 7B
McCoy, Glen	6Y
Munro, Rona	7P
Peel, John	R, T/A, V (2)
Pemberton, Victor	RR
Platt, Marc	7Q, 7N
Pringle, Eric	6M
Robinson, Nigel	C, G, S, GG
Saward, Eric	5X, 6S, 6T
Smith, Andrew	5R
Strutton, Bill	N
Whitaker, David	B, P
Wyatt, Stephen	7E, 7J

3: *WHICH* WHO *IS WHAT*

The purpose of this section is to deal with professional, original *Doctor Who* fiction, and only with professional, original *Doctor Who* fiction. Although only BBC-produced stories are part of the official canon, it is still fascinating to see how many other creators have added their individual touch to the mythos, and used their own imaginations to bring their personal visions to *Doctor Who*.

Because the 'Whoniverse' is a potentially unlimited shared universe, I have endeavoured to list and summarize every bit of professional, original *Doctor Who* fiction I could find.

'Professional' is taken to mean licensed by the BBC and published in a commercial context. This, of course, excludes fan fiction and other amateur publications. This should not be construed as a reflection upon their quality, as in many instances, fan fiction is superior to some of what has been published professionally. The line, however, must be drawn somewhere, and, as much as I would love to, trying to list every piece of *Doctor Who* fan fiction would probably be an impossible task.

'Original' means a new, not repackaged, version of a televised story. You will therefore not find the excellent novelizations of the television series, their albums and/or audiocassette and/or videotape versions. It would be pointless to summarize the same stories again in this book when you can find them listed in the companion volume, *Doctor Who – The Programme Guide*. (Note that all television stories have now been novelized except for EE, LL, 5B, 5H, 6P, 6Z and 7H, which may never be novelized for a variety of legal reasons.)

And '*Doctor Who*' includes not only the Doctor but his companions, villains and anything that is part of the Whoniverse.

Lastly, by 'fiction', I mean just that. You will not find here a list of non-fiction publications (such as *The Doctor Who Pattern Book*, *The Making of Doctor Who*, and so on), magazines, toys or videotapes. This is not a catalogue of *Doctor*

Who merchandise. Again, the purpose of this listing is to emphasize the imagination that goes into *Doctor Who*, not compile a sterile list of products.

For practical reasons this section has been divided according to the format of the fiction considered, such as motion pictures, stage plays, books, comic-books, short stories and so on.

THE MISSING SEASON

The following unproduced stories were scheduled to take place between stories 6Z and 7A when the programme was placed on hold by the BBC in 1985. The BBC regards these stories as official, and therefore as part of the Whoniverse. This, and Shada (5M), already listed in *Doctor Who – The Programme Guide*, are therefore the only exceptions to the general rule that non-televised stories are not part of the *Doctor Who* canon.

THE NIGHTMARE FAIR
Writer
Graham Williams
Story: The Doctor and Peri are drawn to Blackpool. There, the Doctor confronts the Celestial Toymaker, who is revealed to be a being from another universe. The Toymaker is planning to use a monstrous new videogame to enslave mankind. The Doctor eventually defeats the Toymaker's game, and imprisons the evil immortal in a trap powered by his own brain.
Book: Doctor Who – The Nightmare Fair by Graham Williams.

MISSION TO MAGNUS
Writer
Philip Martin
Story: The Doctor is forcibly drawn to the temperate world of Magnus by Anzor, a Time Lord who used to bully him at school. Magnus is a former Earth colony where a virus has ravaged the

male population, leaving the women to rule. The Doctor defeats a plot by the Ice Warriors to move Magnus's orbit and turn the planet into an ice world, thwarting the exiled Sil's business plans in the process. Freed of its virus, Magnus's female leaders contemplate reconciliation with the males of their brother planet, Salvak.

Book: Doctor Who – Mission to Magnus by Philip Martin.

PENACASATA
Writer
Christopher H Bidmead
Story: Not available.

THE ULTIMATE EVIL
Writer
Wally K Daly
Story: The evil Dwarf Mordant, one of the Salankans, a race of ruthless cosmic traders, uses a hate ray to start a war between the peace-loving nation of Tranquela and the computer-controlled society of Ameleria in order to sell them weapons. The Doctor stumbles across the plot while looking for a good spot for a vacation, and convinces Mordant to leave by threatening him with the Time Lords' wrath, if they learn that the crystal balls he gave them are spying devices.

Book: Doctor Who – The Ultimate Evil by Wally K Daly.

THE MOTION PICTURES

Two *Doctor Who* feature films have been made. Their stories are variations of existing television stories and therefore cannot be considered part of the official Whoniverse. In the late 1970s, a third film project, launched by Tom Baker and Ian Marter and reportedly involving the Doctor meeting Scratchman, never got off the ground. A fourth film project is currently under consideration, but has failed to result in the actual production of a motion picture at the time of going to press.

DOCTOR WHO AND THE DALEKS (1965)
Regal Films and British Lion Films
Executive Producer   *Director*
Joe Vegoda   Gordon Flemyng
Producers   *Screenplay*
Milton Subotsky and   Milton Subotsky
Max J Rosenberg
Based on the BBC TV serial by Terry Nation
Cast: Peter Cushing (Dr Who); Roy Castle (Ian Chesterton); Jennie Linden (Barbara); Roberta Tovey (Susan); Barrie Ingham (Alydon); Geoffrey Toone (Temmosus); Mark Petersen (Elyon); John Bown (Antodus); Yvonne Antrobus (Dyoni); Michael Coles (Ganatus); Ken Garady, Michael Lennox, Virginia Tyler, Bruce Wells, Sharon Young, Nicolas Head, Jack Waters, Jane Lumb, Martin Grace, Garry Wyler (Thals); Bruno Castagnoli, Michael Dillon, Brian Hands, Robert Jewell, Kevin Manser, Eric McKay, Len Saunders, Gerald Taylor (Daleks).
Story: Doctor Who is an elderly, absent-minded British scientist who has invented a space-time machine called TARDIS. Accompanied by his two granddaughters, Barbara (who is in her early twenties) and Susan (who is in her early teens), and Barbara's boyfriend, Ian, he travels to Skaro where they meet the blue-skinned Thals and the evil Daleks. After a series of adventures somewhat identical to those chronicled in the original television story, they defeat the Daleks and leave Skaro. But they rematerialize in the path of a Roman legion.

DALEKS – INVASION EARTH 2150 AD (1966)
Aaru Production and British Lion Films
Executive Producer   *Director*
Joe Vegoda   Gordon Flemyng
Producers   *Screenplay*
Milton Subotsky and   Milton Subotsky
Max J Rosenberg
Additional material by David Whitaker
Based on the BBC TV serial by Terry Nation
Cast: Peter Cushing (Dr Who); Bernard Cribbins (Tom Campbell); Roberta Tovey (Susan); Jill Curzon (Louise); Ray Brooks (David); Godfrey Quigley (Dortmun); Andrew Keir (Wyler);

Roger Avon (Wells); Keith Marsh (Conway); Philip Madoc (Brockley); Eddie Powell (Thompson); Kenneth Watson (Craddock); Steve Peters, Geoffrey Cheshire (Robomen); Peter Reynolds (Man on Bicycle); Bernard Spear (Man with Carrier Bag); Sheila Staefel (Young Woman); Eileen Way (Old Woman); John Wreford (Robber); Robert Jewell (Leader Dalek Operator).

Story: Policeman Tom Campbell enters the TARDIS while trying to stop a jewel robbery. There, he meets Doctor Who, his niece Louise, and his granddaughter Susan. When they step out, they're in AD 2150, where they fight the Daleks, who have conquered Earth. Eventually, as in the original television story, they discover the Daleks' plan to turn Earth into a mobile base, but are able to thwart it. The Daleks and their saucer are destroyed. Doctor Who takes Tom far enough back in time for him to arrest the robbers.

THE STAGE PLAYS

The Doctor, his enemies and his companions have been the subject of several successful stage plays whose stories, while all approved by the BBC, could not be considered part of the official Whoniverse. One stage play, *The Inheritors of Time*, by American writer John Ostrander, never became an actual production.

THE CURSE OF THE DALEKS (1965)
Premiered at Wyndham's Theatre, London, 21 December

Producers	*Writers*
John Gale and	David Whitaker and
Ernest Hecht	Terry Nation
Director	*Designer*
Gillian Howell	Hutchinson Scott

Cast: Colin Miller (Sline); John Line (Ladiver); David Ashford (Bob); Nicholas Hawtrey (Captain Redway); Edward Gardener (Rocket); John Moore (Professor Vanderlyn); Hilary Tindall

(Marion); Nicholas Bennett (Dexion); Suzanne Mockler (Ijayna).

Story: The time is AD 2179. The *Starfinder*, an Earth spaceship commanded by Captain Redway, and carrying two prisoners, Sline and Ladiver, is forced to land on Skaro. There, the humans meet the Thals, led by Dexion and his sister, Ijayna. One of the prisoners reactivates the dormant Daleks, thinking he can use them to enslave the galaxy, but the Daleks have their own plans. Eventually, they are defeated by the crew and the Thals.

DOCTOR WHO AND THE DALEKS IN SEVEN KEYS TO DOOMSDAY (1974)

Premiered at the Adelphi Theatre, London, 16 December

Production Supervisor	*Writer*
Trevor Mitchell	Terrance Dicks
Director	*Designer*
Mick Hughes	John Napier

Cast: Trevor Martin (the Doctor); Wendy Padbury (Jenny); James Mathews (Jimmy); Ian Ruskin (Jedak); Patsy Dermott (Tara); Anthony Garner (Garm); Simon Jones (Master of Karn); Jacquie Dubin (Dalek Emperor); Robin Browne (Marco); Peter Jolley, Mo Kiki, Peter Whitting (Clawrentulars); Peter Jolley (Dalek voices).

Story: The Doctor regenerates on stage and, with two new companions from the audience, Jimmy and Jenny, returns to the planet Karn where he was sent by the Time Lords to gather the seven crystals which together make up the Crystal of All Power. Back on Karn, they meet resistance fighters Jedak, Tara and Garm, and the monstrous Clawrentulars, who turn out to be working for the Daleks, who want the crystal to power their ultimate weapon. The Doctor defeats the last surviving Master of Karn in a mental duel, and manages to collect all the crystals, but is later forced to turn them over to the Daleks. But he has managed to alter the molecular structure of the seventh crystal, which explodes, destroying the Daleks and their weapon.

RECALL UNIT (or THE GREAT T-BAG MYSTERY) (1984)

Premiered at Moray House Theatre, Edinburgh, 17 August

Producer	Writer
Richard Franklin	Richard Franklin and
	George A Cairns
Director	Designer
Richard Franklin	James Helps

Cast: Richard Franklin (Yates); John Levene (Benton); Graham Smith (Alistair); Lene Lindewall (Miss Bergbo); Paul Holness (Silent Stephen); Richard Kettles (Major Molesworth); David Roylance (Hamish); Liam Rudden (Jimmy); Kevin Philpotts (Tim); Glynn Dack (Stallion); Nicholas Courtney (Voice of the Brigadier); John Scott Martin (Supreme Dalek).

Story: A mysterious Miss Bergbo rents a theatre to hold auditions for a show to be performed for the army and the politicians in the Falklands. With Alistair, her stage manager, she interviews several acts, including unemployed television actors Franklin and Levene. A blend of fictional sketches with topical review follows, featuring the return of UNIT, tea, the Master, the Falkland Islands, Mrs Thatcher and a musical pantomime, until the final confrontation with the evil Dragoids and the Supreme Dalek.

DOCTOR WHO – THE ULTIMATE ADVENTURE (1989)
Premiered at Wimbledon Theatre, London, 23 March

Producer	Designer
Mark Furness	Paul Staples
Director	Creative Consultant
Carole Todd	John Nathan-Turner
Writer	
Terrance Dicks	

Cast: Jon Pertwee (the Doctor); Rebecca Thornhill (Crystal); Graeme Smith (Jason); David Banks (Karl); Judith Hibbert (Delilah, Mrs T, French Woman); Chris Beaumont (US Envoy, Hairy Alien, Dalek Scientist, Dalek Voice, French Man); Claudia Kelly (Envoy's Wife, Ant Person, Insect Man, Ragamuffin); David Bingham (MC, Vervoid, Dalek, Execution Victim); Stephanie Colburn (Zog, Bell Boy); Wolf Christian (Cyberleader, Draconian, Duelling Guard); Paula Tappenden (Chief Dalek, Cyberman, Chicken-Headed Alien, French Woman); Oliver Gray (Dalek, Cyberman, Cybermen Voices,

French Man); Troy Webb (Emperor Dalek, Insect Man, Mercenary, Bodyguard, Dalek Voice, French Man); Alison Reddihough (Insect Man, Mercenary, Executioner); Terry Walsh (Mercenary, Duelling Guard); Deborah Hecht (Waitress, Bodyguard, Dalek, French Woman).

Story: The Doctor is summoned to 10 Downing Street and charged to search the universe for the kidnappers of an Ameri-can envoy. It appears that alien forces are concerned that Earth people are moving towards peaceful co-existence. By kidnapping the envoy, they hope to trigger a war that will make Earth an easy target for invasion from space. Following a set of clues, the Doctor locates the mercenaries and, with them, the Cybermen. But behind the entire plot is the Emperor Dalek, who sees this plan as an opportunity to destroy the Doctor as well.

Note: The role of the Doctor was later assumed by Colin Baker and (for one performance only) by David Banks.

THE RADIO PLAYS

There really is only one real *Doctor Who* radio play – Eric Saward's *Slipback* – whose story is unlikely to be part of the official Whoniverse, if only because it contradicts the events told in the televised story 6G. Readers will note that we have drawn from Mr Saward's novelization of his play as well as from the play itself for the summary.

THE TIME MACHINE (4 October 1976)
Radio 4 Special, 20 minutes

Producer	*Writer*
Mike Howarth	Bernard Venables
Production	
David Lyttle	

Cast: Tom Baker (the Doctor); Elisabeth Sladen (Sarah Jane Smith); John Westbrook (Megron).
Story: The Doctor and Sarah travel back four thousand million

years to the time when Earth is being created, and save our planet from Megron, who wants the newly formed world to remain a place of chaos.

Note: This programme was part of the geography series *Exploration Earth* and was intended to present a dramatic version of the creation of Earth.

SLIPBACK (25 July, 1 August and 8 August 1985)
Radio 4 Special, six 10-minute episodes

Producer	*Writer*
Paul Spencer	Eric Saward

Cast: Colin Baker (the Doctor); Nicola Bryant (Peri Brown); Jane Carr (Computer); Jon Glover (Shellingborne Grant); Nick Revell (Bates, Snatch); Alan Thompson (Maston Mutant, Steward, Droid, Time Lord); Valentine Dyall (Slarn); Ron Pember (Seedle).

Story: The TARDIS materializes on board the *Vipod Mor*, a galactic survey ship captained by the repulsive Slarn. Grant, one of the ship's officers, turns out to be a galactic conman who tried to escape the law (in the persons of officers Seedle and Snatch) by having his brain transplanted into another person's body. Meanwhile, the ship's computer has developed a schizophrenic personality, and wants to travel back in time to put the galaxy to rights. The Doctor is unable to stop the computer, but later is told by renegade Time Lord Vipod Mor that it is the ship's explosion at the beginning of time that is responsible for the Big Bang.

Book: Doctor Who – Slipback by Eric Saward.

RECORDS AND TAPES

Over the years, there have been numerous *Doctor Who* albums and tapes, either music ones, like the 1964 *Doctor Who Theme Music* (BBC) or the 1979 *Doctor Who – Mankind* (Pinnacle), to quote but two, or audio adaptations of televised stories (such as 4E and 5P), but there has only been one original full-length story, which is very probably not part of the official Who-niverse.

DOCTOR WHO AND THE PESCATONS (1976)
Argo Records (Decca)

Producer	*Engineers*
Don Norman	Kevin Daly (voices); Robert
Directors	Parker, Brian Hodgson
Harvey Usill (voices); Don	(effects and music)
Norman (effects and music)	*Narrator*
Writer	Tom Baker
Victor Pemberton	

Cast: Tom Baker (the Doctor); Elisabeth Sladen (Sarah Jane Smith); Bill Mitchell (Zor).

Story: The Doctor and Sarah Jane Smith encounter the shark-like Pescatons, whose planet is threatened with destruction as its orbit gets closer to its sun. Their leader, the monstrous Zor, leads an invasion of Earth. Sarah discovers the aliens are vulnerable to high frequency sound when the Doctor plays his piccolo. The Doctor then lures Zor into a trap. Once the Pescaton leader is eliminated the invasion falls apart and, soon afterwards, the aliens' planet is destroyed.

Book: Doctor Who and the Pescatons by Victor Pemberton.

THE ARCHIVE TAPES (1989)
Silver Fist in association with Who Dares
Written and read by
David Banks

Origins of the Cybermen	The Cyber Nomads
The Early Cybermen	The Ultimate Cybermen

Note: This series of audiocassettes contains a fictionalized version of David Banks' history of the Cybermen, as published in his book, *Cybermen*, read by the author.

VIDEO

The BBC is releasing numerous *Doctor Who* televised stories (such as B, XX, ZZ, 4D, 4K, 6K and so on) on videocassettes which, like the records above, are not listed here. Fans may also want to look up the wonderful *Myth Makers* series of video interviews (featuring Colin Baker, David Banks, Victor Pemberton and so on) which have done an excellent job of often intermingling reality with light touches of fiction. Nevertheless, the only original *Doctor Who* video production so far involves not the Doctor but one of his companions.

WARTIME (1987)
Reeltime Pictures Production
Myth Makers Presentation

Producer	*Writers*
Keith Barnfather	Andrew Lane and
Director	Helen Stirling
Keith Barnfather	

Cast: John Levene (Sergeant Benton); Michael Wisher (Benton's Father); Mary Greenhalgh (Benton's Mother); Paul Greenhalgh (Chris); Steven Stanley (Johnnie); Peter Noad (Willis); Paul Flanagan (Man); Nicholas Briggs (Soldier).

Story: Sergeant Benton exorcises his past as he confronts the ghosts of his father, a sergeant who was killed during the Second World War, whose approval he desperately wanted, and of his younger brother, Chris, whose accidental death he feels guilty about. He then stops a criminal from hijacking a UNIT shipment of radioactive material.

GAMES

By their very nature, computer games' stories (when they exist) are bound to be limited. It would therefore be unfair to compare these with other, more plot-intensive media. FASA and *Find Your Fate* stories are listed under novels.

DOCTOR WHO – THE FIRST ADVENTURE (1983)

Publisher	*Nature*
BBC	Arcade games

Story: The game is divided into four episodes and is accompanied by a booklet containing a fictional scenario. In *Episode 1 – The Labyrinth of Death*, the Doctor has to travel through an underground maze to collect the three segments of the Key to Time. The maze is also inhabited by poisonous worms. In *Episode 2 – The Prison*, the Doctor must carry explosives across three defences (a highway, a moat and a forecourt) to blow up the wall of the prison. *Episode 3 – The Terrordactyls*, sees the Doctor trying to fly a spaceship through swarms of Terrordactyls to reach the TARDIS. And in *Episode 4 – The Box of Tantalus*, the Doctor must detect and destroy invisible aliens in a grid of space.

DOCTOR WHO AND THE WARLORD (1985)

Publisher	*Nature*
BBC	Text-based game

Story: First, you must traverse a strange planet in search of the Doctor. Then, the TARDIS takes you and the Doctor back to the battle of Waterloo where you must defeat both Napoleon and the Warlord.

DOCTOR WHO AND THE MINES OF TERROR (1986)

Publisher	*Nature*
Micropower	Ladders and levels game

Story: The object is for you (as the Doctor) to infiltrate the mining complex and stop the Master from using your brain to create a chaos weapon. The Doctor is aided by an invisible electronic cat called Splinx and must halt the production of heatonite, a time-warping mineral, disable the Time Instant Replay Unit and regain the plans to the complex.

THE NOVELS

There are few original *Doctor Who* novels, but this state is bound to change soon with Virgin Publishing's plans for such a line. Again, the novelization of televised stories have not been listed, with the exception of the K9 special novelization (for easy reference) and the non-fiction books.

Needless to say, these stories (with the exception of the K9 special), while approved by the BBC, are not part of the official Whoniverse.

THE COMPANIONS OF DOCTOR WHO

HARRY SULLIVAN'S WAR (1986)

Writer	*Publisher*
Ian Marter	WH Allen

Story: Harry, now working for NATO, is reluctant to move to Biological Weapons Research at Yarra. His ethical objections make him a prime suspect when the site is infiltrated by an anti-chemical hazard group with sinister backers. Suspicion also falls on Brigadier Lethbridge-Stewart.

TURLOUGH AND THE EARTHLINK DILEMMA (1986)

Writer	*Publisher*
Tony Attwood	WH Allen

Story: Now a folk hero on Trion, Turlough attempts to discover why the Gardsormr, former allies of the regime of the evil Rehctaht who exiled him, have signed a peace treaty with the new government. He builds a time machine that attracts the attention of a renegade Time Lord. He also discovers Rehctaht is not dead, but merely hiding.

K9 AND COMPANY (1987)

Writer	*Publisher*
Terence Dudley	WH Allen

Story: See *Doctor Who – The Programme Guide.*

THE ADVENTURES OF K9

K9 AND THE TIME TRAP (1980)
Writer   *Publisher*
Dave Martin   Arrow Books
Story: K9 investigates the disappearance of a spacecraft into a time trap created by Omegon (sic), the engineer who first gave the Time Lords time travel, and thwarts the renegade Time Lord's plan to use the stolen ships to destroy Gallifrey.

K9 AND THE ZETA RESCUE (1980)
Writer   *Publisher*
Dave Martin   Arrow Books
Story: The Time Lords send K9 to save a galaxy from being destroyed by a great war between two space empires. He helps set up a hospital for the survivors.

K9 AND THE BEASTS OF VEGA (1980)
Writer   *Publisher*
Dave Martin   Arrow Books
Story: K9 defeats the Vegans, intelligent energy beings who, in order to defend themselves from the negative effects of lasers used in human terraforming operations, project frightening images into the minds of the space crews.

K9 AND THE MISSING PLANET (1980)
Writer   *Publisher*
Dave Martin   Arrow Books
Story: K9 discovers that a missing planet has been transported into another, more advanced universe. He agrees to keep his discovery secret to protect that universe from Earth's ruthless exploitation.

FIND YOUR FATE

1 SEARCH FOR THE DOCTOR (1986)
Writer   *Publisher*
David Martin   Severn (UK), Ballantine (US)
Story: In AD 2056 California, renegade Time Lord Drax and K9 join forces to help the Doctor fight Omega.

2 CRISIS IN SPACE (1986)

Writer   *Publisher*
Michael Holt   Severn (UK), Ballantine (US)

Story: The Doctor and Turlough fight Garth Hadeez, Overlord of the Golons, and his dark servants, the Neroids, who plot to release a black hole in the solar system.

3 GARDEN OF EVIL (1986)

Writer   *Publisher*
David Martin   Severn (UK), Ballantine (US)

Story: The Doctor must locate scientist-prophet Ellis before the evil Maker can fill the universe with obedient machines.

4 MISSION TO VENUS (1986)

Writer   *Publisher*
William Emms   Severn (UK), Ballantine (US)

Story: The Doctor materializes inside a ship inhabited by a villainous crew and mysterious plant lifeforms – and on a collision course with Venus.

5 INVASION OF THE ORMAZOIDS (1986)

Writer   *Publisher*
Philip Martin   Severn (UK), Ballantine (US)

Story: In the 25th century, on the rim worlds, the Doctor must prevent the evil Darval and his unstoppable Ormazoids' plans of conquest.

6 RACE AGAINST TIME (1986)

Writers   *Publisher*
Pip and Jane Baker   Severn (UK), Ballantine (US)

Story: The Doctor and Peri must escape Time Limbo to defuse the Destabilizer that threatens the universe.

SOLO-PLAY ADVENTURE GAMES

1 DOCTOR WHO AND THE VORTEX CRYSTAL (1986)

Writer   *Publisher*
William H Keith, Jr   FASA

Story: On planet Gathwyr, the Doctor, Sarah Jane Smith and Harry Sullivan fight the Daleks for the possession of the Vortex Crystal, whose power threatens the universe.

2 DOCTOR WHO AND THE REBEL'S GAMBLE (1986)

Writer	*Publisher*
William H Keith, Jr	FASA

Story: The Doctor, Peri and Harry Sullivan travel back to the American Civil War to stop a Confederate soldier from changing the course of time.

GAME MODULES

9201: THE IYTEAN MENACE
Publisher
FASA
Story: The Doctor and his companions arrive in Victorian London and unravel a web of mystery that leads to the awakening of an ancient evil.

9202: THE LORDS OF DESTINY
Publisher
FASA
Story: The Doctor arrives on the world-ship of Ydar and must prevent its collision with the galaxy of man.

9203: COUNTDOWN
Publisher
FASA
Story: The Doctor arrives on a spaceship of the Earth empire on an emergency mission to deliver a plague antidote. A gravity bubble threatens as does the ship's paranoid computer, space pirates and an attack by androids.

9204: THE HARTLEWICK HORROR
Publisher
FASA

Story: The Doctor arrives on Earth in 1923 when the archaeological excavation of a druidic mound in the village of Hartlewick unleashes an energy force that threatens the Earth.

9205: THE LEGIONS OF DEATH
Publisher
FASA
Story: An evil renegade Time Lord allies himself with British tribesmen to lure a Roman army and emperor into a trap. History will be changed unless the Doctor can save the day.

9206: CITY OF GOLD
Publisher
FASA
Story: The Doctor and his companions investigate a violent revolution in an age of turmoil and stumble across a plot that could end human history.

9207: THE WARRIOR'S CODE
Publisher
FASA
Story: The Doctor becomes embroiled in a battle of wits in Japan as Samurai warlords fight for supremacy.

THE SHORT STORIES

Professionally commissioned and published *Doctor Who* short stories have appeared mostly in the licensed annuals and in the *Doctor Who Magazine*. More often than not, these were not credited and, sadly, the names of their authors are therefore unknown. (Any information will be greatly appreciated.) A number of these stories deviate from established continuity, and therefore could not be part of the official Whoniverse.

Also included in this listing are other notable short stories that have appeared in books or magazines over the years. Only the first appearance of each story is listed, not reprints.

I am particularly indebted to Jeremy Bentham, David Howe, Shaun Ley and John Peel for their invaluable assistance in researching this section.

DOCTOR WHO MAGAZINES

The following short stories appeared in Marvel Comics' magazine *Doctor Who Weekly*, later *Doctor Who Monthly*, and currently *Doctor Who Magazine*.

THE TWO-TIMER (1980)
Issue: 26
Story: The Doctor finds himself in court, faced with the charge of parking in an illegal time zone.

STOWAWAY (1980)
Issue: 27
Story: The Doctor and K9 defeat a spore creature aboard the TARDIS.

EVIL EGG (1980)
Issue: 28
Story: The Doctor and K9 meet two emotion vampires in an alien egg.

SANDS OF TIME (1980)
Issue: 29–30
Story: The Doctor travels back in time to save the Kristellans.

MIND-JUMP (1980)
Issue: 31
Story: The Doctor encounters a mind parasite.

THE HOLE TRUTH (1980)
Issue: 32
Story: The Doctor discovers what lies on the other side of a freak hole in space.

BREAKDOWN (1980)
Issue: 33
Story: Creatures from fiction materialize inside the TARDIS.

CATALOGUE OF EVENTS (1983)
Writer
Alan McKenzie
Issue:
Summer Special 1983
Story: The Doctor visits the Events Library which controls events in the universe.

POWER TO THE PEOPLE (1986)
Writer
Ian Marchant
Issue: 114
Story: The Doctor meets the creator of the universe.

THE HEAT-SEEKERS (1986)
Writer
Andrew Lowes
Issue: 117
Story: The Doctor defeats the alien Ronans at the Dead Sea.

HALL OF MIRRORS (1986)
Writer
Alan McKee
Issue: 119
Story: The Doctor and Peri meet a schizophrenic alien.

BIRD OF FIRE (1987)
Writer
Stephen Moxon
Issue: 122
Story: The Doctor defeats a phoenix.

SCREAM OF THE SILENT (1988)
Issue: 25th Anniversary Special
Story: The Doctor recombines a species that evolved into two different lifeforms.

THE INFINITY SEASON (1989)
Writer
Dan Abnett
Issue: 151

Story: An unscrupulous reporter fakes an alien story to boost his ratings.

LIVING IN THE PAST (1990)
Writer
Andy Lane
Issue: 162
Story: The Doctor rescues Ace from a strange entity on primeval Earth, intent on speeding up evolution.

TEENAGE KICKS (1990)
Writer
Paul Cornell
Issue: 163
Story: Nothing dangerous can be found in a British public house – unless you're the Doctor and Ace.

DOCTOR WHO ANNUALS

First Doctor

DOCTOR WHO AND THE INVASION FROM SPACE (1966)
Publisher
World International
Story: The Doctor is joined by the Mortimer family, fleeing the Great Fire of London. The TARDIS rematerializes on the spaceship of the One, a super-computer. It is carrying survivors from Andromeda who are preparing to invade our galaxy. The One is destroyed by a bowl of food thrown by the Mortimers' daughter.

1966
Writer   *Publisher*
David Whitaker   World International

THE LAIR OF THE ZARBI SUPREMO
Story: A giant, intelligent Zarbi moves Vortis into the solar system. The Doctor teams up with the Menoptera to prevent an invasion of Earth.

THE SONS OF THE CRAB

Story: After tampering with their germ-plasm, the Yend of the Crab Nebula are doomed to a permanent existence of shape-changing.

THE LOST ONES

Story: During his very first visit to Vortis, the Doctor encounters survivors of Atlantis.

THE MONSTERS FROM EARTH

Story: The Doctor and two Earth children confront the Sensorites over their feeding of criminals to the hideous, yet sacred, spider-like Zilgan.

PERIL IN MECHANISTRIA

Story: The Doctor lands on a world where machines have enslaved men. He takes one of its denizens, Drako, back to the past so that he may prevent his world from evolving into Mechanistria.

THE FISHMEN OF KANDALINGA

Story: The Doctor prevents the Voord, who have been exiled from Marinus, from taking over a water world and enslaving its inhabitants.

1967
Publisher
World International

THE CLOUD EXILES

Story: The Doctor helps the cloud-like Ethereals regain their bodies and defeat the robotic Baggolts.

THE SONS OF GREKK

Story: The Doctor sides with peaceful non-human aliens against the evil genius Deemon and the humanoid sons of Grekk.

TERROR ON TIRO

Story: The Doctor returns to Tiro to save the Staggs from the evil Klarimo.

THE DEVIL-BIRDS OF CORBO
Story: On Corbo, the Doctor helps stranded space explorer Dr Strong and his children defeat Ulla and his robot birds.

THE PLAYTHINGS OF FO
Story: The Doctor helps the natives of Rhoos to get rid of Fo, a space cyclops.

JUSTICE OF THE GLACIANS
Story: The Doctor exposes a tyrant who buried peaceful aliens under ice to make himself ruler of the ice-world of Bruhl.

TEN FATHOM PIRATES
Story: The Doctor escapes underwater pirates who have caught the TARDIS in a force field-like net.

Second Doctor

1968
Publisher
World International

THE SOUR NOTE
Story: The Doctor finds his recorder an invaluable aid to control a giant mechanical insect he suspects may have killed Ben.

THE DREAM MASTERS
Story: On the planet Dorada, dreams are used as a means of controlling the workers, who are secretly dominated by a race of giant brains.

THE WORD OF ASIRIES
Story: The Doctor is mistaken as an emissary of the Galactic Ruler by Queen Qar, who is seeking permission to exterminate a race of primitives.

ONLY A MATTER OF TIME
Story: A fleet of refugee spaceships is on course for Earth. Though the people aboard are peaceful, their machines could be used for war.

PLANET OF BONES
Story: The planet Harmony appears to be a paradise, until the

Doctor discovers how its inhabitants use the minds and bodies of space travellers.

WHEN STARLIGHT GROWS COLD
Story: Polly saves the Doctor when his curiosity moves him to investigate a collection of creatures floating without space suits between the galaxies.

HMS TARDIS
Story: The TARDIS lands on the deck of the HMS *Victory* and the travellers are brought before Lord Nelson, whom the Doctor helps win the Battle of Trafalgar.

THE KING OF GOLDEN DEATH
Story: Exploring an ancient Egyptian tomb, the time travellers thwart a raid by grave robbers. The Doctor reseals the tomb, to leave it safe for Howard Carter in 1922.

1969
Publisher
World International

LORDS OF THE GALAXY
Story: Slug-like aliens threaten the Doctor to learn the secret of invisibility.

FOLLOW THE PHANTOMS
Story: Jamie follows a line of marching wraiths into a cloud, which takes him into another dimension. There, a warrior race believes he has come to lead them into battle.

MASTERMIND OF SPACE
Story: Victoria gives a lesson in compassion to seven creatures which exist only as pure thought. Realizing what they have lost, the aliens embark upon a new evolutive cycle.

THE CELESTIAL TOYSHOP
Story: The TARDIS lands in a place where all dimensions overlap. Venturing through infinitely regressing gateways, the Doctor fears he is losing reality as he draws nearer the source of light.

VALLEY OF DRAGONS
Story: When the TARDIS is stolen, the time travellers are unable to explain their arrival to a race of hostile bird-like aliens, who throw them into an arena to face a dragon.

PLANET FROM NOWHERE
Story: The Doctor believes he has done the right thing when he wakes the Salonians from suspended animation. But they turn out to be future Earthmen, who still carry within them the seeds of war.

HAPPY AS QUEEG
Story: The power of the Doctor's mind is needed to defeat Queeg, the master of an alien world.

WORLD OF ICE
Story: On a frozen planet, Victoria is hunted by savage robot Cogwens wanting access to the TARDIS. She then discovers the Doctor and Jamie have been replaced by robot duplicates.

THE MICROTRON MEN
Story: The Doctor is puzzled by a feudal world where astronomy is impossible because the stars keep changing. He discovers this world is just a specimen under a microscope – and shortly due to end.

DEATH TO MUFL
Story: The Doctor falls into a shaft leading him to an underworld. The hypnotic effect of the Doctor's pipe saves Mufl from being killed by the traitorous J'nk.

1970
Publisher
World International

THE DRAGONS OF KEKOKRO
Story: The Doctor, Jamie and Zoe land during prehistoric times and witness one of the last, great battles between lizard-kind and emerging apemen.

THE SINGING CRYSTALS
Story: The travellers appear to be attacked by protoplasmic

creatures, while crystals are growing on the TARDIS walls. The Doctor realizes the crystals are their true enemy, not the blob-like lifeforms.

THE MYSTERY OF THE *MARIE CELESTE*
Story: The Doctor lands on a metallic world and becomes the prisoner of two scientists, Eretz and Lantis, who have also captured a sea serpent and the crew of the *Marie Celeste.*

GRIP OF ICE
Story: Cosmos, a space criminal, is harvesting thought energy to power an invincible spaceship.

MAN FRIDAY
Story: The Doctor and Zoe rescue Jamie, who has been made prisoner by a race of Lava People and their robot servants, the Blikks.

SLAVES OF SHRAN
Story: The Doctor is hypnotized by Shran, a powerful super-computer. His rescuer, Ekk, wants his help in overthrowing Shran.

RUN THE GAUNTLET
Story: The TARDIS lands on a world inhabited by apemen with advanced technology and at war with their neighbours.

A THOUSAND AND ONE DOORS
Story: The travellers are captured by dimensional explorers, who are preparing to dissect them.

Third Doctor

1971
Publisher
World International

THE MIND EXTRACTORS
Story: Alien invaders from another dimension have come to Earth to steal knowledge from men – and from the Doctor.

SOLDIERS FROM ZOLTA
Story: A Mars Probe mission discovers the alien Zoltans on the

red planet. Mankind looks forward to a peaceful contact, until the spaceship brings back deadly insects.

THE GHOULS OF GRESTONSPEY
Story: The Doctor is taken inside an inert spacecraft from Cassiopeia, which is refuelling itself by draining power from UNIT's Grestonspey nuclear reactor in Scotland.

CAUGHT IN THE WEB
Story: Dr Rossi believes he has discovered a new source of life when he begins analyzing an alien dust. Only the Doctor realizes that it is lethal when exposed to ultraviolet light.

INVADERS INVISIBLE
Story: A UFO deposits a blob of mud-like matter which enslaves Liz Shaw's mind. The Brigadier faces a full-scale mutiny, unless the Doctor finds a way to defeat the microscopic invaders.

THE DARK PLANET
Story: Dying aliens are infiltrating the minds and bodies of Earthmen, gradually reconditioning them to become their next evolutionary step.

CAVERNS OF HORROR
Story: The Doctor and UNIT investigate the appearances of giant insects deep in a complex of caves.

A UNIVERSE CALLED FRED
Story: The Doctor receives a distress call from inner space. Two microscopic civilizations face destruction from a dying blue star. The Doctor and Liz visit the two worlds, but are accused of being spies. They return to Earth knowing that this universe in a jar will soon cease to be.

1973
Publisher
World International

DARK INTRUDERS
Story: The Doctor defeats Minoan brain stealers who have infiltrated a Mars space probe.

WAR IN THE ABYSS
Story: The oil-dependent robotic Klatris, who live underground, plan to move Earth closer to the sun to get rid of mankind.

HUNT TO THE DEATH
Story: The alien robot Kelad is trapped by his pursuers in a Yorkshire pot hole.

DOORWAY INTO NOWHERE
Story: The Master steals a multi-dimensional gateway invented by physicist Giles Winston.

THE CLAW
Story: The Doctor encounters a shape-changing time-traveller who has disguised his craft as a lobster pot.

SAUCER OF FATE
Story: The Triolites use a transporter to take people back to their spaceship as hostages.

THE PHASER ALIENS
Story: Invisible aliens with the ability to phase through matters steal diamonds to worship them.

1974
Publisher
World International

LISTEN – THE STARS!
Story: The Master uses ionic vibrations to exploit the power of an alien mind trapped in the body of a UNIT cleaning lady.

OUT OF THE GREEN MIST
Story: The Doctor is taken outside of the universe.

THE FATHOM TRAP
Story: A race of serpentoids use the Brigadier as a model in order to heal two humans found at sea. In return, the Doctor repairs their spaceship.

TALONS OF TERROR
Story: The Doctor is mistaken for Premier Lutz and becomes a pawn in the conflict opposing two races from the future.

OLD FATHER SATURN
Story: The Doctor encounters alien survivors from a world whose explosion helped form the rings of Saturn.

GALACTIC GANGSTER
Story: A huge alien conqueror plans to use Earth as a space base.

1975
Publisher
World International

THE HOUSE THAT JACK BUILT
Story: The Doctor and Jo are kidnapped by a computer which tests games and trials of particular planets on unfortunate subjects.

REVENGE OF THE PHANTOMS
Story: A body-snatching spirit seeks to capture the Doctor for its new incarnation.

THE TIME THIEF
Story: The Doctor and Sarah defeat a renegade Time Lord who wishes to run the world from the beginning of time.

FUGITIVES FROM CHANCE
Story: Fugitives from various Earth eras are forced to fight to provide the bird-like Melovians with gambling opportunities.

THE BATTLE WITHIN
Story: The Doctor fights the evil within himself.

BEFORE THE LEGEND
Story: In Earth's past, the Doctor confronts the alien Lantans.

SCORCHED EARTH
Story: The Doctor uses salt to fight a viral infection that scorches the ground.

Fourth Doctor

THE AMAZING WORLD OF DOCTOR WHO (1976)
Publisher
World International

THE VAMPIRES OF CRELLIUM
Story: The Doctor encounters a Drakkam psychic parasite attempting to invade the souls of the Yulian.

ON THE SLIPPERY TRAIL
Story: The Doctor uses salt to free the Anthrons from the Jannosaur, a giant slug.

1976
Publisher
World International

A NEW LIFE
Story: The Doctor must help the Lexopterans, who have turned themselves into plants to avoid an enemy attack.

THE HOSPITALITY ON HANKUS
Story: The Doctor mistakenly materializes the TARDIS at one thousandth of its expected size.

THE SINISTER SPONGE
Story: An alien sponge-like entity attacks the male Inscrutans.

AVAST THERE!
Story: The Doctor lands on a space galleon.

THE MISSION
Story: A giant robot plans to pilot a planet into a more hospitable part of the solar system.

1977
Publisher
World International

WAR ON ACQUATICA
Story: Three kingdoms are fighting over glyt-mines.

CYCLONE TERROR
Story: A race which hates weapons uses a giant wind machine in its plans of conquest.

THE TIME SNATCH
Story: Aliens trying to recover their crystal from UNIT send the Doctor into Earth's prehistory.

THE EYE-SPIDERS OF PERGROSS
Story: The Doctor travels back in time to save an old friend from becoming an Eye-Spider.

DETOUR TO DIAMEDES
Story: The Doctor helps another old friend to see his homeland again before he dies.

DOUBLE TROUBLE
Story: A member of the Disciplinary Council of Dumok uses Sarah's body to pursue a criminal to Earth.

SECRET OF THE BALD PLANET
Story: The irrational behaviour of their ruler, Gresk, threatens the Parads' world – unless his psyche is transported to another world.

1978
Publisher
World International

THE SLEEPING BEAST
Story: The Doctor discovers that the Sphinx is a giant robot waiting to be activated.

THE SANDS OF TYMUS
Story: Aliens use Sarah's body as a model to replace the females of their species.

A NEW LIFE
Story: The Doctor convinces an alien race to return to the surface of its planet, once infected by a deadly gas.

THE SEA OF FACES
Story: The Kendorian population is so large that many members live their lives through gas-induced dreams rather than in their confined spaces.

1979
Publisher
World International

FAMINE ON PLANET X
Story: The Doctor ends the Octopoids' persecution of the children of Rha and ends the planet's famine.

THE PLANET OF DUST
Story: The Doctor helps a peaceful vegetal lifeform by helping a crashed Larkal spaceman leave its world.

TERROR ON TANTALOGUS
Story: The Doctor and Leela arrive on a living planet inhabited by cannibals.

FLASHBACK
Story: A Pendorian criminal controls the subconscious minds of a space beacon crew that makes them cause much damage.

THE CROCODILES FROM THE MIST
Story: Radioactive poison leaking from a crashed spaceship affects the evolution of crocodiles.

1980
Publisher
World International

X-RANI AND THE UGLY MUTANTS
Story: X-Rani has banished from her planet all those who do not live up to her physical ideals.

LIGHT FANTASTIC
Story: Romana reduces a renegade Time Lord to pulsar-like radiation.

RELUCTANT WARRIORS
Story: The Doctor destroys a fear machine on the planet Banto.

RETURN OF THE ELECTRIDS
Story: The worm-like Electrids kill their master, the disgruntled Zedon, and replace him with a more amiable clone.

THE SLEEPING GUARDIANS
Story: The Valerians are under attack, but they cannot find the key that activates their robot army.

1981
Publisher
World International

COLONY OF DEATH
Story: Lured from an overcrowded Earth, human colonists find themselves working as mining slaves.

ALIEN MIND GAMES
Story: A robot satellite tries to delude the Doctor into believing that he is in anti-space.

A MIDSUMMER'S NIGHTMARE
Story: An alien energy source hopes to gain a youthful body on Earth.

THE VOTON TERROR
Story: The Votons plot to use the voice of an ambassador to trigger a bomb at a galactic peace conference.

SWEET FLOWER OF UTHE
Story: A war computer on Uthe 3 continues to fight a war a century after it has ended.

1982
Publisher
World International

INTER-GALACTIC CAT
Story: Genesis III, a super-powerful computer, uses a Composition Adjustment Teleport to create a planet on a single carbon atom and lures travellers there, intending to turn them into a deadly army.

CONUNDRUM
Story: The TARDIS becomes lost in a portion of space that functions like a Möbius strip.

PLANET OF PARADISE
Story: Adric disarms service robots which had taken over a planet.

149

JUST A SMALL PROBLEM
Story: The Doctor defeats a giant beast who is swallowing the population of Xiter.

Fifth Doctor

1982 CONTINUED

THE KEY OF VAGA
Story: The Vagans want to have a last look at their home planet but their ship cannot exist at the same time as the Doctor's without destroying the planet.

PLANET OF FEAR
Story: Ixos-4 defends itself through feeding off the subconscious fears of any arrivals.

1983
Publisher
World International

DANGER DOWN BELOW
Story: The Doctor defeats an alien who is diverting the food supply to Aronassus 49.

THE GOD MACHINE
Story: Pirates use a 'god machine' to extract gems from the natives.

THE ARMAGEDDON CHRYSALIS
Story: The TARDIS is attacked by a grub that feeds off energy.

THE HAVEN
Story: The Doctor disturbs the peace of Carnak, who has taken over the bodies of cryogenically frozen people.

THE PENALTY
Story: The Doctor contracts Ponassan fever.

NIGHT FLIGHT TO NOWHERE
Story: The Master plans to replace high-ranking people with androids.

1984
Publisher
World International

THE OXAQUA INCIDENT
Story: The damming of water on Oxaqua has upset natural balance and the relationship between two races.

WINTER ON MESIQUE
Story: A harsh winter creates a food problem on Mesique.

THE CREATION OF CAMELOT
Story: The Master poses as Merlin and attempts to change the course of history.

CLASS 4 RENEGADE
Story: A robot discovers his master's supply of Antherack and hopes to trade it to buy its freedom.

THE VOLCANIS DEAL
Story: The people of Ilium banish their criminals to Earth after removing their memories.

THE NEMERTINES
Story: Toxic waste causes the mutation of the Nemertines, who the Doctor defeats with salt.

FUNGUS
Story: The Doctor uses a high frequency whistle to eliminate a deadly fungus.

Sixth Doctor

1985
Publisher
World International

BATTLE PLANET
Story: The Doctor and Peri rescue a blue rock which contains all the secrets of the sister planets of Belstar.

DAY OF THE DRAGON
Story: Qualar, Grand Master of Fire, returns to menace Earth but is defeated by an explosion engineered by the Doctor.

THE REAL HEREWARD
Story: The Doctor discovers that Saxon outlaw Hereward the Wake was in fact King Harold.

THE DEADLY WEED
Story: The Doctor destroys an alien weed that turns people into zombies.

VORTON'S REVENGE
Story: The alien Vorton plots to use the Doctor to gain revenge on the Time Lords.

THE TIME SAVERS
Story: The Master persuades a Cambridge scientist to build a time machine, but is thwarted by soldiers from the future.

THE MYSTERY OF THE RINGS
Story: Aliens from Varliark attempt to colonise Earth through a circle of standing stones.

1986
Publisher
World International

THE FELLOWSHIP OF QUAN
Story: The Master uses the Doctor to revive Quan, an ancient mining robot.

TIME WAKE
Story: The alien Tasq, stranded on Earth, aims to replace all British Prime Ministers throughout history with androids to boost space research and build a ship that he could then steal.

INTERFACE
Story: The Time Lords want the Doctor to deal with a time convergence.

BEAUTY AND THE BEAST
Story: On an alien world, those who pass a test at age ten live in a beautiful castle, while those who fail become their drones.

RETRIBUTION
Story: An alien race seeks revenge for the crash of an Earth ship which killed millions of its people.

DAVARRK'S EXPERIMENT
Story: Davarrk plots to use humans to reconstitute his body, so that his flesh will be as durable as an android's.

THE RADIO WAVES
Story: The Master uses the Telecom Tower to beam a radio signal to incite London's population to murder Britain's political leaders.

K9 ANNUAL 1983
Publisher
World International

POWERSTONE
Story: When a witch's skeleton is discovered behind the walls of Aunt Lavinia's house, the coven believes its lost powerstone may be with it.

THE SHROUD OF AZAROTH
Story: A film production company on the location of the Azaroth Cult experiences strange accidents – the revenge of a woman whose parents disappeared after attending one of the coven's meetings.

HOUND OF HELL
Story: Sarah Jane attempts an exposé of satanists in the druid's ring on Bodmin Marshes, but not before damage to K9's memory banks causes it to act like the devil hound, Ragok.

THE MONSTER OF CRAG
Story: The Laird of Castle Crag uses a mini-submarine to keep people away and to protect his smuggling operations.

HORROR HOTEL
Story: Sarah Jane and K9 save a young woman from being forced to succeed her father as leader of the coven.

THE CURSE OF KANBO-ALA
Story: An Indian sect seeks to recover an idol taken from them by Sarah Jane's late uncle, African Smith.

DALEK ANNUALS

THE DALEK BOOK 1965 (1964)

Writers   *Publisher*
David Whitaker and   Souvenir
Terry Nation

RED FOR DANGER
Story: The Daleks have attacked the Earth colony on Venus. Andy Stone rescues his brother, Jeff, from a plant where the Daleks are experimenting with ways to toughen their casings.

THE SECRET OF THE MOUNTAIN
Story: The Dalek invaders on Venus have mysteriously disappeared. Jeff and Andy discover their hidden base beneath a mountain.

MESSAGE OF MYSTERY
Story: Susan lands on Skaro and helps the Daleks decode a mysterious deep space message.

THE SMALL DEFENDER
Story: A small mole inadvertently defeats a covert advance landing party of Daleks on Earth.

BREAK-THROUGH
Story: The Daleks are routed and forced to retreat back to Skaro. The space fleet from Earth finds the planet protected by an unbreachable force field.

THE OIL WELL
Story: Jeff and Andy attack a Dalek oil installation to rescue Mary and to thwart the Daleks' efforts to speed up the fuelling of their space craft.

THE DALEK OUTER SPACE BOOK 1967 (1966)

Writers   *Publisher*
David Whitaker and   Souvenir
Terry Nation

THE OUTLAW PLANET
Story: The origins of the SSS, the Space Security Service, and

how Sara Kingdom defeated a Dalek attack on the planet Barzilla.

THE LIVING DEATH
Story: The Daleks intend to use the Harwicke Elixir, a rejuvenating drug, to defeat the human race.

DIAMOND DUST
Story: The Daleks have developed a method of refining and directing a cloud of deadly diamond dust at Earth. But Jeff Stone turns the tables on them.

TERRY NATION'S DALEK ANNUAL 1976
Publisher
World International

TERROR TASK FORCE
Story: Shaw, Seven and Shavron of the Anti-Dalek Force battle the Daleks on Skaro itself.

EXTERMINATE! EXTERMINATE! EXTERMINATE!
Story: On the planet Omegon, the ADF arrives too late to save the city from destruction by the Daleks.

NIGHTMARE
Story: Under the influence of the drug Psycroton, Gil Tranter tells the ADF of his encounters with Daleks in human form.

TIMECHASE
Story: Two boys break into their uncle's Time Conveyor and unwittingly give the secret away to the Daleks.

1977
Publisher
World International

THE DOOMSDAY MACHINE
Story: The Anti-Dalek Force destroys a miniaturizing machine set up by the Daleks.

REPORT FROM AN UNKNOWN PLANET
Story: The Daleks have hidden an army on an unknown planet. An unfortunate archaeologist sends a taped warning.

THE FUGITIVE
Story: A Venusian prisoner of the Daleks escapes to 1977 Earth, where two boys help him escape his pursuers.

1978
Publisher
World International

THE CASTAWAY
Story: After three years of solitude on the planet Knossos, Agent Shannon at last finds life – Daleks!

THE SEEDS OF DESTRUCTION
Story: In search of the famous scientist Lambray, Kramer finds a trail of destruction in the Pacific. The Daleks have captured Lambray and want his secret.

ASSASSINATION SQUAD
Story: Secret documents have been stolen from ADF headquarters and the criminal is discovered to be in the control of the Daleks.

1979
Publisher
World International

BLOCKADE
Story: Ed Cowley is attacked by Daleks outside a black hole, and is forced to land on a planet inhabited by monstrous creatures with strange healing powers.

THE SOLUTION
Story: The ADF attempts to rescue a ship under attack by Daleks. Members of the ADF are captured and discover Igo, a robot designed to overcome any invading army.

THE PLANET THAT CRIED WOLF!
Story: Murderers imprisoned on Penal Planet X26 claim to be attacked by Daleks. The ADF investigate and are captured by the prisoners who try to force them to help them leave the planet.

THE DALEK WORLD
Publisher
World International

THE SECRET STRUGGLE
Story: Agent Meric attempts to assassinate Defence Minister Yorke, who turns out to be only a humanoid under the control of the Daleks.

THE LOG OF THE GYPSY JOE
Story: Sent to survey the planet Esmera, Ron Marlowe is attacked by Daleks. He manages to escape the ship and finds an Orbitus, which he programs to obey him.

MANHUNT
Story: Meric and four others are captured by Daleks and subjected to a gruesome endurance test, only to discover that one of his companions has been replaced by a humanoid in control of the Daleks.

DR WHO'S SPACE ADVENTURE BOOK
Story: The Doctor lands on Zaos, a familiar planet now threatened by Daleks. He signals Earth and Commander Clay comes to the rescue with his new, lethal weapon.

MISCELLANEOUS FICTION

WE ARE THE DALEKS! (1973)
Writer   *Publisher*
Terry Nation   BBC
Appeared in: Radio Times Doctor Who 10th Anniversary Special
Story: Man is revealed to be more intimately related to the Daleks than he ever realized.

DALEKS: THE SECRET INVASION (1979)
Writer   *Publisher*
Terry Nation   WH Allen

Appeared in: Terry Nation's Dalek Special
Story: A group of children defeats the Daleks, who have placed neutronic charges in the London underground.

DOCTOR WHO – QUIZ BOOK OF DINOSAURS (1982)
DOCTOR WHO – QUIZ BOOK OF MAGIC (1983)
DOCTOR WHO – QUIZ BOOK OF SCIENCE (1983)
DOCTOR WHO – QUIZ BOOK OF SPACE (1983)

Writer	*Publisher*
Michael Holt	Magnet (Methuen)

Illustrations
Rowan Barnes-Murphy
Note: This series of books contains thematic fictional elements featuring the Fifth Doctor, Nyssa and Tegan.

BIRTH OF A RENEGADE (1983)

Writer	*Publisher*
Eric Saward	BBC

Appeared in: Radio Times Doctor Who 20th Anniversary Special
Story: The Gallifreyan origins of the Doctor and Susan are revealed, as the Doctor defeats the Master and the Cybermen.

GENESIS OF THE CYBERMEN (1988)

Writer	*Publisher*
Gerry Davis	Silver Fist in association with Who Dares

Appeared in: Doctor Who – Cybermen
Story: The Doctor and Felicity land on Mondas where King Dega has initiated the creation of the Cybermen.
Note: This book contains a fictional history of the Cybermen written by David Banks, illustrated by Andrew Skilleter with additional material by Adrian Rigelsford and consultant Jan Vincent-Rudzki.

THE OFFICIAL DOCTOR WHO AND THE DALEKS
BOOK (1988)

Writers	*Publisher*
John Peel and Terry Nation	St Martin's Press

Note: This book contains a fictional history of the Daleks by John Peel, as well as *The Survivors*, by Terry Nation the original story line which became the first televised Dalek story.

THE COMICS

Listing all the *Doctor Who* stories that have appeared in comics would have been an impossible task if not for the dedicated help of Jeremy Bentham, Shaun Ley and Eric Hoffman.

All titles of the *TV Comic* stories featuring the First, Second and Third Doctors (up to and including *The Kingdom Builders*) and *The Dalek Chronicles* stories are by Jeremy Bentham or the author. These did not appear on the strips, and are there purely to tie stories together in defined blocks.

The *Doctor Who* comics stories, even more so than the novels or the short stories, deviate wildly from the television series' continuity and are therefore not part of the official *Doctor Who* universe.

Again, only the first appearance, not reprints, of each story have been listed.

TV COMIC

First Doctor

THE KLEPTON PARASITES (1965)
Writer/Artist   *Publisher*
Neville Main   TV Publications Ltd
Issues: 674-683
Story: The Doctor and his grandchildren, John and Gillian, travel to the 29th century and help the peaceful Thains overthrow the alien Kleptons who live in an underwater city.

THE THEROVIAN QUEST (1965)
Writer/Artist   *Publisher*
Neville Main   TV Publications Ltd

Issues: 684-689
Story: The TARDIS crew and Grig, a Therovian astronaut, travel to planet Ixos to find an alien moss that might prove to be the antidote to the disease that is ravaging the people of Theros.

THE HIJACKERS OF THRAX (1965)

Writer/Artist	*Publisher*
Neville Main	TV Publications Ltd

Issues: 690-692
Story: In 2075, the Doctor fights space pirate Anastas aboard a giant, invisible space station between Earth and Venus.

RETURN TO THE WEB PLANET aka DOCTOR WHO ON THE WEB PLANET (1965)

Writer/Artist	*Publisher*
Neville Main	TV Publications Ltd

Issues: 693-698
Story: The Doctor returns to Vortis to help the Menoptera who are once more threatened by the Zarbi, this time directed by the evil Skirkons. Disguised as flying Zarbi, they have come to steal the rare mineral Galvinium X.

THE GYROS INJUSTICE (1965)

Writer/Artist	*Publisher*
Neville Main	TV Publications Ltd

Issues: 699-704
Story: The TARDIS crew restores justice on a distant world, where the threat of plague has divided the population into land dwellers and old men living in mechanised cities, under the domination of the robotic Gyros.

CHALLENGE OF THE PIPER (1965)

Writer/Artist	*Publisher*
Neville Main	TV Publications Ltd

Issues: 705-709
Story: The Doctor fights a battle of wits with the magical Pied Piper to persuade him to return the children of Hamelin.

MOON LANDING aka MOONSHOT (1965)
Writer/Artist   *Publisher*
Neville Main   TV Publications Ltd
Issues: 710–712
Story: The first American astronauts land on the Moon in July 1970 – only to discover the TARDIS.

TIME IN REVERSE (1965)
Writer/Artist   *Publisher*
Neville Main   TV Publications Ltd
Issues: 713–715
Story: The TARDIS lands near a rocket base in eastern Europe, but time is running backwards and the travellers must guess the sequence of events that will lead them back to the beginning.

DINOSAUR WORLD aka LIZARDWORLD (1965)
Writer/Artist   *Publisher*
Neville Main   TV Publications Ltd
Issues: 716–719
Story: The TARDIS arrives on a planet inhabited by giant, hostile lizards who capture the time travellers. In order to escape, the Doctor hypnotizes a dinosaur.

THE ORDEALS OF DEMETER (1965)
Writer/Artist   *Publisher*
Bill Mevin   TV Publications Ltd
Issues: 720–723
Story: The Doctor helps the Roman-like world of Demeter to fight back the attacks of its neighbouring planet Bellus.

ENTER: THE GO-RAY aka BURN-OUT (1965)
Writer/Artist   *Publisher*
Bill Mevin   TV Publications Ltd
Issues: 724–727
Story: The Go-Ray robots accuse the Doctor of depleting their supply of cadmium.

SHARK BAIT (1965)
Writer/Artist   *Publisher*
Bill Mevin   TV Publications Ltd
Issues: 728–731
Story: The Doctor meets the Ancient Mariner, as he seeks to save a race of intelligent frog creatures from a giant shark.

A CHRISTMAS STORY aka A STORY FOR CHRISTMAS (1965)
Writer/Artist   *Publisher*
Bill Mevin   TV Publications Ltd
Issues: 732–735
Story: The Doctor helps Santa Claus save his toys from the Demon Magician.

THE DIDUS EXPEDITION (1966)
Writer/Artist   *Publisher*
Bill Mevin   TV Publications Ltd
Issues: 736–739
Story: The Doctor and his grandchildren brave the perils of an alien jungle to find the last of the Didus birds.

SPACE STATION Z-7 (1966)
Writer/Artist   *Publisher*
Bill Mevin   TV Publications Ltd
Issues: 740–743
Story: The Doctor must warn Earth that fanatical rebels have seized a space battle station and are preparing to attack the galaxy.

PLAGUE OF THE BLACK SCORPI (1966)
Writer/Artist   *Publisher*
Bill Mevin   TV Publications Ltd
Issues: 744–747
Story: On a drought-ravaged planet, the Doctor helps save a plantation from a deadly species of black scorpi, then is instrumental in getting the rains to fall again.

THE TRODOS TYRANNY (1966)

Writer/Artist   *Publisher*
John Canning   TV Publications Ltd
Issues: 748–752
Story: The Doctor encounters the robotic Trods who have overthrown their human creators and plot to enslave the universe. But the controlling Super-Trod is only a puppet directed by a megalomaniacal villain.

THE SECRETS OF GEMINO (1966)

Writer/Artist   *Publisher*
John Canning   TV Publications Ltd
Issues: 753–757
Story: To help the starving Geminians, survivors of an interplanetary war, the Doctor runs a gauntlet of traps in a mechanized city to unlock the Vaults of Plenty.

THE HAUNTED PLANET aka SPACE GHOST (1966)

Writer/Artist   *Publisher*
John Canning   TV Publications Ltd
Issues: 758–762
Story: On the mythical 'haunted planet', the Doctor confronts Zentor, Master of the Supernatural Abode, who is in reality a mad scientist plotting to poison the universe with a deadly gas.

THE HUNTERS OF ZEROX (1966)

Writer/Artist   *Publisher*
John Canning   TV Publications Ltd
Issues: 763–767
Story: The Doctor is the quarry in a hunt to the death by the warriors of a gaming Emperor. He manages to get back to the TARDIS and gains the Emperor's respect.

THE UNDERWATER ROBOT aka UNDERWATER ADVENTURE (1966)

Writer/Artist   *Publisher*
John Canning   TV Publications Ltd
Issues: 768–771

Story: The TARDIS crew defeats two insane inventors, who use a giant underwater robot to plunder surface ships.

RETURN OF THE TRODS (1966)

Writer/Artist	*Publisher*
John Canning	TV Publications Ltd

Issues: 772–775
Story: The TARDIS returns to Trodos where a megalomaniacal space traveller has reactivated the deadly robots.

THE GALAXY GAMES (1966)

Writer/Artist	*Publisher*
John Canning	TV Publications Ltd

Issues: 776–779
Story: John is invited to compete in the Galaxy Games, but a rival team, the Klondites, intends he should fail.

THE EXPERIMENTERS (1966)

Writer/Artist	*Publisher*
John Canning	TV Publications Ltd

Issues: 780–783
Story: A so-called Master Race is developing space flight using humans as guinea pigs.

Second Doctor

THE EXTORTIONER aka VOLCANO (1967)

Writer/Artist	*Publisher*
John Canning	TV Publications Ltd

Issues: 784–787
Story: The villainous Extortioner intends to fire missiles at every civilized world from his hidden volcano base. The Doctor foils his plan by reawakening the volcano.

THE TRODOS AMBUSH aka AMBUSH (1967)

Writer/Artist	*Publisher*
John Canning	TV Publications Ltd

Issues: 788–791
Story: The Doctor travels to Trodos to make peace with the

Trods. But the Daleks have already defeated the Trods and are now laying a trap for the Doctor.

THE DOCTOR STRIKES BACK aka FIGHT-BACK (1967)
Writer/Artist   *Publisher*
John Canning   TV Publications Ltd
Issues: 792-795
Story: Determined to destroy the Daleks, the Doctor infiltrates a Dalek base in a stolen casing and, imitating the Black Dalek, orders the garrison to self-destruct.

THE ZOMBIES (1967)
Writer/Artist   *Publisher*
John Canning   TV Publications Ltd
Issues: 796-798
Story: The Doctor fights the alien Zagbors, who have turned the population of London into zombies.

MASTER OF THE SPIDERS (1967)
Writer/Artist   *Publisher*
John Canning   TV Publications Ltd
Issues: 799-802
Story: Testing an anti-Dalek weapon on a swampy world, the TARDIS crew are pursued by a spider-like vehicle operated by the villainous Master of the Spiders, who wants to feed them to his arachnid pets.

THE EXTERMINATOR (1967)
Writer/Artist   *Publisher*
John Canning   TV Publications Ltd
Issues: 803-806
Story: The Doctor derails a super-train carrying a Dalek team and a giant exterminator gun with which the Daleks plan to destroy the Earth.

THE MONSTERS OF NEW YORK (1967)
Writer/Artist   *Publisher*
John Canning   TV Publications Ltd
Issues: 807-811

Story: The Doctor, John and Gillian are vacationing in 1960s New York when a mad scientist uses a drug to bring several museum dinosaur exhibits back to life.

GODS OF THE JUNGLE aka INDIAN ATTACK (1967)
Writer/Artist   *Publisher*
John Canning   TV Publications Ltd
Issues: 812–815
Story: The time travellers are mistaken for gods by a South American tribe, and are then expected to defeat a rival, unfriendly tribe which is prepared to attack.

ROBOT WAR aka SPACE WAR TWO (1967)
Writer/Artist   *Publisher*
John Canning   TV Publications Ltd
Issues: 816–819
Story: The Doctor must stop super-villain Aborge Quince who is preparing to attack Earth for the second time with an army of war robots.

EGYPTIAN ESCAPADE (1967)
Writer/Artist   *Publisher*
John Canning   TV Publications Ltd
Issues: 820–823
Story: The TARDIS is captured by the soldiers of the Mahadi in Egypt in 1880. The Doctor sets out to warn the British garrison at Fort Cavendish of the Mahadi's plans for attack.

THE COMING OF THE CYBERMEN aka RETURN OF THE CYBERMEN (1967)
Writer/Artist   *Publisher*
John Canning   TV Publications Ltd
Issues: 824–827
Story: Trapped aboard a space carrier, the Doctor must outwit the Cybermen and destroy their powerful flying bomb, whose target is Earth.

SABOTAGE (1967)
Writer/Artist   *Publisher*
John Canning   TV Publications Ltd

Issues: 828–831

Story: In 1988 Arizona, the Doctor uncovers enemy spies in a base hidden under the desert sands and out to disrupt secret US Air Force tests.

FLOWER POWER (1967)

Writer/Artist	*Publisher*
John Canning	TV Publications Ltd

Issues: 832–836

Story: Dead Cybermats are discovered on a peaceful, meadowed world. An eccentric butterfly collector, Professor Grant, helps the Doctor defeat the Cybermen.

THE WITCHING HOUR (1968)

Writer/Artist	*Publisher*
John Canning	TV Publications Ltd

Issues: 837–841

Story: With gadgets from his utility belt, the Doctor puts on an impressive display as the Wizard of Omega to disperse a gathering of witches on planet Vargo.

CYBER-MOLE (1968)

Writer/Artist	*Publisher*
John Canning	TV Publications Ltd

Issues: 842–845

Story: Using a mole machine, the Cybermen steal Earth's Doomsday Bomb, then issue an ultimatum from the Earth's crust: surrender or they will blow up the planet.

ATTACK OF THE PRIMATES (1968)

Writer/Artist	*Publisher*
John Canning	TV Publications Ltd

Issues: 846–849

Story: The time travellers help a weird zoologist, who has invented a miracle substance called Squidge, escape from hostile sabre-toothed gorillas.

EMPIRE OF THE CYBERMEN (1968)

Writer/Artist	*Publisher*
John Canning	TV Publications Ltd

Issues: 850-853
Story: The TARDIS lands in the heart of the Cybermen's Empire. The Doctor fights the Cyber-Controller to free thousands of human slaves.

THE DYRONS (1968)
Writer/Artist   *Publisher*
John Canning   TV Publications Ltd
Issues: 854-858
Story: After their ship crashes, the Doctor helps school expedition defeat the carnivorous Dyrons.

ZARCUS OF NEON aka THE SPACE PIRATES (1968)
Writer/Artist   *Publisher*
John Canning   TV Publications Ltd
Issues: 859-863
Story: The Doctor helps Zarcus, ruler of Neon, to thwart Captain Burglass' pirate raids on his supply ships.

THE CAR OF THE CENTURY (1968)
Writer/Artist   *Publisher*
John Canning   TV Publications Ltd
Issues: 864-867
Story: To make amends for causing a racing accident, the Doctor builds an indestructible car using material from the TARDIS, but it is stolen by a master criminal.

THE JOKERS (1968)
Writer/Artist   *Publisher*
John Canning   TV Publications Ltd
Issues: 868-871
Story: The TARDIS lands on the planet Comedy, where the time travellers encounter the deadly Jokers, four hideous gnomes who delight in playing dangerous practical jokes. With the help of a little snuff, the Doctor turns the tables on them.

INVASION OF THE QUARKS (1968)
Writer/Artist   *Publisher*
John Canning   TV Publications Ltd

Issues: 872-876

Story: John and Gillian enrol at the university on planet Zebadee. The Doctor travels to Scotland and, with the help of Jamie, foils a Quark invasion.

THE KILLER WASPS (1968)

Writer/Artist	*Publisher*
John Canning	TV Publications Ltd

Issues: 877-880

Story: The Quarks develop a strain of giant wasp and dispatch the creatures to destroy the Doctor and Jamie on the planet Gano, but the deadly insects turn against their creators.

THE ICE PRIMATES aka THE ICE APES (1968)

Writer/Artist	*Publisher*
John Canning	TV Publications Ltd

Issues: 881-884

Story: Aliens plan to throw Earth off its axis by detonating a giant, underground bomb, but are foiled by a race of ice primates who live under the pole.

HUNTED BY THE QUARKS aka THE HUNTED (1968)

Writer/Artist	*Publisher*
John Canning	TV Publications Ltd

Issues: 885-889

Story: The Doctor and Jamie use stampeding elephants to survive a hunt by the vengeful Quarks.

THE TEMPLE OF TIME (1969)

Writer/Artist	*Publisher*
John Canning	TV Publications Ltd

Issues: 890-894

Story: The TARDIS arrives in the abode of Father Time, who is furious to see others meddling in his domain.

TERROR OF THE QUARKS aka ROBOT REIGN OF TERROR (1969)

Writer/Artist	*Publisher*
John Canning	TV Publications Ltd

Issues: 895–898
Story: An American tycoon markets the Doctor's latest invention: household robots dubbed 'Marthas', but a radio signal from the Quarks turns the Marthas into deadly killer robots.

THE DUELLISTS (1969)
Writer/Artist   *Publisher*
John Canning   TV Publications Ltd
Issues: 899–902
Story: On planet Hekton, the Doctor faces the deadly Quarks, and a band of cruel Regency gentlemen who subject him to a series of duels.

CYBERMEN ON ICE aka CONFLICT ON ICE (1969)
Writer/Artist   *Publisher*
John Canning   TV Publications Ltd
Issues: 903–906
Story: The Cybermen have landed on an ice planet. The Doctor teams up with Joe, an eskimo inventor, to drive them back.

CRASH-DRIVE (1969)
Writer/Artist   *Publisher*
John Canning   TV Publications Ltd
Issues: 907–910
Story: A rocket crashes into the seabed of planet Nook. The Doctor enlists the help of a giant squid to rescue the astronauts.

OPERATION WURLITZER (1969)
Writer/Artist   *Publisher*
John Canning   TV Publications Ltd
Issues: 911–915
Story: The Doctor leads a mission to rescue Jason Wurlitzer, one of the richest men in the galaxy, from a gang of dwarf kidnappers.

THE TEARAWAYS (1969)
Writer/Artist   *Publisher*
John Canning   TV Publications Ltd
Issues: 916–920

Story: Exiled to Earth by the Time Lords, the Doctor must save three spoiled boys who have run afoul of nuclear fuel thieves.

THE MARK OF TERROR (1969)

Writer/Artist   *Publisher*
John Canning   TV Publications Ltd
Issues: 921–924
Story: The Doctor helps a medical team save a man in a coma, but his condition is due to the Nazi-like Blenhims.

THE BROTHERHOOD (1969)

Writer/Artist   *Publisher*
John Canning   TV Publications Ltd
Issues: 925–928
Story: Living in a West End hotel, the Doctor passes his exile lecturing at London University. But he attracts the attention of the Brotherhood, a Mafia-like organization that intends to use his skills to unearth a buried treasure.

THE QUOTRON RESCUE aka RESCUE (1969)

Writer/Artist   *Publisher*
John Canning   TV Publications Ltd
Issues: 929–933
Story: Via a young radio ham, the Doctor learns of a Quotron spaceship stranded on Earth. He must repair the craft before the authorities learn of its existence.

THE NIGHT WALKERS (1969)

Writer/Artist   *Publisher*
John Canning   TV Publications Ltd
Issues: 934–936
Story: The Doctor investigates the mysteries of walking scarecrows, who turn out to be servants of the Time Lords who have come to Earth to complete the Doctor's sentence – the changing of his physical appearance.

Third Doctor

THE ARKWOOD EXPERIMENTS (1970)
Writer/Artist   *Publisher*
John Canning   Polystyle Publications
Issues: 944–949
Story: A clever but wicked ten-year-old perfects a gas that turns quiet school boys into maniacal hooligans.

THE MULTI-MOBILE (1970)
Writer/Artist   *Publisher*
John Canning   Polystyle Publications
Issues: 950–954
Story: Foreign agents hijack the invincible Multi-Mobile, intent on destroying the Nuclear Defence Centre.

THE INSECTS aka INSECT (1970)
Writer/Artist   *Publisher*
John Canning   Polystyle Publications
Issues: 955–959
Story: The Brigadier and UNIT are called to stop a swarm of giant insects. The Doctor locates the cause: an accident at an insecticide refinery.

THE METAL EATERS (1970)
Writer/Artist   *Publisher*
John Canning   Polystyle Publications
Issues: 960–964
Story: A fallen meteorite disgorges a metal-eating virus, which must then be fought by the Doctor, Liz Shaw and the Brigadier.

THE FISHMEN OF CARPANTHA (1970)
Writer/Artist   *Publisher*
John Canning   Polystyle Publications
Issues: 965–970
Story: The Doctor and Liz encounter the undersea Carpanthans whose city was unwittingly blown up during a UNIT depth charge test, and who are out for revenge.

SUBTERFUGE (1970)

Writer/Artist   *Publisher*
John Canning   Polystyle Publications
Issues: 971–976

Story: At a space centre, Dr Logan falsely claims to have landed men on Venus.

ROBOT RAMPAGE (1970)

Writer/Artist   *Publisher*
John Canning   Polystyle Publications
Issues: 977–984

Story: Professor Readon's new robot, Robbie, goes on an inexplicable rampage. The Doctor finds the culprit, Readon's assistant.

TRIAL OF FIRE (1970)

Writer/Artist   *Publisher*
John Canning   Polystyle Publications
Issues: 985–991

Story: A vengeful scientist makes contact with a rebel band of Fire Demons who live under the Earth, and plans to help them attack the human race.

THE KINGDOM BUILDERS (1971)

Writer/Artist   *Publisher*
John Canning   Polystyle Publications
Issues: 992–999

Story: A prototype time machine travels to 2971 when Britain is a backward country torn apart by two rival slave kingdoms, one of them ruled by the descendant of the time machine's inventor.

CHILDREN OF THE EVIL EYE (1973)

Writer/Artist   *Publisher*
Gerry Haylock   Polystyle Publications
Issues: 1133–1138

Story: The Doctor arrives on Earth in the 32nd century to find a world dominated by children, who are led by the young genius Oswald and his mind-destroying machine, the Eye.

NOVA (1973)
Writer/Artist   *Publisher*
Gerry Haylock   Polystyle Publications
Issues: 1139–1147
Story: The Doctor and Arnold, a boy from the previous story, must defeat the Spidrons, arachnid creatures who prey on the primitive humans sharing their world.

THE AMATEUR (1974)
Writer/Artist   *Publisher*
Gerry Haylock   Polystyle Publications
Issues: 1148–1154
Story: After returning Arnold to the 32nd century, the Doctor must escort a crippled prototype time machine back to the 19th century, but ends up in 1914.

THE DISINTEGRATOR (1974)
Writer/Artist   *Publisher*
Martin Asbury   Polystyle Publications
Issues: 1155–1159
Story: The CID asks the Doctor to investigate gangland boss Sylvester. The Time Lord discovers he is secretly in the employ of the Daleks.

IS ANYONE THERE? (1974)
Writer/Artist   *Publisher*
Gerry Haylock   Polystyle Publications
Issues: 1160–1169
Story: A new Earth device for sending messages into deep space unwittingly almost destroys planet Morrax, which then plans to retaliate.

SIZE CONTROL (1974)
Writer/Artist   *Publisher*
Gerry Haylock   Polystyle Publications
Issues: 1170–1176
Story: The Doctor confronts the insect-like Manti who have perfected size control. They want knowledge of time travel to defeat their former Tyrryxian masters.

THE MAGICIAN (1974)

Writer/Artist   *Publisher*
Gerry Haylock   Polystyle Publications
Issues: 1177–1183
Story: In the Middle Ages, the Doctor is wrongly accused and imprisoned. An evil magician, Sigmus, then plans to steal his body.

THE METAL EATERS (1974)

Writer/Artist   *Publisher*
Gerry Haylock   Polystyle Publications
Issues: 1184–1190
Story: Professor McTurk creates a new species of metal-eating insects, but is killed by foreign agents. Alerted by McTurk's daughter, the Doctor is able to kill the bugs by turning Blackpool Tower into a giant magnet.

LORDS OF THE ETHER (1974)

Writer/Artist   *Publisher*
Gerry Haylock   Polystyle Publications
Issues: 1191–1197
Story: An American astronaut is mysteriously turned to stone. The Doctor and CIA agent Harry Godino discover the tomb of one of the Lords of the Ether on the moon.

THE WANDERERS (1975)

Writer/Artist   *Publisher*
Gerry Haylock   Polystyle Publications
Issues: 1198–1203
Story: In hibernation, the Thusian race is journeying to a new world. But the young and unstable Zeros awakens and plans conquest.

Fourth Doctor

DEATH FLOWER (1975)

Writer/Artist   *Publisher*
Gerry Haylock   Polystyle Publications
Issues: 1204–1214

Story: The Doctor and Sarah investigate Vegpro, a firm manufacturing a sinister new breed of plant life, the Sarricoids.

RETURN OF THE DALEKS (1975)
Writer/Artist   *Publisher*
Martin Asbury   Polystyle Publications
Issues: 1215-1222
Story: Shazar, a renegade Time Lord, allies himself with the Daleks, to steal the Doctor's TARDIS.

THE WRECKERS (1975)
Writer/Artist   *Publisher*
Martin Asbury   Polystyle Publications
Issues: 1223-1231
Story: The Vogans (from *Countdown* 15-22) are behind a plot to drag cargo ships to their doom on the moons of Gorgas.

THE EMPEROR'S SPY (1975)
Writer/Artist   *Publisher*
John Canning   Polystyle Publications
Issues: 1232-1238
Story: In 19th century England, the Doctor helps the Admiralty perfect a submarine for use against Napoleon, and runs afoul of a French spy.

THE SINISTER SEA (1975)
Writer/Artist   *Publisher*
John Canning   Polystyle Publications
Issues: 1239-1244
Story: The Doctor discovers an alien spaceship that is causing tidal waves on the North Sea.

THE SPACE GHOST (1975)
Writer/Artist   *Publisher*
John Canning   Polystyle Publications
Issues: 1245-1250
Story: On the Yorkshire moors, the Doctor and Sarah solve an ancient riddle to rid a tracking station of ghosts.

THE DALEK REVENGE (1976)
Writer/Artist *Publisher*
John Canning Polystyle Publications
Issues: 1251–1258
Story: The Time Lords send the Doctor to Ercos to thwart a Dalek plan to turn the entire planet into a missile aimed at Earth.

VIRUS (1976)
Writer/Artist *Publisher*
John Canning Polystyle Publications
Issues: 1259–1265
Story: The Doctor and Sarah are carriers of a deadly virus, but the language barrier prevents them from warning their Bandriggen captors.

TREASURE TRAIL (1976)
Writer/Artist *Publisher*
John Canning Polystyle Publications
Issues: 1266–1272
Story: In Italy during the Second World War, the Doctor and Sarah help an Italian priest save his monastery's treasures from retreating Nazi soldiers.

HUBERT'S FOLLY (1976)
Writer/Artist *Publisher*
John Canning Polystyle Publications
Issues: 1273–1279
Story: Julian Hubert excavates a site beneath his family's ancestral folly and unleashes a terrible force.

COUNTER-ROTATION (1976)
Writer/Artist *Publisher*
John Canning Polystyle Publications
Issues: 1280–1286
Story: A Martian Scartig infiltrates a space project and launches a device in orbit which will stop Earth's rotation unless his demands are met.

MIND SNATCH (1976)

Writer/Artist   *Publisher*
John Canning   Polystyle Publications
Issues: 1287–1290
Story: Meekle, lord of the evil Goablins, intends to save his race from extinction by possessing the Doctor's mind.

THE HOAXERS (1976)

Writer/Artist   *Publisher*
John Canning   Polystyle Publications
Issue: 1291
Story: The Doctor and Sarah disguise themselves as aliens to persuade a millionaire miser and UFO spotter to make a donation to charity.

THE MUTANT STRAIN (1976)

Writer/Artist   *Publisher*
John Canning   Polystyle Publications
Issues: 1292–1297
Story: The Doctor and a reporter must stop Professor Braun, a mad scientist who has mutated several animals into giants.

DOUBLE TROUBLE (1976)

Writer/Artist   *Publisher*
John Canning   Polystyle Publications
Issues: 1298–1304
Story: The evil Vartheks create a double of the Doctor to frame him in the eyes of the Time Lords.

THE INTRUDERS (1977)

Writer/Artist   *Publisher*
John Canning   Polystyle Publications
Issues: 1305–1311
Story: A Crayton spaceship makes an emergency landing on Earth, but when the aliens try to make peaceful contact, they are attacked by the US Navy.

THE FALSE PLANET (1977)

Writer/Artist   *Publisher*
John Canning   Polystyle Publications

Issues: 1312–1317
Story: The Diloons need the Doctor's aid to find a new fuel source to power their hibernation space fleet.

THE FIRE FEEDERS (1977)
Writer/Artist   *Publisher*
John Canning   Polystyle Publications
Issues: 1318–1325
Story: The Doctor and Detective Inspector Keel use bags of soot to defeat the Zandans and their deadly heat projector.

SHADOW OF THE DRAGON (1977)
Writer/Artist   *Publisher*
John Canning   Polystyle Publications
Issues: 1326–1333
Story: On planet Earthos, the Doctor helps the Braggen defeat their oppressors, the Klings, a Shogun-like civilization.

THE ORB (1977)
Writer/Artist   *Publisher*
John Canning   Polystyle Publications
Issues: 1334–1340
Story: The Doctor and Leela discover a Stracton invasion force inside a hollow asteroid.

THE MUTANTS (1977)
Writer/Artist   *Publisher*
John Canning   Polystyle Publications
Issues: 1341–1347
Story: The Doctor and Leela help the Meerags defeat mutant insects created by pollution.

THE DEVIL'S MOUTH (1977)
Writer/Artist   *Publisher*
John Canning   Polystyle Publications
Issues: 1348–1352
Story: After an accident at Devil's Mouth, a pot-holer turns into a lizard-like Vrakon.

THE AQUA-CITY (1978)
Writer/Artist   *Publisher*
John Canning   Polystyle Publications
Issues: 1353–1360
Story: The Doctor and Leela are rescued from the super-strong Cyeran robots by Kwella, one of the robots' Atlantean creators and who are now victims.

THE SNOW DEVILS (1978)
Writer/Artist   *Publisher*
John Canning   Polystyle Publications
Issues: 1361–1365
Story: The Doctor discovers the Snow Devils threatening a Himalayan monastery are in reality Kurugs, aliens stranded on Earth.

THE SPACE GARDEN (1978)
Writer/Artist   *Publisher*
John Canning   Polystyle Publications
Issues: 1366–1370
Story: The Doctor helps the Dovans to get rid of a huge, mutated plant and a bunch of space pirates.

THE EERIE MANOR (1978)
Writer/Artist   *Publisher*
John Canning   Polystyle Publications
Issues: 1371–1372
Story: Meteorite fragments animate suits of armour at Darke Manor.

THE GUARDIAN OF THE TOMB (1978)
Writer/Artist   *Publisher*
John Canning   Polystyle Publications
Issues: 1373–1379
Story: An unexploded bomb turns out to be an alien space tomb, which releases a mist that takes control of men and machinery.

THE IMAGE MAKERS (1978)
Writer/Artist   *Publisher*
John Canning   Polystyle Publications

Issues: 1380-1385
Story: The Turags are stranded on the planet of the Bukats and use deadly image-projecting technology to protect themselves, in turn leading the Bukats to believe them to be hostile.

THE DUELLISTS
Issues: 1386-1389
Redrawn version of the story originally published in issues 899-902.

THE AMATEUR
Issues: 1390-1396
Redrawn version of the story originally published in issues 1148-1154.

THE MAGICIAN
Issues: 1397-1403
Redrawn version of the story originally published in issues 1177-1183.

THE WANDERERS
Issues: 1404-1408
Redrawn version of the story originally published in issues 1198-1203.

THE METAL EATERS
Issues: 1409-1415
Redrawn version of the story originally published in issues 1184-1190.

MOON EXPLORATION aka LORDS OF THE ETHER
Issues: 1416-1423
Redrawn version of the story originally published in issues 1191-1197.

SIZE CONTROL
Issues: 1424-1430
Redrawn version of the story originally published in issues 1170-1176.

Third Doctor

THE GEMINI PLAN (1971)
Writer/Artist   *Publisher*
Harry Lindfield   Polystyle Publications
Issues: 1–5
Story: An abortive flight in the TARDIS lands the Doctor in Australia, where a catastrophic plan to deflect the path of Venus with a nuclear explosion is set to go off.

TIMEBENDERS (1971)
Writer/Artist   *Publisher*
Harry Lindfield   Polystyle Publications
Issues: 6–13
Story: In 1942, Professor Verdun is forced to work on a crude trans-mat device by the Nazis. His device reaches through time and recalls the Doctor, who must stop the Germans.

THE VOGAN SLAVES (1971)
Writer/Artist   *Publisher*
Harry Lindfield   Polystyle Publications
Issues: 15–22
Story: The Doctor discovers a cryogenic suspension ship operated by the evil Vogans, who are bringing mining slaves to their world. The Doctor defeats the Vogans and finds a new home for the sleepers.

THE CELLULOID MIDAS (1971)
Writer/Artist   *Publisher*
Harry Lindfield   Polystyle Publications
Issues: 23–32
Story: The molecular transformation of a BBC film crew into plastic, brings the Doctor in conflict with mad scientist Professor Midas.

BACKTIME (1971)
Writer/Artist   *Publisher*
Frank Langford   Polystyle Publications

Issues: 33–39
Story: The TARDIS's backtime facility lands the Doctor first in Victorian London, then at the height of the American Civil War.

THE ETERNAL PRESENT (1971)
Writer/Artist   *Publisher*
Harry Lindfield (40–41) Polystyle Publications
and Gerry Haylock (42–46)
Issues: 40–46
Story: The Doctor must stand trial by the Time Police in the year 3550 where he is branded a criminal.

SUB-ZERO (1972)
Writer/Artist   *Publisher*
Gerry Haylock   Polystyle Publications
Issues: 47–54
Story: The Daleks hijack an atomic submarine, then stage an attack on Sidney, planning to convert the survivors into Daleks.

THE PLANET OF THE DALEKS (1972)
Writer/Artist   *Publisher*
Gerry Haylock   Polystyle Publications
Issues: 55–62
Story: Using a Time Vector Generator, the Daleks divert the TARDIS to Skaro where they intend to turn the Doctor into a Dalek. The Doctor escapes and must fight for his life in the jungle.

A STITCH IN TIME (1972)
Writer/Artist   *Publisher*
Gerry Haylock   Polystyle Publications
Issues: 63–70
Story: A super-nova propels the TARDIS to AD 5000 where the primitive Noms battle with the super-human Mutes whose secret weapon is an airship.

THE ENEMY FROM NOWHERE (1972)
Writer/Artist   *Publisher*
Gerry Haylock   Polystyle Publications

Issues: 71–78
Story: The Doctor fights the Zerons, anti-matter creatures who want to exterminate mankind.

THE UGRAKKS (1972)

Writer/Artist   *Publisher*
Gerry Haylock   Polystyle Publications
Issues: 78–88
Story: The Doctor helps an old professor escape the fungus-like Ugrakks with help from the Zama flies.
Note: Ugrakks created by Ian Fairnington.

STEEL FIST (1972)

Writer/Artist   *Publisher*
Gerry Haylock   Polystyle Publications
Issues: 89–93
Story: The Steelfist Gang kidnaps a nuclear physicist.

ZERON INVASION (1973)

Writer/Artist   *Publisher*
Gerry Haylock   Polystyle Publications
Issues: 94–100
Story: The Doctor tries to warn government officials about an imminent space invasion but finds the people of London are already pawns of the aliens.

THE DEADLY CHOICE (1973)

Writer/Artist   *Publisher*
Gerry Haylock   Polystyle Publications
Issues: 101–103
Story: The evil abbot of Mai Sung uses a nerve gas to kidnap the world's leading scientists.

WHO IS THE STRANGER? (1973)

Writer/Artist   *Publisher*
Gerry Haylock   Polystyle Publications
Issue: 104
Story: In France during the Second World War, the Doctor

helps the Reynard Resistance Group to smuggle a German scientist to England.

THE GLEN OF SLEEPING (1973)
Writer/Artist   *Publisher*
Gerry Haylock   Polystyle Publications
Issues: 107–111
Story: The Master awakens a band of fierce Highland warriors asleep since 1745 and uses them to hijack a Polaris submarine. The Doctor takes the submarine back into the past where the Redcoats give the Master a lesson.

THE THREAT FROM BENEATH (1973)
Writer/Artist   *Publisher*
Gerry Haylock   Polystyle Publications
Issue: 112
Story: The Doctor traces the destruction of spy satellites to a submerged Dalek flying saucer.

BACK TO THE SUN (1973)
Writer/Artist   *Publisher*
Gerry Haylock   Polystyle Publications
Issues: 116–119
Story: Sir Lomax, the director of a solar energy plant, is in league with alien invaders who plot to turn Earth into an inferno.

THE LABYRINTH (1973)
Writer/Artist   *Publisher*
Gerry Haylock   Polystyle Publications
Issue: 120
Story: The Doctor must undergo a series of tests on a dying planet, when he is assessed for his suitability to be entrusted with taking the world's doomed children to a new home.

THE SPOILERS (1973)
Writer/Artist   *Publisher*
Gerry Haylock   Polystyle Publications
Issue: 123
Story: Lord Soton of planet Farraf tries to trick the Doctor into

helping him in his insane war against the neighbouring world of Raffar.

THE VORTEX (1973)
| *Writer/Artist* | *Publisher* |
| Gerry Haylock | Polystyle Publications |

Issues: 125–129
Story: An organic world uses a trans-mat beam to capture the Doctor and a young boy as zoo specimens.

THE UNHEARD VOICE (1973)
| *Writer/Artist* | *Publisher* |
| Gerry Haylock | Polystyle Publications |

Issue: 131
Story: The Doctor must track down and disable a malfunctioning satellite that is destroying buildings.

THE HUNGRY PLANET
TV ACTION ANNUAL 1974
| *Writer/Artist* | *Publisher* |
| Gerry Haylock | Polystyle Publications |

Story: The Doctor and a stranded spaceman defeat a living planet.

TV 21

The Dalek Chronicles aka The Dalek Tapes

GENESIS OF EVIL (1965)
Writers	*Publisher*
David Whitaker and	City Publications
Terry Nation	

Artist
Richard Jennings
Issues: 1–3
Story: An alternative history of the Daleks, who are revealed to be mutations of creatures created by Dal scientist Yarvelling.

POWER PLAY (1965)
| *Writer* | *Publisher* |
| David Whitaker | City Publications |

Richard Jennings
Issues: 4–10
Story: The Daleks steal a Krattorian spaceship, thereby gaining access to space.

DUEL OF THE DALEKS (1965)
Writer	*Publisher*
David Whitaker	City Publications

Artist
Richard Jennings
Issues: 11–17
Story: Zeg, a Dalek made stronger by his discovery of an indestructible alloy, challenges the Emperor Dalek, but loses.

THE AMARYLL CHALLENGE aka OUT INTO SPACE (1965)
Writer	*Publisher*
David Whitaker	City Publications

Artist
Richard Jennings
Issues: 18–24
Story: The Daleks fight the vegetal Amarylls on Alvega, and eventually destroy the planet when they find they cannot conquer it.

THE PENTA RAY FACTOR (1965)
Writer	*Publisher*
David Whitaker	City Publications

Artist
Richard Jennings
Issues: 25–32
Story: The Daleks attack Solturis where a human traitor offers them the key to the deadly Penta Ray.

PLAGUE OF DEATH (1965)
Writer	*Publisher*
David Whitaker	City Publications

Artist
Richard Jennings

Issues: 33–39
Story: A mysterious radioactive dust cloud attacks the Daleks.

THE MENACE OF THE MONSTRONS aka ATTACK OF THE MONSTRONS (1965)

Writer	*Publisher*
David Whitaker	City Publications

Artist
Richard Jennings
Issues: 40–46
Story: The Monstrons invade Skaro, but are defeated by Dalek sacrifice and a volcanic eruption.

EVE OF THE WAR (1965)

Writer	*Publisher*
David Whitaker	City Publications

Artists
Richard Jennings and Ron Turner
Issues: 47–51
Story: The Mechanoids use a hypnotic ray to attack the Daleks.

THE ARCHIVES OF PHRYNE (1966)

Writer	*Publisher*
David Whitaker	City Publications

Artist
Eric Eden
Issues: 52–58
Story: Searching for new weapons, the Daleks invade Phryne, the Hidden Planet.

ROGUE PLANET (1966)

Writer	*Publisher*
David Whitaker	City Publications

Artist
Ron Turner
Issues: 59–62
Story: A rogue planet named Skardal threatens Skaro. The Daleks plan to use it against the Mechanoids.

IMPASSE (1966)
Writer   *Publisher*
David Whitaker   City Publications
Artist
Ron Turner
Issues: 63–69
Story: The Zerovians dispatch Robot 2K to Skaro, then to Mechanus, and trick the two species into a truce.

THE TERRORKON HARVEST (1966)
Writer   *Publisher*
David Whitaker   City Publications
Artist
Ron Turner
Issues: 70–75
Story: The Dalek Emperor must locate the whereabouts of a Terrorkon lizard that is carrying a nuclear missile.

LEGACY OF YESTERYEAR (1966)
Writer   *Publisher*
David Whitaker   City Publications
Artist
Ron Turner
Issues: 76–85
Story: Three survivors of the old humanoid Daleks are found. One knows the whereabouts of Earth.

SHADOW OF HUMANITY (1966)
Writer   *Publisher*
David Whitaker   City Publications
Artist
Ron Turner
Issues: 86–89
Story: A Dalek questions an order. The Emperor must find the source of this 'contamination' and eliminate it.

THE EMISSARIES OF JEVO (1966)
Writer   *Publisher*
David Whitaker   City Publications

Artist
Ron Turner
Issues: 90-95
Story: The human factor thwarts the Emperor again when Jevan astronauts choose death instead of surrender.

ROAD TO CONFLICT

Writer	*Publisher*
David Whitaker	City Publications

Artist
Ron Turner
Issues: 96-104
Story: An Earth spaceship crashes on Skaro. The Daleks discover Earth's location from the spaceship's flight recorder.

DOCTOR WHO WEEKLY

Fourth Doctor

DOCTOR WHO AND THE IRON LEGION (1979)

Writers	*Publisher*
Pat Mills and John Wagner	Marvel Comics
(Pat Mills)	

Artist
Dave Gibbons
Issues: 1-8
Story: On an alternative Earth where Rome never fell, robot legions led by General Ironicus are engaged in an eternal war. That Earth is secretly controlled by the evil Malevilus Magog, who poses as Juno, the Emperor's mother. With the help of the robot Vesuvius, the Doctor defeats Magog.

CITY OF THE DAMNED (1980)

Writers	*Publisher*
Pat Mills and John Wagner	Marvel Comics
(John Wagner)	

Artist
Dave Gibbons
Issues: 9-16

Story: In the city of Zombos, ruled by the Brains' Trust, emotion is a crime. The Doctor joins the rebels, but a crazed rebel leader unleashes a man-eating bug. The Doctor discovers that, to save the City, people must be given back their emotions.

TIMESLIP (1980)

Writers	*Publisher*
Dez Skinn (plot) and	Marvel Comics
Paul Neary (script)	

Artist
Paul Neary
Issues: 17–18
Story: A space creature swallows the TARDIS and causes the Doctor to regress through his past.

DOCTOR WHO AND THE STAR BEAST (1980)

Writers	*Publisher*
Pat Mills and John Wagner	Marvel Comics
(Pat Mills)	

Artist
Dave Gibbons
Issues: 19–26
Story: In pursuit of the harmless-looking Meep, the Wrarth turn the Doctor into a living bomb. The Meep turns out to be a bloodthirsty alien, whose black sun stardrive will destroy Earth. The Doctor and Sharon, a young girl from Blackcastle, thwart his plans.

DOCTOR WHO AND THE DOGS OF DOOM (1980)

Writers	*Publisher*
John Wagner and Pat Mills	Marvel Comics
(John Wagner)	

Artist
Dave Gibbons
Issues: 27–34
Story: A space freighter is attacked by the Wereloks. The Doctor, who has briefly turned into a Werelok himself, discovers that the Daleks are behind the attacks. With the help of Brill the Werelock and Sharon, he eventually defeats the Daleks.

DOCTOR WHO AND THE TIME WITCH (1980)
Writer   *Publisher*
Steve Moore   Marvel Comics
Artist
Dave Gibbons
Issues: 35-38
Story: Brimo the Time Witch draws the Doctor and Sharon into her own universe where her every thought becomes reality. The Doctor defeats her by making her think of what she fears the most.

DRAGON'S CLAW (1980)
Writer   *Publisher*
Steve Moore   Marvel Comics
Artist
Dave Gibbons
Issues: 39-45
Story: In 16th century China, the Doctor and Sharon are captured by Shaolin Monks who turn out to have been programmed by the Sontarans to become fierce killers. The Doctor overcomes their conditioning and the monks defeat the Sontarans.

DOCTOR WHO MONTHLY

Fourth Doctor

THE COLLECTOR (1980)
Writer   *Publisher*
Steve Moore   Marvel Comics
Artist
Dave Gibbons
Issue: 46
Story: The Doctor, Sharon and K9 help a stranded alien anthropologist.

DREAMERS OF DEATH (1981)
Writer   *Publisher*
Steve Moore   Marvel Comics

Artist
Dave Gibbons
Issues: 47–48
Story: The Doctor and Sharon land on Uniceptor IV where dreams can be controlled through the telepathic Slinth, who have been secretly feeding on the people's psychic energy. The Doctor uses electricity to destroy a giant Slinth monster. Sharon decides to stay on the planet.

THE LIFE BRINGER (1981)

Writer	*Publisher*
Steve Moore	Marvel Comics

Artist
Dave Gibbons
Issues: 49–50
Story: The Doctor frees Prometheus and meets the Gods of Olympus. After escaping Olympus, he helps Prometheus spread life throughout the universe.

WAR OF THE WORDS (1981)

Writer	*Publisher*
Steve Moore	Marvel Comics

Artist
Dave Gibbons
Issue: 51
Story: The Doctor tricks the alien Vromyx and Garynths into abandoning their war over Biblios, a library planet.

SPIDER-GOD (1981)

Writer	*Publisher*
Steve Moore	Marvel Comics

Artist
Dave Gibbons
Issue: 52
Story: The Doctor cannot prevent a well-meaning human survey team from killing a giant spider, which turns out to be an intrinsic part in a lifechain which produced beautiful butterfly humanoids.

THE DEAL (1981)
Writer   *Publisher*
Steve Parkhouse   Marvel Comics
Artist
Dave Gibbons
Issue: 53
Story: The Doctor encounters, and is used by, a fierce mercenary killer.

END OF THE LINE (1981)
Writer   *Publisher*
Steve Parkhouse   Marvel Comics
Artist
Dave Gibbons
Issues: 54-55
Story: In a bleak, industrial, hopelessly polluted world, the Doctor becomes caught up in a war between underground cannibals and guardian angels.

DOCTOR WHO AND THE FREE-FALL WARRIORS
(1981)
Writer   *Publisher*
Steve Parkhouse   Marvel Comics
Artist
Dave Gibbons
Issues: 56-57
Story: The Doctor meets Doctor Asimoff and the Freefall Warriors and becomes involved in a space race which turns into a space battle.

JUNKYARD DEMON (1981)
Writer   *Publisher*
Steve Parkhouse   Marvel Comics
Artists
Mike McMahon and Adolfo Buylla
Issues: 58-59
Story: A Mondasian Cyberman becomes reactivated and hijacks the TARDIS and Jetsam, the mechanic of a galactic junkyard,

whom he wants to revive Zogroan, an ancient Cyberleader, but instead Jetsam turns him into a super-butler.

THE NEUTRON KNIGHTS (1982)
Writer   *Publisher*
Steve Parkhouse   Marvel Comics
Artist
Dave Gibbons
Issue: 60
Story: Merlin draws the Doctor to a future time when he and King Arthur are about to be defeated by the forces of Catavolcus and his Neutron Knights.

Fifth Doctor

THE TIDES OF TIME (1982)
Writer   *Publisher*
Steve Parkhouse   Marvel Comics
Artist
Dave Gibbons
Issues: 61–67
Story: The demon Melanicus takes control of the Event Synthesizer, which enables him to create chaos through time and space. Rassilon, Merlin and other High Evolutionaries enlist the Doctor's help. With Justin, a knight, and Shayde, a Matrix agent sent by Rassilon, the Doctor travels into a white hole where he meets the powerful civilization of Althrace from which Melanicus originally comes. Eventually, the High Evolutionaries achieve a reversal of time, which enables the Doctor and Justin to defeat the demon.

STARS FELL ON STOCKBRIDGE (1982)
Writer   *Publisher*
Steve Parkhouse   Marvel Comics
Artist
Dave Gibbons
Issues: 68–69
Story: The Doctor and Maxwell Edison, who believes in UFOs, discover a haunted starship.

THE STOCKBRIDGE HORROR (1983)
Writer   *Publisher*
Steve Parkhouse   Marvel Comics
Artists
Steve Parkhouse, Paul Neary, Mick Austin
Issues: 70–75
Story: The TARDIS becomes possessed by the elemental spirit of the haunted spacecraft. Having failed to expunge it, the Doctor faces trial on Gallifrey, but is eventually cleared by Shayde.

LUNAR LAGOON (1983)
Writer   *Publisher*
Steve Parkhouse   Marvel Comics
Artist
Mick Austin
Issues: 76–77
Story: On a Pacific Island, the Doctor becomes involved in a conflict between Americans and Japanese in the Second World War. Yet, the year is 1963.

FOUR-DIMENSIONAL VISTAS (1983)
Writer   *Publisher*
Steve Parkhouse   Marvel Comics
Artist
Mick Austin
Issues: 78–83
Story: The Doctor leaves the alternative 1963 with Angus Goodman, the American fighter pilot, as his new companion and discovers that the Meddling Monk and the Ice Warriors have been manipulating time from their Arctic Base. The Doctor succeeds in defeating them with some help from the paramilitary SAG commando.

THE MODERATOR (1984)
Writer   *Publisher*
Steve Parkhouse   Marvel Comics
Artist
Steve Dillon

Issue: 84
Story: The Doctor and Angus run afoul of Josiah W Dogbolter, a ruthless froglike tycoon who wants to buy the TARDIS.

DOCTOR WHO MAGAZINE

Fifth Doctor

THE MODERATOR (continued) (1984)
Writer	*Publisher*
Steve Parkhouse	Marvel Comics

Artist
Steve Dillon
Issues: 86–87
Story: When the Doctor refuses to sell the TARDIS, Dogbolter sends the Moderator, a hired killer, after him. Angus shoots the Moderator, who then kills him.

Sixth Doctor

THE SHAPE SHIFTER (1984)
Writer	*Publisher*
Steve Parkhouse	Marvel Comics

Artist
John Ridgway
Issues: 88–89
Story: Dogbolter puts a price on the Doctor's head. Frobisher, the shape-changing Whifferdill and the Doctor team up to trick him out of the reward.

THE VOYAGER (1984)
Writer	*Publisher*
Steve Parkhouse	Marvel Comics

Artist
John Ridgway
Issues: 90–94
Story: The Doctor and Frobisher the Whifferdill (now in the shape of a three-foot high penguin) meet Astrolabus, the Time Thief, who once stole star charts from the mysterious Lord of Life, Voyager, who now asks the Doctor for their return.

POLLY THE GLOT (1985)
Writer   *Publisher*
Steve Parkhouse   Marvel Comics
Artist
John Ridgway
Issues: 95-97
Story: The Doctor and Frobisher team up with Dr Asimoff to save the beautiful Zyglots, hunted by the dull Akkers, while having another encounter with Astrolabus, who kidnaps Frobisher.

ONCE UPON A TIME LORD (1985)
Writer   *Publisher*
Steve Parkhouse   Marvel Comics
Artist
John Ridgway
Issues: 98-99
Story: The Doctor pursues Astrolabus through a land of nightmarish fantasies. He eventually discovers that the star charts Astrolabus stole are tattooed on his body. Voyager comes and reclaims his charts.

WAR-GAME (1985)
Writer   *Publisher*
Alan McKenzie   Marvel Comics
Artist
John Ridgway
Issues: 100-101
Story: On a savage, primitive planet, the Doctor and Frobisher become involved in a war between a stranded Draconian and a Barbarian warlord.

FUNHOUSE (1985)
Writer   *Publisher*
Alan McKenzie   Marvel Comics
(as Max Stockbridge)
Artist
John Ridgway

Issues: 102–103
Story: The Doctor and Frobisher defeat a creature that looks like an old house and lives in the time vortex.

KANE'S STORY (1985)

ABEL'S STORY (1985)

THE WARRIOR'S STORY (1985)

FROBISHER'S STORY (1985)

Writer	*Publisher*
Alan McKenzie	Marvel Comics
(as Max Stockbridge)	
Artist	
John Ridgway	

Issues: 104, 105, 106, 107 respectively
Story: Six champions are drafted to save the galaxy from the Skeletoids: the Doctor, Peri, Frobisher, a Draconian, Kane and Abel Gantz, the alchemist, who sacrifices his life.

EXODUS (1986)

REVELATION (1986)

GENESIS (1986)

Writer	*Publisher*
Alan McKenzie	Marvel Comics
Artist	
John Ridgway	

Issues: 108, 109, 110 respectively
Story: The Doctor encounters fleeing farmers whose story leads him to Sylvaniar where a mad scientist has been reconstructing a host of Cybermen. Frobisher discovers he is now stuck in penguin shape.

NATURE OF THE BEAST (1986)

Writer	*Publisher*
Simon Furman	Marvel Comics
Artist	
John Ridgway	

Issues: 111–113
Story: The Doctor and Peri encounter a wolf-like creature who turns out to be the transformed wife of an alien warlord.

TIME BOMB (1986)

Writer	Publisher
Jamie Delano	Marvel Comics

Artist
John Ridgway
Issues: 114–116
Story: The Doctor and Frobisher help save the alien Hedrons who have unwittingly disposed of their genetically impure material by warping it back to primeval Earth, where it created an advanced society which in turn brought about the Hedrons' destruction.

SALAD DAZE (1986)

Writer	Publisher
Simon Furman	Marvel Comics

Artist
John Ridgway
Issue: 117
Story: Peri goes through a personal reality warp and ends up in her own version of Alice's Wonderland.

CHANGES (1986)

Writer	Publisher
Grant Morrison	Marvel Comics

Artist
John Ridgway
Issues: 118–119
Story: A shape-shifting chimera gains entry to the TARDIS. The Doctor, Peri and Frobisher must search the ship for it.

PROFITS OF DOOM (1987)

Writer	Publisher
Mike Collins	Marvel Comics

Artist
John Ridgway
Issues: 120–122
Story: On their way to the peace-loving world of Arcadia, the Doctor, Peri and Frobisher encounter the *Mayflower*, a space-

craft carrying colonists from an overcrowded Earth to a new planet. It is attacked by profit-minded, slug-like aliens. The Doctor discovers that the evil immortal Seth is behind the scheme. He defeats the aliens and helps the colonists relocate to the world that will one day become Arcadia.

THE GIFT (1987)
Writer	Publisher
Jamie Delano	Marvel Comics

Artists
John Ridgway and Tim Perkins (inks, 126 only)
Issues: 123–126
Story: To rid the planet Zazz of a breed of self-replicating robots unwittingly brought back by a crazy scientist's space probe, the Doctor resorts to the Pied Piper's trick.

THE WORLD SHAPERS (1987)
Writer	Publisher
Grant Morrison	Marvel Comics

Artists
John Ridgway and Tim Perkins
Issues: 127–129
Story: Responding to a distress signal from another TARDIS, the Doctor and Peri land on Marinus. The Voords have used a time-altering, world-changing device to turn the planet into an arid world (later to be known as Planet 14, then Mondas) and evolve themselves into Cybermen. The Doctor seeks help from an ageing Jamie, who sacrifices himself to destroy the world-shaper. The Time Lords refuse to stop the creation of the Cybermen because they know that, someday, they will evolve into a disembodied, benevolent intelligence.

Seventh Doctor

A COLD DAY IN HELL (1988)
Writer	Publisher
Simon Furman	Marvel Comics

Artists
John Ridgway and Tim Perkins

Issues: 130–133
Story: The Ice Warriors turn A-Lux, a pleasure planet, into an iceworld, from which they plan to attack the Federation. The Doctor teams up with a Dreilyn heat vampire to defeat them. Afterwards, Frobisher chooses to stay on the planet.

REDEMPTION (1988)
Writer   *Publisher*
Simon Furman   Marvel Comics
Artists
Kevin Hopgood and Tim Perkins
Issue: 134
Story: The young Dreilyn picked up by the Doctor in the previous story is revealed to be a heat vampire.

THE CROSSROADS OF TIME (1988)
Writer   *Publisher*
Simon Furman   Marvel Comics
Artist
Geoff Senior
Issue: 135
Story: The Doctor's TARDIS collides with bounty-hunter Death-Head in the Vortex.

CLAWS OF THE KLATHI
Writer   *Publisher*
Mike Collins   Marvel Comics
Artists
Kevin Hopgood and Dave Hine
Issues: 136–138
Story: The 1851 Great Exhibition in London provides the power source for a crashed alien ship attempting to leave Earth, but in the process thousands could die.

CULTURE SHOCK (1988)
Writer   *Publisher*
Grant Morrison   Marvel Comics
Artist
Bryan Hitch
Issue: 139

Story: The Doctor helps the Syntelligence to escape from a virus.

KEEPSAKE (1988)
Writer   *Publisher*
Simon Furman   Marvel Comics
Artist
John Higgins
Issue: 140
Story: The Doctor saves a medic in distress and provides a little action and romance for a scavenger.

PLANET OF THE DEAD (1988)
Writer   *Publisher*
John Freeman   Marvel Comics
Artist
Lee Sullivan
Issues: 141–142
Story: The Doctor encounters the parasitic, shape-changing Gwanzulum who disguise themselves as his previous incarnations and many of his former companions in the hope he will take them off the planet.

ECHOES OF THE MOGOR (1989)
Writer   *Publisher*
Dan Abnett   Marvel Comics
Artist
John Ridgway
Issues: 143–144
Story: The Doctor helps a Foreign Hazard Duty team solve a series of murders: the victims died of fright when they beheld the images of monstrous creatures retained by a planet's peculiar geology.

TIME AND TIDE (1989)
Writers   *Publisher*
Richard Alan and   Marvel Comics
John Carnell
Artists
Dougie Braithwaite and Dave Elliott

Issues: 145–146
Story: The Doctor persuades the one warrior of the fatalistic Tojanan race to leave his planet before his race is wiped out.

FOLLOW THAT TARDIS (1989)

Writer	*Publisher*
John Carnell	Marvel Comics

Artists
Andy Lanning, John Higgins, Kevin Hopgood, Dougie Braithwaite and Dave Elliott
Issue: 147
Story: The Doctor and the Sleeze Brothers team up to stop the Meddling Monk from tampering with history.

INVADERS FROM GANTAC (1989)

Writer	*Publisher*
Alan Grant	Marvel Comics

Artists
Martin Griffiths and Cam Smith
Issues: 148–150
Story: Body lice from the unwanted vagrant Leapy help destroy alien invaders.

NEMESIS OF THE DALEKS (1989)

Writers	*Publisher*
Richard Alan (plot) and	Marvel Comics
Steve Alan (script)	

Artist
Lee Sullivan
Issues: 152–155
Story: The Doctor teams up with Abslom Daak to confront the Emperor Dalek and stave off Operation Genocide. Daak sacrifices his life to destroy the Daleks' Death Wheel.

STAIRWAY TO HEAVEN (1990)

Writers	*Publisher*
Paul Cornell (plot) and	Marvel Comics
John Freeman (script)	

Artists
Gerry Dolan (pencils) and Rex Ward (inks)

Issue: 156
Story: The Doctor becomes part of living art when he meets Garg Ardoniquist, the genetic sculptor.

HUNGER FROM THE ENDS OF TIME (1990)

Writer	*Publisher*
Dan Abnett	Marvel Comics
Artist	
John Ridgway	

Issues: 157-158
Story: The Doctor meets a Foreign Hazard Duty team on the planet Catalog where, to save space, the archives are stored in different times. But bugs are eating up the information, so the Doctor is forced to bring everything back to the present.

TRAIN FLIGHT (1990)

Writers	*Publisher*
Andrew Donkin and	Marvel Comics
Graham S Brand	
Artist	
John Ridgway	

Issues: 159-161
Story: The Doctor and Sarah Jane Smith encounter renegade Kaliks, insect-like aliens who hunt humans.

DOCTOR CONKEROR (1990)

Writer	*Publisher*
Ian Rimmer	Marvel Comics
Artist	
Mike Collins	

Issue: 162
Story: The Doctor seeks more conkers for his game. Some Vikings have a different idea about conquering.

FELLOW TRAVELLERS (1990)

Writer	*Publisher*
Andrew Cartmel	Marvel Comics
Artist	
Arthur Ranson	

Issues: 164–166
Story: The Doctor and Ace are pursued by Hitchers through the time vortex, and eventually confront the creatures in a strange country mansion.

DARKNESS FALLING (1990)
DISTRACTIONS (1991)
THE MARK OF MANDRAGORA (1991)

Writer	*Publisher*
Dan Abnett	Marvel Comics

Artist
Lee Sullivan
Issues: 167, 168 and 169–172 respectively
Story: A UNIT soldier is in trouble, as mysterious forces gather for a final confrontation. The Doctor finally realizes what has been bothering him about his recent Earthbound adventures: the Mandragora Helix still infects the TARDIS after all these years.

PARTY ANIMALS (1991)

Writer	*Publisher*
Gary Russell	Marvel Comics

Artists
Mike Collins and Steve Pini
Issue: 173
Story: The Doctor and Ace finally reach Maruthea for Bonjaxx's party, but they're not the only ones who have been delayed.

THE GOOD SOLDIER (1991)

Writer	*Publisher*
Andrew Cartmel	Marvel Comics

Artists
Mike Collins and Steve Pini
Issues: 175–177
Story: America in the 1950s, flying saucers, virulent anti-communism, and a mysterious spaceship in orbit around the moon all add up to a deadly puzzle for the Doctor and Ace.

BACK-UP FEATURE AND SPECIALS

THE RETURN OF THE DALEKS (1979)

Writer
Steve Moore

Publisher
Marvel Comics

Artists
Paul Neary and David Lloyd

Issues: 1–4

Story: On planet Anhaut, movie studio owner Glax unwittingly brings back the Daleks, who had been defeated 800 years ago. The actor playing the role of the one who defeated them and a former Dalek agent help defeat them again.

THROWBACK (THE SOUL OF A CYBERMAN) (1979)

Writer
Steve Moore

Publisher
Marvel Comics

Artist
Steve Dillon

Issues: 5–7

Story: On Mondaran, junior Cyberleader Kroton turns out to have emotions. He befriends the human rebel leader, even saving him from the other Cybermen, and eventually leaves the planet for the solitude of space.

THE FINAL QUEST (1979)

Writer
Steve Moore

Publisher
Marvel Comics

Artist
Paul Neary

Issue: 8

Story: Vicious Sontaran warrior Katsu looks for the ultimate weapon and eventually discovers it is a deadly plague, which kills him.

THE STOLEN TARDIS (1979)

Writer
Steve Moore

Publisher
Marvel Comics

Artist
Steve Dillon

Issues: 9–11
Story: Reptilian alien Sillarc steals a TARDIS, unaware that young Time Lord mechanic Plutar is on board. Plutar eventually outwits Sillarc, and gets promoted to full Time Lordship.

K-9'S FINEST HOUR (1980)
Writer   *Publisher*
Steve Moore   Marvel Comics
Artist
Paul Neary
Issue: 12
Story: Space villain Rolgof is hired by the Sontarans to kill the Doctor but is instead defeated by K9.

WARLORD OF THE OGRONS (1980)
Writer   *Publisher*
Steve Moore   Marvel Comics
Artist
Steve Dillon
Issues: 13–14
Story: Villainous Dr Leofrix uses brain implants to turn Gnork the Ogron into a super-Ogron, but Gnork steals his ship and abandons him on the Ogron planet.

DEATHWORLD (1980)
Writer   *Publisher*
Steve Moore   Marvel Comics
Artist
David Lloyd
Issues: 15–16
Story: Looking for Trisilicate, the Ice Warriors land on Yama-10. There, they fight the Cybermen to mutual extermination.

ABSLOM DAAK, DALEK-KILLER (1980)
Writer   *Publisher*
Steve Moore   Marvel Comics
Artist
Steve Dillon
Issues: 17–20

Story: Abslom Daak, a convicted criminal of the 26th century, chooses to become a Dalek-killer rather than face capital punishment. Exiled to planet Mazam, he helps Princess Tayin get rid of the Daleks, but a surviving Dalek kills her. Daak swears revenge on the entire Dalek race.

TWILIGHT OF THE SILURIANS (1980)
Writer	*Publisher*
Steve Moore	Marvel Comics
Artist	
David Lloyd	

Issues: 21–22
Story: In the last days of the Silurians, early hominids get their revenge upon Silurian scientist Nagara who mistreated them.

SHIP OF FOOLS (1980)
Writer	*Publisher*
Steve Moore	Marvel Comics
Artist	
Steve Dillon	

Issues: 23–24
Story: A spaceship caught in a time warp picks up rebel Cyberman Kroton, which frees the ship, but time catches up with the humans and everyone on board dies, leaving Kroton alone once more.

THE OUTSIDER (1980)
Writer	*Publisher*
Steve Moore	Marvel Comics
Artist	
David Lloyd	

Issues: 25–26
Story: Skrant the Sontaran lands on Braktilis and enlists the help of Demimon, a local astrologer, who ends up killing him to save his daughter.

STAR TIGERS (1980)
Writer	*Publisher*
Steve Moore	Marvel Comics

Artist
Steve Dillon
Issues: 27–30
Story: Prince Salander of Draconia teams up with Abslom Daak, Dalek-killer, and is forced to flee from his planet. The two of them embark on an expedition to recruit more companions.

YONDER ... THE YETI (1980)
Writer   *Publisher*
Steve Moore   Marvel Comics
Artist
David Lloyd
Issues: 31–34
Story: The Great Intelligence and its Yeti attack three travellers in Tibet, but are defeated by the monk Gampo and his real Yeti.

BLACK LEGACY (1980)
Writer   *Publisher*
Alan Moore   Marvel Comics
Artist
David Lloyd
Issues: 35–38
Story: On Goth, the Cybermen meet the Apocalypse Device of the long-dead Deathsmiths, which turns out to be a deadly synthetic creature. The last surviving Cyberman sacrifices himself to imprison the monster.

BUSINESS AS USUAL (1980)
Writer   *Publisher*
Alan Moore   Marvel Comics
Artist
David Lloyd
Issues: 40–43
Story: The Autons turn out to be behind a line of action figures plastic toys, but are found out by an industrial spy.

STAR TIGERS (1980)
Writer   *Publisher*
Steve Moore   Marvel Comics

Artist
Steve Dillon
Issues: 44–46
Story: Abslom Daak and Salander recruit Harma, an Ice Warrior, as well as Mercurius, Daak's old rival, whom he snatches away from an army of robot killers. Together, they then defeat a Dalek space commando unit.

STAR DEATH (1980)

Writer	*Publisher*
Alan Moore	Marvel Comics

Artist
David Lloyd
Issue: 47
Story: Fenris the Hellbringer, a master saboteur from the future, tries to prevent the creation of the Time Lords. He is stopped by Rassilon, but only after he has already caused Omega's doom.

THE TOUCHDOWN ON DENEB 7 (1981)

Writer	*Publisher*
Paul Neary	Marvel Comics

Artist
David Lloyd
Issue: 48
Story: K9 meets five ancient robots who explain the disappearance of Deneb 7.

VOYAGE TO THE EDGE OF THE UNIVERSE (1981)

Writers	*Publisher*
Paul Neary and David Lloyd	Marvel Comics

Artist
David Lloyd
Issue: 49
Story: Azal the Daemon confronts another, identical universe at the edge of ours.

CRISIS ON KALDOR (1981)

Writer	*Publisher*
Steve Moore	Marvel Comics

Artist
John Stokes
Issue: 50
Story: A human agent disguises himself as a robot to thwart a rebellion by the Robots of Death but is later killed by the other robots, which think he's suffering from a malfunction.

THE 4-D WAR (1981)
Writer   *Publisher*
Alan Moore   Marvel Comics
Artist
David Lloyd
Issue: 51
Story: Time Lady Jodelex and Wardog retrieve Fenris and discover he was sent by the Order of the Black Sun, whose members then lead an attack upon Gallifrey to silence him.

THE GREATEST GAMBLE (1981)
Writer   *Publisher*
John Peel   Marvel Comics
Artist
Mike McMahon
Issue: 56
Story: The Celestial Toymaker punishes a Mississippi riverboat gambler who cheats.

BLACK SUN RISING (1981)
Writer   *Publisher*
Alan Moore   Marvel Comics
Artist
David Lloyd
Issue: 57
Story: A Sontaran tricks a Time Lady into killing a member of the Order of the Black Sun, thus leading to the future war between the order and Gallifrey. But she is avenged by Wardog.

SKYWATCH-7 (1981)
Writer   *Publisher*
Alan McKenzie   Marvel Comics
(as Max Stockbridge)

Artist
Mick Austin
Issues: 58 and Winter Special 1981
Story: UNIT's remote radar post Skywatch-7 is attacked by a shape-changing Zygon.

MINATORIUS (1981)
Writer   *Publisher*
Alan McKenzie   Marvel Comics
(as Max Stockbridge)
Artist
John Stokes
Issue: Winter Special 1981
Story: Young Time Lord Cargan and his robot companion, Orb, save the galaxy from a power-draining complex at the cost of their own lives.

THE GODS WALK AMONG US (1981)
Writer   *Publisher*
John Peel   Marvel Comics
Artist
David Lloyd
Issue: 59
Story: A Sontaran is found buried in an ancient Egyptian tomb.

DEVIL OF THE DEEP (1982)
Writer   *Publisher*
John Peel   Marvel Comics
Artist
John Stokes
Issue: 61
Story: In the 17th century, pirates encounter a Sea Devil.

THE FIRES DOWN BELOW (1982)
Writer   *Publisher*
John Peel   Marvel Comics
Artist
John Stokes
Issue: 64

Story: UNIT troops encounter a Dominator inside an Icelandic volcano.

THE FABULOUS IDIOT (1982)

| *Writer* | *Publisher* |
| Steve Parkhouse | Marvel Comics |

Artists
Steve Parkhouse and Geoff Senior
Issue: Summer Special 1982
Story: SF writer Dr Ivan Asimoff meets his cover artist.

HULK PRESENTS

Seventh Doctor

ONCE IN A LIFETIME (1989)

| *Writer* | *Publisher* |
| John Freeman | Marvel Comics |

Artist
Geoff Senior
Issue: 1
Story: The Doctor is pestered by a nosy reporter.

HUNGER FROM THE ENDS OF TIME (1989)
Issues: 2-3
See *Doctor Who Magazine* 157-158.

WAR WORLD (1989)

| *Writer* | *Publisher* |
| John Freeman | Marvel Comics |

Artists
Art Weatherell and Dave Harwood
Issue: 4
Story: The Doctor lands in the middle of a centuries-old war.

TECHNICAL HITCH (1989)

| *Writer* | *Publisher* |
| Dan Abnett | Marvel Comics |

Artists
Art Weatherell and Dave Harwood
Issue: 5
Story: On a strange planet, the Doctor seeks to help a man who has lost its entire population.

A SWITCH IN TIME (1989)

Writer   *Publisher*
John Freeman   Marvel Comics
Artist
Geoff Senior
Issue: 6
Story: The Doctor is caught up in a bizarre chase between dimensions.

THE SENTINEL (1989)

Writer   *Publisher*
John Tomlinson   Marvel Comics
Artist
Andy Wildman
Issue: 7
Story: A genetic scientist seeks to create a new race of Time Lords, using the Doctor as guinea pig.

WHO'S THAT GIRL (1989)

Writer   *Publisher*
Simon Furman   Marvel Comics
Artists
John Marshall and Steven Baskerville
Issues: 8-9
Story: A girl impersonates the Doctor to assassinate a warlord.

THE ENLIGHTENMENT OF LI-CHEE (1980)

Writer   *Publisher*
Simon Jowett   Marvel Comics
Artist
Andy Wildman
Issue: 10
Story: The Doctor answers a holy man's life-long question.

SLIMMER! (1989)
Writers   *Publisher*
Mike Collins and   Marvel Comics
Tim Robbins
Artist
Geoff Senior
Issue: 11
Story: The Doctor investigates some mysterious happenings on a health farm.

NINEVEH! (1989)
Writer   *Publisher*
John Tomlinson   Marvel Comics
Artist
Cam Smith
Issue: 12
Story: Summoned to a graveyard of TARDISes, the Doctor is told his life is at an end.

DEATH'S HEAD

Seventh Doctor

TIME BOMB (1989)
Writer   *Publisher*
Steve Parkhouse   Marvel Comics
Artists
Art Weatherell and Steve Parkhouse
Issue: 8
Story: Dogbolter hires Death's Head to steal the TARDIS and kill the Doctor.

DOCTOR WHO ANNUALS

First Doctor

1967
Writer   *Publisher*
David Whitaker   World International

MISSION FOR DUH
Story: Returning to the planet Birr, the Doctor resolves a misunderstanding between the Rostrows and the native plant Verdants.

Second Doctor

1968
Publisher
World International

THE TESTS OF TREFUS
Story: The Doctor shows the rulers of Trefus that those with fair hair are not inferior to dark-haired ones.

WORLD WITHOUT NIGHT
Story: A sunlit civilization destroys itself in a fit of madness because they have never known an eclipse.

1969
Publisher
World International

FREEDOM BY FIRE
Story: To save a starving tribe from plant creatures, the Doctor teaches them how to make fire.

ATOMS INFINITE
Story: At the heart of an atom, the Doctor finds worlds threatened by atomic fission.

1970
Publisher
World International

THE VAMPIRE PLANTS
Story: A botanist on Venus, Dr Vane, is searching for a rare plant he thinks has been stolen. But it has mutated into something deadly.

THE ROBOT KING
Story: The Doctor travels to a future Earth where robots are the sole survivors of a holocaust.

Third Doctor

1974
Publisher
World International

THE TIME THIEF
Story: The Master uses a time transporter to send invaders to any place on Earth.

MENACE OF THE MOLAGS
Story: Demon-like creatures return to warn Earth of the awakening of the Molags, seed-based mindless monsters which will drain the planet of all life.

1975
Publisher
World International

DEAD ON ARRIVAL
Story: Jo is sucked through a time warp to an alternative Earth.

AFTER THE REVOLUTION
Story: The Doctor returns to a post-revolution world whose ruler has now created robots controlled by him to fulfil his view of perfection after the failure of his new world.

Fourth Doctor

1976
Publisher
World International

THE PSYCHIC JUNGLE
Story: A planet protects itself by projecting the fears that visitors carry in their minds.

NEURONIC NIGHTMARE
Story: Neuroids try to use the TARDIS crew to absorb neuronic energy which threatens their existence.

1977
Publisher
World International

THE BODY SNATCHER
Story: The Doctor's body is taken over, but by storing his soul in Sarah's body, the Time Lord retains control of his own.

MENACE ON METALUPITER
Story: Metalupiter is being fused into a giant crystal, but the process threatens the entire solar system.

1978
Publisher
World International

THE RIVAL ROBOTS
Story: Two types of robots fight to protect their masters from the perceived threat of the other type.

THE TRAITOR
Story: The Doctor is forced to betray a group of escapees to keep them on a planet that nullifies their deformities.

1979
Publisher
World International

THE POWER
Story: The ruling princess of Shem decides to give the power to all the Shemians.

EMSONE'S CASTLE
Story: The Doctor fights Emsone, who wishes to incorporate a Time Lord's brain in the heart of a machine.

1980
Publisher
World International

TERROR ON XABOI
Story: The Doctor reluctantly destroys a large beast to allow the evolution of the Xaboi to continue.

THE WEAPON
Story: The Doctor destroys a weapon which threatened to alter the everlasting fight between good and evil.

1981
Publisher
World International

EVERY DOG HAS HIS DAY
Story: K9 reprograms a war computer.

1982
Publisher
World International

PLAGUE WORLD
Story: The Druden unleash a plague on a human colony to obtain human flesh for their young.

Fifth Doctor

1983
Publisher
World International

ON THE PLANET ISOPTERUS
Story: The Doctor uses a dream machine to divert giant termites.

DALEK ANNUALS

THE DALEK BOOK 1965 (1964)

Writers	*Publisher*
Terry Nation and David Whitaker	Souvenir

INVASION OF THE DALEKS
Story: Skaro moves into the solar system. The Daleks attack the Earth colony on Venus. Scientists Jeff and Mary Stone are taken prisoners. Their brother, Andy, swears to free them and rid Venus of the invaders.

CITY OF THE DALEKS
Story: Jeff Stone infiltrates the Dalek city on Skaro. He takes back to Earth a secret document showing the anatomy of a Dalek.

THE HUMANOIDS
Story: Mary, Jeff and Andy, looking for Daleks on Mars, uncover a plot to flood the Earth with android replicas.

MONSTERS OF GURNIAN
Story: Captured by the Daleks, Andy and Mary Stone must survive on the dreaded planet Gurnian. They find the savage, twin-headed Horrorkon monsters unusual allies against the Daleks.

BATTLE FOR THE MOON
Story: The Dalek Emperor signs a peace treaty, but on the Moon, a Dalek unit is preparing to bombard Earth with moondust.
Note: This book also contains the following photo-novel, which uses frames from the television story B.

THE DALEK OUTER SPACE BOOK 1967 (1966)

Writers	*Publisher*
David Whitaker and Terry Nation	Souvenir

THE DALEK TRAP
Story: The Daleks kidnap two astronauts and force them to trek

into the caves of Skaro in search of a mineral that will increase their firepower.

SARA KINGDOM, SPACE SECURITY AGENT
Story: Sara rescues a top scientist being held at a slave colony and whose knowledge of metallurgy is needed by the Daleks.

THE SUPER SUB
Story: Jeff Stone discovers the wreck of a Dalek submarine at the bottom of the sea.

SECRET OF THE EMPEROR
Story: The Dalek Emperor orders that a gigantic, static casing be built for him in the heart of the Dalek city.

THE SEA MONSTERS
Story: Off the coast of Spain, a marine rescue brigade tracks down and kills a mutated species of reptiles.
Note: Filler story unconnected with the Daleks.

THE UNWILLING TRAVELLER
Story: A burglar breaks into a research centre and accidentally gets locked inside a time machine.
Note: Filler story unconnected with the Daleks.

CHRIS WELKIN, PLANETEER
Story: A young boy helps Planeteer Chris Welkin defeat a hijacker intent on stealing a magnetically-powered spaceship.
Note: Filler story unconnected with the Daleks.

THE BRAIN TAPPERS
Story: The Daleks put a vessel into Earth's orbit with a device aboard that can read human minds.

TERRY NATION'S DALEK ANNUAL 1976
Publisher
World International

PLANET OF SPIDERS
Story: Reb Shavron crashes on Terroth to be confronted in turn by swamp creatures and by Daleks.

FLOOD!!!
Story: The world's cities are threatened by catastrophic flooding as the Daleks melt the polar ice caps.

1977
Publisher
World International

THE ENVOYS OF EVIL
Story: The Daleks invade the peaceful planet of Solturis. Although they appear friendly, they intend to exterminate the people and seize their weapon, the penta ray.

THE MENACE OF THE MONSTRONS
Story: Monstrons, a highly advanced race, land on Skaro and plan to enslave the Daleks as Engibrain soldiers wreak havoc on the planet.

THE QUEST
Story: The Daleks strike back at the Monstrons from the depth of a volcano and instead attack the people of Phryne.

1978
Publisher
World International

THE ROGUE PLANET (1)
Story: A new planet controlled by the Mechanoids is heading towards Skaro, while the Zeroan robot 2K is dispatched to fight both the Mechanoids and the Daleks.

THE ROGUE PLANET (2)
Story: 2K is discovered by the Daleks and escapes in a rocket heading for Earth and for the rogue planet.

1979
Publisher
World International

THE HUMAN BOMBS
Story: The Daleks prepare to launch their new Geiga bombs at Earth and a special ADF force is prepared to fight them.

ISLAND OF HORROR
Story: In the Pacific, Japanese fishermen find scientists hideously mutilated by the Daleks into savage psychopaths.

THE DALEK WORLD
Publisher
World International

THE MECHANICAL PLANET
Story: Threatened by a mechanical planet, Earth has no choice but to rearm the Daleks who, after victory is achieved, vow once more to conquer Earth.

TREASURE OF THE DALEKS
Story: Two men stow away on Brit's ship and force her to take them to Skaro where the Daleks' treasure is stored under the protection of the hideous Dredly monster.

THE INVISIBLE INVADER
Story: An invisible enemy attacks the Dalek's compressed-water factory, threatening all of Skaro in the process.

THE ORBITUS
Story: For his birthday, Roger is given an Orbitus, a wonderful Dalek creation that will obey his every order, and that eventually saves his life.

THE WORLD THAT WAITS
Story: Mechanus, a planet ruled by Mechanoids, is attacked by the Daleks - who seem at last to have met their equals in power.

MASTERS OF THE WORLD
Story: Unispace agent Meric investigates an underwater city full of humanoid copies of Earth leaders.

INDEX OF FICTION

This index is provided for anyone who remembers a story title, but does not know where (or when) it first appeared. It is also interesting to be able to see the mind-boggling diversity of *Doctor Who* adventures at a glance.

Note that the words 'Doctor Who' have usually been eliminated when they precede a title, but do not otherwise seem to serve a useful function, for example, *Doctor Who – The Ultimate Adventure* is listed as *Ultimate Adventure, The*. Entries such as *K9 and the Zeta Rescue* are double-listed under *K9* and *Zeta Rescue*.

For these originally untitled comics stories, both Jeremy Bentham's and our made-up titles have been listed: *Robot Reign of Terror* and *Terror of the Quarks*, for example, refer to the same story.

Each title is followed by the category under which the story is listed: *Motion Picture*, *Novel*, *Short Story*, *Comics* and so on. For categories such as *Short Stories* and *Comics*, where further listing is virtually required to locate the desired story, the following abbreviations have been used:

A77 – *Doctor Who* Annual 1977
DA77 – *Dalek* Annual 1977
DWM26 – *Doctor Who* Magazine, issue 26
HULK – Hulk Presents
K9A83 – *K9* Annual 1983
TVA10 – TV Action, issue 10
TVC694 – TV Comic, issue 694
TV21/9 – TV 21, issue 9, and so on.

STORY	CATEGORY AND REFERENCE
4-D War, The	*Comics* DWM51
Abel's Story	*Comics* DWM105
Abslom Daak, Dalek-Killer	*Comics* DWM17-20
After the Revolution	*Comics* A75
Alien Mind Games	*Short Story* A81
Amaryll Challenge, The	*Comics* TV21/18-24

STORY	CATEGORY AND REFERENCE
Amateur, The	*Comics* TVC1148–1154, TVC1390–1396
Ambush	See Trodos Ambush, The
Aqua-City, The	*Comics* TVC1353–1360
Archive Tapes, The	*Tape*
Archives of Phryne, The	*Comics* TV21/52–58
Arkwood Experiments, The	*Comics* TVC944–949
Armageddon Chrysalis, The	*Short Story* A83
Assassination Squad	*Short Story* DA78
Atoms Infinite	*Comics* A69
Attack of the Monstrons	See Menace of the Monstrons, The
Attack of the Primates	*Comics* TVC846–849
Avast There!	*Short Story* A76
Backtime	*Comics* TVA33–39
Back to the Sun	*Comics* TVA116–119
Battle for the Moon	*Comics* DA65
Battle Planet	*Short Story* A85
Battle Within, The	*Short Story* A75
Beasts of Vega, The	See K9 and the Beasts of Vega
Beauty and the Beast	*Short Story* A86
Before the Legend	*Short Story* A75
Bird of Fire	*Short Story* DWM122
Birth of a Renegade	*Short Story* Radio Times
Black Legacy	*Comics* DWM35–38
Black Sun Rising	*Comics* DWM57
Blockade	*Short Story* DA79
Body Snatcher, The	*Comics* A77
Brain Tappers, The	*Comics* DA67
Breakdown	*Short Story* DWM33
Break-Through	*Short Story* DA65
Brotherhood, The	*Comics* TVC925–928
Burn-Out	See Enter: the Go-Ray
Business as Usual	*Comics* DWM40–43
Car of the Century, The	*Comics* TVC864–867
Castaway, The	*Short Story* DA78
Catalogue of Events	*Short Story* DWM Summer Special 1983
Caught in the Web	*Short Story* A71
Caverns of Horror	*Short Story* A71
Celestial Toyshop, The	*Short Story* A69
Celluloid Midas, The	*Comics* TVA23–32
Challenge of the Piper	*Comics* TVC705–709
Changes	*Comics* DWM118–119
Children of the Evil Eye	*Comics* TVC1133–1138
Christmas Story, A	*Comics* TVC732–735
Chris Welkin, Planeteer	*Comics* DA67

STORY	CATEGORY AND REFERENCE
City of the Daleks	*Comics* DA65
City of the Damned	*Comics* DWM9–16
City of Gold	*Game Module* FASA
Class 4 Renegade	*Short Story* A84
Claw, The	*Short Story* A73
Claws of the Klathi	*Comics* DWM136–138
Cloud Exiles, The	*Short Story* A66
Cold Day in Hell, A	*Comics* DWM130–133
Collector, The	*Comics* DWM46
Colony of Death	*Short Story* A81
Coming of the Cybermen	*Comics* TVC824–827
Conflict on Ice	See Cybermen on Ice
Conundrum	*Short Story* A82
Countdown	*Game Module* FASA
Counter-Rotation	*Comics* TVC1280–1286
Crash-Dive	*Comics* TVC907–910
Creation of Camelot, The	*Short Story* A84
Crisis in Space	*Novel* Find Your Fate
Crisis on Kaldor	*Comics* DWM50
Crocodiles from the Mist, The	*Short Story* A79
Crossroads of Time, The	*Comics* DWM135
Culture Shock	*Comics* DWM139
Curse of Kanbo-Ala, The	*Short Story* K9A83
Curse of the Daleks, The	*Stage Play*
Cyber Nomads, The	*Tape*
Cyber-Mole	*Comics* TVC842–845
Cybermen on Ice	*Comics* TVC903–906
Cyclone Terror	*Short Story* A77
Dalek Revenge, The	*Comics* TVC1251–1258
Dalek Trap, The	*Comics* DA67
Daleks – Invasion Earth 2150 AD	*Motion Picture*
Daleks: The Secret Invasion	*Short Story* Dalek Special
Danger Down Below	*Short Story* A83
Dark Intruders	*Short Story* A73
Dark Planet, The	*Short Story* A71
Darkness Falling	*Comics* DWM167
Davarrk's Experiment	*Short Story* A86
Day of the Dragon	*Short Story* A85
Dead on Arrival	*Comics* A75
Deadly Choice, The	*Comics* TVA101–103
Deadly Weed, The	*Short Story* A85
Deal, The	*Comics* DWM53
Death Flower	*Comics* TVC1204–1214
Death to Mufl	*Short Story* A69
Deathworld	*Comics* DWM15–16
Detour to Diamedes	*Short Story* A77

STORY	CATEGORY AND REFERENCE
Devil of the Deep	*Comics* DWM61
Devil's Mouth, The	*Comics* TVC1348-1352
Devil-Birds of Corbo, The	*Short Story* A66
Diamond Dust	*Short Story* DA67
Didus Expedition, The	*Comics* TVC736-739
Dinosaur World	*Comics* TVC716-719
Disintegrator, The	*Comics* TVC1155-1159
Distractions	*Comics* DWM168
Doctor Conkeror	*Comics* DWM162
Doctor Strikes Back, The	*Comics* TVC792-795
Doctor Who and the Daleks	*Motion Picture*
Doctor Who's Space Adventure	*Short Story* DWSA book
Dogs of Doom, The	*Comics* DWM27-34
Doomsday Machine, The	*Short Story* DA77
Doorway into Nowhere	*Short Story* A73
Double Trouble	*Comics* TVC1298-1304
Double Trouble	*Short Story* A77
Dragon's Claw	*Comics* DWM39-45
Dragons of Kekokro, The	*Short Story* A70
Dream Masters, The	*Short Story* A68
Dreamers of Death	*Comics* DWM47-48
Duel of the Daleks	*Comics* TV21/11-17
Duellists, The	*Comics* TVC899-902, TVC1386-1389
Dryons, The	*Comics* TVC854-858
Early Cybermen, The	*Tape*
Earthlink Dilemma, The	See Turlough and the Earthlink Dilemma
Echoes of the Mogor	*Comics* DWM143-144
Eerie Manor, The	*Comics* TVC1371-1372
Egyptian Escapade	*Comics* TVC820-823
Emissaries of Jevo, The	*Comics* TV21/90-95
Emperor's Spy, The	*Comics* TVC1232-1238
Empire of the Cybermen	*Comics* TVC850-853
Emsone's Castle	*Comics* A79
End of the Line	*Comics* DWM54-55
Enemy from Nowhere, The	*Comics* TVA71-78
Enlightenment of Li-Chee, The	*Comics* HULK10
Enter: The Go-Ray	*Comics* TVC724-727
Envoys of Evil, The	*Comics* DA77
Eternal Present, The	*Comics* TVA40-46
Eve of the War	*Comics* TV21/47-51
Every Dog Has His Day	*Comics* A81
Evil Egg	*Short Story* DWM28
Exodus	*Comics* DWM108
Experimenters, The	*Comics* TVC780-783

STORY	CATEGORY AND REFERENCE
Exterminate! Exterminate! Exterminate!	*Short Story* DA76
Exterminator, The	*Comics* TVC803-806
Extortioner, The	*Comics* TVC784-787
Eye-Spiders of Pergross, The	*Short Story* A77
Fabulous Idiot, The	*Comics* DWM Summer Special 1982
False Planet, The	*Comics* TVC1312-1317
Famine on Planet X	*Short Story* A79
Fathom Trap, The	*Short Story* A74
Fellow Travellers	*Comics* DWM164-166
Fellowship of Quan, The	*Short Story* A86
Fight-Back	See Doctor Strikes Back, The
Final Quest, The	*Comics* DWM8
Fire Feeders, The	*Comics* TVC1318-1325
Fires Down Below, The	*Comics* DWM64
First Adventure, The	*Videogame*
Fishmen of Carpantha, The	*Comics* TVC965-970
Fishmen of Kandalinga, The	*Short Story* A65
Flashback	*Short Story* A79
Flood!!!	*Comics* DA76
Flower Power	*Comics* TVC832-836
Follow that Tardis	*Comics* DWM147
Follow the Phantoms	*Short Story* A69
Four-Dimensional Vistas	*Comics* DWM78-83
Free-Fall Warriors, The	*Comics* DWM56-57
Freedom by Fire	*Comics* A69
Frobisher's Story	*Comics* DWM107
Fugitive, The	*Short Story* DA77
Fugitives from Chance	*Short Story* A75
Fungus	*Short Story* A84
Funhouse	*Comics* DWM102-103
Galactic Gangster	*Short Story* A74
Galaxy Games, The	*Comics* TVC776-779
Garden of Evil	*Novel* Find Your Fate
Gemini Plan, The	*Comics* TVA1-5
Genesis	*Comics* DWM110
Genesis of Evil	*Comics* TV21/1-3
Genesis of the Cybermen	*Short Story* Cybermen
Ghouls of Grestonspey, The	*Short Story* A71
Gift, The	*Comics* DWM123-126
Glen of Sleeping, The	*Comics* TVA107-111
God Machine, The	*Short Story* A83
Gods of the Jungle	*Comics* TVC812-815
Gods Walk Among Us, The	*Comics* DWM59
Good Soldier, The	*Comics* DWM175-177

STORY	CATEGORY AND REFERENCE
Great T-Bag Mystery, The	*Stage Play*
Greatest Gamble, The	*Comics* DWM56
Grip of Ice	*Short Story* A70
Guardian of the Tomb, The	*Comics* TVC1373–1379
Gyros Injustice, The	*Comics* TVC699–704
HMS Tardis	*Short Story* A68
Hall of Mirrors	*Short Story* DWM119
Happy as Queeg	*Short Story* A69
Harry Sullivan's War	*Novel*
Hartlewick Horror, The	*Game Module* FASA
Haunted Planet, The	*Comics* TVC758–762
Haven, The	*Short Story* A83
Heat-Seekers, The	*Short Story* DWM117
Hijackers of Thrax, The	*Comics* TVC690–692
History of the Daleks, The	*Short Story* Daleks Book
Hoaxers, The	*Comics* TVC1291
Hole Truth, The	*Short Story* DWM32
Horror Hotel	*Short Story* K9A83
Hospitality on Hankus, The	*Short Story* A76
Hound of Hell	*Short Story* K9A83
House that Jack Built, The	*Short Story* A75
Hubert's Folly	*Comics* TVC1273–1279
Human Bomb, The	*Comics* DA79
Humanoids, The	*Comics* DA65
Hunger from the Ends of Time	*Comics* DWM157–158
Hungry Planet, The	*Comics* TVA Annual 74
Hunt to the Death	*Short Story* A73
Hunted by the Quarks	*Comics* TVC885–889
Hunted, The	See Hunted by the Quarks
Hunters of Zerox, The	*Comics* TVC763–767
Ice Apes, The	See Ice Primates, The
Ice Primates, The	*Comics* TVC881–884
Image Makers, The	*Comics* TVC1380–1385
Impasse	*Comics* TV21/63–69
Indian Attack	See Gods of the Jungle
Infinity Season, The	*Short Story* DWM151
Insect	See Insects, The
Insects, The	*Comics* TVC955–959
Inter-Galactic Cat	*Short Story* A82
Interface	*Short Story* A86
Intruders, The	*Comics* TVC1305–1311
Invaders from Gantac	*Comics* DWM148–150
Invaders Invisible	*Short Story* A71
Invasion from Space, The	*Short Story*
Invasion of the Daleks	*Comics* DA65
Invasion of the Ormazoids	*Novel* Find Your Fate

STORY	CATEGORY AND REFERENCE
Invasion of the Quarks	*Comics* TVC872–876
Invisible Invader, The	*Comics* Dalek World
Iron Legion, The	*Comics* DWM1–8
Is Anyone There?	*Comics* TVC1160–1169
Island of Horror	*Comics* DA79
Iytean Menace, The	*Game Module* FASA
Jokers, The	*Comics* TVC868–871
Junkyard Demon	*Comics* DWM58–59
Just a Small Problem	*Short Story* A82
Justice of the Glacians	*Short Story* A66
K9 and Company	*Novel*
K9 and the Beasts of Vega	*Novel*
K9 and the Missing Planet	*Novel*
K9 and the Time Trap	*Novel*
K9 and the Zeta Rescue	*Novel*
K9's Finest Hour	*Comics* DWM12
Kane's Story	*Comics* DWM104
Keepsake	*Comics* DWM140
Key of Vaga, The	*Short Story* A82
Killer Wasps, The	*Comics* TVC877–880
King of Golden Death, The	*Short Story* A68
Kingdom Builders, The	*Comics* TVC992–999
Klepton Parasites, The	*Comics* TVC674–683
Labyrinth, The	*Comics* TVA120
Lair of the Zarbi Supremo, The	*Short Story* A65
Legacy of Yesteryear	*Comics* TV21/76–85
Legions of Death, The	*Game Module* FASA
Life Bringer, The	*Comics* DWM49–50
Light Fantastic	*Short Story* A80
Listen – The Stars!	*Short Story* A74
Living Death, The	*Comics* DA67
Living in the Past	*Short Story* DWM162
Lizardworld	See Dinosaur World
Log of the Gypsy Joe, The	*Short Story* Dalek World
Lords of Destiny, The	*Short Story* Dalek World
Lords of the Ether	*Comics* TVC1191–1197, TVC1416–1423
Lords of the Galaxy	*Short Story* A69
Lost Ones, The	*Short Story* A65
Lunar Lagoon	*Comics* DWM76–77
Magician, The	*Comics* TVC1177–1183, TVC1397–1403
Manhunt	*Short Story* Dalek World
Man Friday	*Short Story* A70
Mark of Mandragora, The	*Comics* DWM169–172
Mark of Terror, The	*Comics* TVC921–924

STORY	CATEGORY AND REFERENCE
Master of the Spiders	*Comics* TVC799–802
Mastermind of Space	*Short Story* A69
Masters of the World	*Comics* Dalek World
Mechanical Planet, The	*Comics* Dalek World
Menace of the Molags	*Comics* A74
Menace of the Monstrons, The	*Comics* DA77
Menace on Metalupiter	*Comics* A77
Message of Mystery	*Photo-Novel* DA65
Metal Eaters, The	*Comics* TVC960–964
Metal Eaters, The	*Comics* TVC1184–1190, TVC1409–1415
Microtron Men, The	*Short Story* A69
Midsummer's Nightmare, A	*Short Story* A81
Minatorius	*Comics* DWM Winter Special 1981
Mind Extractors, The	*Short Story* A71
Mind Snatch	*Comics* TVC1287–1290
Mind-Jump	*Short Story* DWM31
Mines of Terror, The	*Videogame*
Missing Planet, The	See K9 and the Missing Planet
Mission for Duh	*Comics* A66
Mission to Magnus	*Missing Season*
Mission to Venus	*Novel* Find Your Fate
Mission, The	*Short Story* A76
Moderator, The	*Comics* DWM84, 86–87
Monster of Crag, The	*Short Story* K9A83
Monsters From Earth, The	*Short Story* A65
Monsters of Gurnian	*Comics* DA65
Monsters of New York, The	*Comics* TVC807–811
Moon Exploration	See Lords of the Ether
Moon Landing	*Comics* TVC710–712
Moonshot	See Moon Landing
Multi-Mobile, The	*Comics* TVC950–954
Mutant Strain, The	*Comics* TVC1292–1297
Mutants, The	*Comics* TVC1341–1347
Mystery of the *Marie Celeste*, The	*Short Story* A70
Mystery of the Rings, The	*Short Story* A85
Nature of the Beast	*Comics* DWM111–113
Nemertines, The	*Short Story* A84
Nemesis of the Daleks	*Comics* DWM152–155
Neuronic Nightmare	*Comics* A76
Neutron Knights, The	*Comics* DWM60
New Life, A	*Short Story* A76
New Life, A	*Short Story* A78
Night Flight to Nowhere	*Short Story* A83
Night Walkers, The	*Comics* TVC934–936
Nightmare	*Short Story* DA76

STORY	CATEGORY AND REFERENCE
Nightmare Fair, The	*Missing Season*
Nineveh!	*Comics* HULK12
Nova	*Comics* TVC1139–1147
Oil Well, The	*Comics* DA65
Old Father Saturn	*Short Story* A74
On the Planet Isopterus	*Comics* A83
On the Slippery Trail	*Short Story* Amazing World
Once in a Lifetime	*Comics* HULK1
Once Upon a Time Lord	*Comics* DWM98–99
Only a Matter of Time	*Short Story* A68
Operation Wurlitzer	*Comics* TVC911–915
Orb, The	*Comics* TVC1334–1340
Orbitus, The	*Comics* Dalek World
Ordeals of Demeter, The	*Comics* TVC720–723
Origins of the Cybermen	*Tape*
Out into Space	See Amaryll Challenge, The
Outlaw Planet, The	*Short Story* DA67
Out of the Green Mist	*Short Story* A74
Outsider, The	*Comics* DWM25–26
Oxaqua Incident, The	*Short Story* A84
Party Animals	*Comics* DWM173
Penacasata	*Missing Season*
Penalty, The	*Short Story* A83
Penta Ray Factor, The	*Comics* TV21/25–32
Peril in Mechanistria	*Short Story* A65
Pescatons, The	*Record*
Phaser Aliens, The	*Short Story* A73
Plague of Death	*Comics* TV21/33–39
Plague of the Black Scorpi	*Comics* TVC744–747
Plague World	*Comics* A82
Planet from Nowhere	*Short Story* A69
Planet of Bones	*Short Story* A68
Planet of Dust, The	*Short Story* A79
Planet of Fear	*Short Story* A82
Planet of Paradise	*Short Story* A82
Planet of the Daleks, The	*Comics* TVA55–62
Planet of the Dead	*Comics* DWM141–142
Planet that Cried Wolf, The	*Short Story* DA79
Playthings of Fo, The	*Short Story* A66
Polly the Glot	*Comics* DWM95–97
Power Play	*Comics* TV21/4–10
Power to the People	*Short Story* DWM114
Power, The	*Comics* A79
Powerstone	*Short Story* K9A83
Profits of Doom	*Comics* DWM120–122
Psychic Jungle, The	*Comics* A76

STORY	CATEGORY AND REFERENCE
Quest, The	*Comics* DA77
Quiz Book of Dinosaurs	*Novel*
Quiz Book of Magic	*Novel*
Quiz Book of Science	*Novel*
Quiz Book of Space	*Novel*
Quotron Rescue, The	*Comics* TVC929-933
Race Against Time	*Novel* Find Your Fate
Radio Waves, The	*Short Story* A86
Real Hereward, The	*Short Story* A85
Rebel's Gamble, The	*Novel* FASA
Recall Unit	*Stage Play*
Red for Danger	*Short Story* DA65
Redemption	*Comics* DWM134
Reluctant Warriors	*Short Story* A80
Report from an Unknown Planet	*Short Story* DA77
Rescue	See Quotron Rescue, The
Retribution	*Short Story* A86
Return of the Cybermen	See Coming of the Cybermen, The
Return of the Daleks	*Comics* TVC1215-1222
Return of the Daleks, The	*Comics* DWM1-4
Return of the Electrids	*Short Story* A80
Return of the Trods	*Comics* TVC772-775
Return to the Web Planet	*Comics* TVC693-698
Revelation	*Comics* DWM109
Revenge of the Phantoms	*Short Story* A75
Rival Robots, The	*Comics* A78
Road to Conflict	*Comics* TV21/96-104
Robot King, The	*Comics* A70
Robot Rampage	*Comics* TVC977-984
Robot Reign of Terror	See Terror of the Quarks
Robot War	*Comics* TVC816-819
Rogue Planet	*Comics* TV21/59-62
Rogue Planet, The	*Comics* DA78
Run the Gauntlet	*Short Story* A70
Sabotage	*Comics* TVC828-831
Salad Daze	*Comics* DWM117
Sands of Time	*Short Story* DWM29-30
Sands of Tymus, The	*Short Story* A78
Sara Kingdom, Space Security Agent	*Comics* DA67
Saucer of Fate	*Short Story* A73
Scorched Earth	*Short Story* A75
Scream of the Silent	*Short Story* DWM 25th Anniversary Special
Sea Monsters, The	*Comics* DA67
Sea of Faces, The	*Short Story* A78

STORY	CATEGORY AND REFERENCE
Search for the Doctor	*Novel* Find Your Fate
Secret Invasion, The	See Daleks Secret Invasion, The
Secret of the Bald Planet	*Short Story* A77
Secret of the Emperor	*Comics* DA67
Secret of the Mountain, The	*Short Story* DA65
Secret Struggle, The	*Short Story* Dalek World
Secrets of Gemino, The	*Comics* TVC753-757
Seeds of Destruction, The	*Short Story* DA78
Sentinel, The	*Comics* HULK7
Seven Keys to Doomsday	*Stage Play*
Shadow of Humanity	*Comics* TV21/86-89
Shadow of the Dragon	*Comics* TVC1326-1333
Shape Shifter, The	*Comics* DWM88-89
Shark Bait	*Comics* TVC728-731
Ship of Fools	*Comics* DWM23-24
Shroud of Azaroth, The	*Short Story* K9A83
Singing Crystals, The	*Short Story* A70
Sinister Sea, The	*Comics* TVC1239-1244
Sinister Sponge	*Short Story* A76
Size Control	*Comics* TVC1170-1176, TVC1424-1430
Skywatch-7	*Comics* DWM Winter Special 1981
Slaves of Shran	*Short Story* A70
Sleeping Beast, The	*Short Story* A78
Sleeping Guardians, The	*Short Story* A80
Slimmer!	*Comics* HULK11
Slipback	*Radio Play*
Small Defender, The	*Short Story* DA65
Snow Devils, The	*Comics* TVC1361-1365
Soldiers from Zolta	*Short Story* A71
Solution, The	*Short Story* DA79
Sons of Grekk, The	*Short Story* A66
Sons of the Crab, The	*Short Story* A65
Sour Note	*Short Story* A68
Space Garden, The	*Comics* TVC1366-1370
Space Ghost	See Haunted Planet, The
Space Ghost, The	*Comics* TVC1245-1250
Space Pirates, The	See Zarcus of Neon
Space Station Z-7	*Comics* TVC740-743
Space War Two	See Robot War
Spider-God	*Comics* DWM52
Spoilers, The	*Comics* TVA123
Stairway to Heaven	*Comics* DWM156
Star Beast, The	*Comics* DWM19-26
Star Death	*Comics* DWM47
Star Tigers	*Comics* DWM27-30, DWM44-46

STORY	CATEGORY AND REFERENCE
Stars Fell on Stockbridge	*Comics* DWM68–69
Steel Fist	*Comics* TVA89–93
Stitch in Time, A	*Comics* TVA63–70
Stockbridge Horror, The	*Comics* DWM70–75
Stolen Tardis, The	*Comics* DWM9–11
Story for Christmas, A	See Christmas Story, A
Stowaway	*Short Story* DWM27
Sub-Zero	*Comics* TVA47–54
Subterfuge	*Comics* TVC971–976
Super Sub, The	*Comics* DA67
Sweet Flower of Uthe	*Short Story* A81
Switch in Time, A	*Comics* HULK6
Talons of Terror	*Short Story* A74
Tearaways, The	*Comics* TVC916–920
Technical Hitch	*Comics* HULK5
Teenage Kicks	*Short Story* DWM163
Temple of Time, The	*Comics* TVC890–894
Ten Fathom Pirates	*Short Story* A66
Terror of the Quarks	*Comics* TVC895–898
Terror on Tantalogus	*Short Story* A79
Terror on Tiro	*Short Story* A66
Terror on Xaboi	*Comics* A80
Terrorkon Harvest, The	*Comics* TV21/70–75
Terror Task Force	*Short Story* DA76
Tests of Trefus, The	*Comics* A68
Therovian Quest, The	*Comics* TVC684–689
Thousand and One Doors, A	*Short Story* A70
Threat from Beneath, The	*Comics* TVA112
Throwback (The Soul of a Cyberman)	*Comics* DWM5–7
Tides of Time, The	*Comics* DWM61–67
Timechase	*Short Story* DA76
Time and Tide	*Comics* DWM145–146
Time Bomb	*Comics* Death's Head 8
Time Bomb	*Comics* DWM114–116
Time in Reverse	*Comics* TVC713–715
Time Machine, The	*Radio Play*
Time Savers, The	*Short Story* A85
Time Snatch, The	*Short Story* A77
Time Thief, The	*Comics* A74
Time Thief, The	*Short Story* A75
Time Trap, The	See K9 and the Time Trap
Time Wake	*Short Story* A86
Time Witch, The	*Comics* DWM35–38
Timebenders	*Comics* TVA6–13
Timeslip	*Comics* DWM17–18

STORY	CATEGORY AND REFERENCE
Touchdown on Deneb 7, The	*Comics* DWM48
Train Flight	*Comics* DWM159-161
Traitor, The	*Comics* A78
Treasure of the Daleks	*Comics* Dalek World
Treasure Trail	*Comics* TVC1266-1272
Trial of Fire	*Comics* TVC985-991
Trodos Ambush, The	*Comics* TVC788-791
Trodos Tyranny, The	*Comics* TVC748-752
Turlough and the Earthlink Dilemma	*Novel*
Twilight of the Silurians	*Comics* DWM21-22
Two-Timer, The	*Short Story* DWM26
Ugrakks, The	*Comics* TVA78-88
Ultimate Adventure, The	*Stage Play*
Ultimate Cybermen, The	*Tape*
Ultimate Evil, The	*Missing Season*
Underwater Adventure	See Underwater Robot, The
Underwater Robot, The	*Comics* TVC768-771
Unheard Voice, The	*Comics* TVA131
Universe Called Fred, A	*Short Story* A71
Unwilling Traveller, The	*Comics* DA67
Valley of Dragons	*Short Story* A69
Vampire Plants, The	*Comics* A70
Vampires of Crellium, The	*Short Story* Amazing World
Virus	*Comics* TVC1259-1265
Vogan Slaves, The	*Comics* TVA15-22
Volcanis Deal, The	*Short Story* A84
Volcano	See Extortioner, The
Vortex Crystal, The	*Novel* FASA
Vortex, The	*Comics* TVA125-129
Vorton's Revenge	*Short Story* A85
Voton Terror, The	*Short Story* A81
Voyage to the Edge of the Universe	*Comics* DWM49
Voyager, The	*Comics* DWM90-94
Wanderers, The	*Comics* TVC1198-1203, TVC1404-1408
War in the Abyss	*Short Story* A73
War of the Words	*Comics* DWM51
War on Acquatica	*Short Story* A77
War World	*Comics* HULK4
War-Game	*Comics* DWM100-101
Warlord	*Videogame*
Warlord of the Ogrons	*Comics* DWM13-14
Warrior's Code, The	*Game Module* FASA
Warrior's Story, The	*Comics* DWM106
Wartime	*Video*
We are the Daleks!	*Short Story* Radio Times

STORY	CATEGORY AND REFERENCE
Weapon, The	*Comics* A80
When Starlight Grows Cold	*Short Story* A68
Who is the Stranger?	*Comics* TVA104
Who's that Girl?	*Comics* HULK8-9
Winter on Mesique	*Short Story* A84
Witching Hour, The	*Comics* TVC837-841
Word of Asiries, The	*Short Story* A68
World of Ice	*Short Story* A69
World Shapers, The	*Comics* DWM127-129
World that Waits, The	*Comics* Dalek World
World Without Night	*Comics* A68
Wreckers, The	*Comics* TVC1223-1231
X-Rani and the Ugly Mutants	*Short Story* A80
Yonder . . . The Yeti	*Comics* DWM31-34
Zarcus of Neon	*Comics* TVC859-863
Zeron Invasion	*Comics* TVA94-100
Zeta Rescue, The	See K9 and the Zeta Rescue
Zombies, The	*Comics* TVC796-798

4: ADDENDUM TO
DOCTOR WHO –
THE PROGRAMME GUIDE

Twenty-Sixth Season
Story Summaries for the twenty-sixth season of *Doctor Who* were not available from the BBC at the time *Doctor Who – The Programme Guide* went to press. This involuntary omission is corrected below.

7N
BATTLEFIELD (4 episodes)
Writer
Ben Aaronovitch
Story: Answering a distress signal, the TARDIS is drawn to Cadbury, where a nuclear missile convoy, under the direction of UNIT Brigadier Winifred Bambera, is stopped. Under a neighbouring lake is an extra-dimensional spaceship containing the body of King Arthur and his sword Excalibur. Ancelyn, a knight from that other dimension, arrives on Earth to recover Excalibur, but is followed by the evil Mordred, who summons his mother, the powerful sorceress Morgaine. They all recognize the Doctor as Merlin, one of his future incarnations. A battle erupts between UNIT and Morgaine's men. Hearing of the Doctor's return, Brigadier Lethbridge-Stewart comes out of retirement, and ends up using silver bullets to kill the Destroyer, an otherworldly creature released by Morgaine to devour Earth. Morgaine tries to trigger the explosion of the nuclear missile, but the Doctor shows her there would be no honour in such a victory. Arthur is revealed to have been dead all along. Morgaine and Mordred are remanded to UNIT's custody.
Book: Doctor Who – Battlefield by Ben Aaronovitch.

7Q
GHOST LIGHT
Writer
Marc Platt

Story: The Doctor and Ace arrive in Perivale in 1883, in Gabriel Chase, an evil house that Ace burned down in 1983. The house is built upon an ancient spaceship, and its inhabitants are under the domination of Josiah Samuel Smith, who turns out to be a reptilian alien from the ship who has evolved into a human. Smith is holding prisoner the explorer Redvers Fenn-Cooper, who went mad when he first beheld the ship's true owner, and plots to have him kill Queen Victoria to restore the British Empire to its former glory. Smith's plans are thwarted by Control, another alien who evolves into a woman; Nimrod, his Neanderthal servant; and Ace, who causes the release of a powerful alien named Light. Light once catalogued all of Earth's species, but when he learns that his catalogue has been made obsolete by evolution, he wants to destroy mankind. He disintegrates when the Doctor shows him that no one can stop evolution. Fenn-Cooper, Control and Nimrod leave in the ship.

Book: Doctor Who – Ghost Light by Marc Platt.

7M

THE CURSE OF FENRIC

Writer

Ian Briggs

Story: The Doctor and Ace arrive at a secret naval base off the coast of Northumberland towards the end of the Second World War. There, Dr Judson has built the Ultima Machine, a computer designed to break German ciphers. Base commander Millington, obsessed by Norse mythology, plots to let a Russian commando unit, led by Captain Sorin, steal the Ultima core, which he has booby-trapped with a deadly toxin. Judson uses the Ultima Machine to translate ancient runes, which in turn lead to the release of Fenric, an evil entity from the dawn of time whom the Doctor trapped seventeen centuries ago in a Chinese flask. The flask was later stolen and buried by Vikings. The base is attacked by humans who have become vampiric Haemovores. Fenric takes over Judson's body to challenge the Doctor at chess, and Ace unwittingly helps Fenric win. Fenric then takes over Sorin's body, and plans to release the deadly toxins. But the Doctor succeeds in turning an Ancient Haemvore against Fenric, whose host body is killed by the toxin. The baby of a young woman whom Ace helped escape the Haemovores is revealed to be her mother.

Book: Doctor Who – The Curse of Fenric by Ian Briggs.

7P
SURVIVAL
Writer
Rona Munro

Story: The Doctor takes Ace to Perivale because she wants to look up her old mates, but most of them seem to have disappeared. They have been transported by the cat-like kitlings to the planet of the Cheetah People, descendants of an ancient race which has reverted to savagery and has the ability to teleport through space. The Doctor and Ace are eventually transported to the planet. Ace teams up with Midge and two other old friends, while the Doctor meets the Master, who has drawn him there because he needs the Doctor's help to escape from the doomed planet, whose symbiotic nature is causing the Master to turn into an animal. Midge lets his animal side overcome him, and the Master uses him to teleport to Earth. Ace, who has almost succumbed to the attraction of a Cheetah woman, Karra, gains the same ability and takes the Doctor and the others back to Perivale. There, the Master uses Midge and his friends to go after the Doctor, but Midge dies. The Master kills Karra, who reverts to human form. Overtaken by his animal nature, he drags the Doctor back to the disintegrating Cheetah planet. The Doctor is transported back to Earth when he makes the decision to refuse to fight.

Book: Doctor Who – Survival by Rona Munro.

EPISODE TITLES FOR STORIES A–Z

All the episodes of *Doctor Who* had individual titles until Story AA (*The Savages*). An alphabetical list of these titles is provided here for quick reference. Episode codes are used as follows: M2 means that *All Roads Lead to Rome* is the second episode of story M (*The Romans*).

TITLE	EPISODE CODE	TITLE	EPISODE CODE
Abandoned Planet, The	V11	Edge of Destruction, The	C1
Airlock	T3	End of Tomorrow, The	K4
All Roads Lead to Rome	M2	Escape Switch	V10
		Escape to Danger	N3
Ambush, The	B4	Escape, The	B3
Assassin at Peking	D7	Executioners, The	R1
Bargain of Necessity, A	H5	Expedition, The	B5
Battle of Wits, A	S3	Exploding Planet, The	T4
Bell of Doom	W4	Feast of Steven, The	V7
Bomb, The	X4	Final Phase, The	Q4
Bride of Sacrifice, The	F3	Final Test, The	Y4
Brink of Disaster, The	C2	Firemaker, The	A4
Cave of Skulls, The	A2	Five Hundred Eyes	D3
Celestial Toyroom, The	Y1	Flashpoint	K6
Centre, The	N6	Flight Through Eternity	R3
Change of Identity, A	H3	Forest of Fear, The	A3
Checkmate	S4	Four Hundred Dawns	T1
Conspiracy	M3	Golden Death	V9
Coronas of the Sun	V6	Guests of Madame Guillotine	H2
Counterplot	V5		
Crater of Needles	N4	Hall of Dolls, The	Y2
Crisis	J3	Hidden Danger	G3
Daleks, The	K2	Holiday for the Doctor, A	Z1
Dancing Floor, The	Y3		
Dangerous Journey	J2	Horse of Destruction	U4
Day of Armageddon	V2	Inferno	M4
Day of Darkness, The	F4	Invasion	N5
		Johnny Ringo	Z3
Day of Reckoning	K3	Journey into Terror	R4
Dead Planet, The	B1	Keys of Marinus, The	E6
Death of a Spy	U3	Kidnap	G5
Death of Doctor Who, The	R5	Knight of Jaffa, The	P2
		Land of Fear, A	H1
Death of Time, The	R2	Lion, The	P1
Desperate Measures	L2	Meddling Monk, The	S2
Desperate Venture, A	G6	Mighty Kublai Khan	D6
Destruction of Time	V12	Mission to the Unknown	T/A
Devil's Planet	V3		
Dimensions of Time, The	Q2	Nightmare Begins, The	V1
Don't Shoot the Pianist	Z2	OK Corral, The	Z4
		Ordeal, The	B6

TITLE	EPISODE CODE	TITLE	EPISODE CODE
Plague, The	X2	Watcher, The	S1
Planet of Decision, The	R6	Web Planet, The	N1
Planet of Giants	J1	Wheel of Fortune, The	P3
Powerful Enemy, The	L1	World's End	K1
Priest of Death	W3	Zarbi, The	N2
Prisoners of Conciergerie	H6		
Race Against Death, A	G4		
Rescue, The	B7		
Return, The	X3		
Rider From Shang-Tu	D5		
Roof of the World, The	D1		
Screaming Jungle, The	E3		
Sea Beggar, The	W2		
Sea of Death, The	E1		
Search, The	Q3		
Sentence of Death	E5		
Singing Sands, The	D2		
Slave Traders, The	M1		
Small Prophet, Quick Return	U2		
Snows of Terror, The	E4		
Space Museum, The	Q1		
Steel Sky, The	X1		
Strangers in Space	G1		
Survivors, The	B2		
Temple of Evil, The	F1		
Temple of Secrets	U1		
Traitors, The	V4		
Trap of Steel	T2		
Tyrant of France, The	H4		
Unearthly Child, An	A1		
Unwilling Warriors, The	G2		
Velvet Web, The	E2		
Volcano	V8		
Waking Ally, The	K5		
Wall of Lies, The	D4		
War of God	W1		
War-Lords, The	P4		
Warriors of Death, The	F2		

ERRATA

In spite of everyone's best efforts, some errors have crept into the recently revised and updated edition of *Doctor Who – The Programme Guide*. Here is an exhaustive, and hopefully complete, list of corrections.

PAGE	STORY	CORRECTIONS
16	TABLE	*Vengeance on Varos*: Production code is 6V (not 6U). *The Two Doctors*: Production code is 6W (not 6V).
17	–	Sydney Newman (not Sidney).
23	B	*Story*: static electricity (not eletricity).
27	G	Correct order of episodes is: STRANGERS IN SPACE, THE UNWILLING WARRIORS, HIDDEN DANGER, A RACE AGAINST DEATH, KIDNAP, A DESPERATE VENTURE.
31	L	*Cast*: Ray Barrett played Bennett (not Bennet).
33	N	Correct order of episodes is: THE WEB PLANET, THE ZARBI (not THE ZARBI INVASION), ESCAPE TO DANGER, CRATER OF NEEDLES, INVASION, THE CENTRE.
34	P	*Cast*: Petra Markham (not Pera).
39	V	Correct order of episodes is: THE NIGHTMARE BEGINS, DAY OF ARMAGEDDON, DEVIL'S PLANET, THE TRAITORS, COUNTER PLOT, CORONAS OF THE SUN, THE FEAST OF STEVEN, VOLCANO, GOLDEN DEATH, ESCAPE SWITCH, THE ABANDONED PLANET, DESTRUCTION OF TIME.
41	V	*Correct story summary is*: After a chase across the universe, the TARDIS lands on the volcanic planet Tigus, where the Doctor *meets his old enemy the Meddling Monk, who betrays him to the Daleks.*

PAGE	STORY	CORRECTIONS
		Back on Kembel, the Doctor finally activates the Time Destructor . . . (the italicized words were omitted by mistake).
41	W	*Cast*: Erik Chitty (not Eric).
46	BB	*Number of Episodes*: 4 (not 6); *Cast*: Desmond Cullum-Jones (not Callum-Jones); Eddie Davis (not David); Michael Rathborne (not Rathbone).
51	HH	*Writer*: Gerry Davis, uncredited.
54	LL	*Cast*: Ken Tyllson (not Tyllsen).
56	MM	*Cast*: Michael Kilgarriff played the Cyber Controller.
66	YY	*Cast*: Nik Zaran (not Nick).
70	BBB	*Cast*: Gordon Richardson played Squire (not Square).
71	CCC	*Cast*: Dallas Cavell (not Cavall).
75	GGG	*Cast*: Tim Pigott-Smith (not Piggott-Smith).
77	JJJ	*Cast*: John Joyce (not Jon).
86	SSS	*Note*: None of Paul Bernard's directed work (on QQQ) appears in SSS, but some of David Maloney's directed work (on SSS) is used at the very end of QQQ.
90	YYY	*Cast*: Frank Gatliff (not Gatcliffe).
95	4E	*Cast*: Ivor Roberts played Mogran (not Mogren).
96	4D	*Writer*: Robert Holmes, uncredited; *Cast*: David Collings played Vorus (not Vorus/Wilkins).
102	4L	*Cast*: John Acheson (not Achson).
103	4M	*Cast*: Jon Laurimore (not John); Jay Neill (not Niell); Kathy Wolff (not Wolfit).
104	4N	*Cast*: Robin Hargrave (not Hargreave); John Delieu (not Delein).
108	4S	*Cast*: Penny Lister (not Peggy).
129	5Q	*Cast*: Add the following names: Tony Allef, Ranjit Nakara, Hi Ching, Bruce Callender, John Holland, James Muir

PAGE	STORY	CORRECTIONS
		(Gaztaks); Terence Creasey, Eddie Sommer, Ray Knight, Chris Marks, Stephen Nagy, Sylvia Marriott, Lewis Hooper (Deons); Michael Brydon, David Cleeve (Guards); Stephen Kane, John Laing, David Cole, Howard Barnes (Savants); Michael Gordon Browne, Harry Fielder, Laurie Goode, Peter Gates-Fleming, Geoff Whitestone (Tigellans).
132	5T	*Cast*: Margot Van Der Burgh (not Van De Burgh).
134	K9	*Story*: Lilly Gregson (not Lily).
137	5W	*Cast*: Illarrio Bisi Pedro (not Illario).
141	6B	*Cast*: Michael Gordon Browne (not Brown).
144	6D	*Cast*: Barrie Smith (not Barry).
145	6G	*Cast*: Rachael Weaver (not Rachel).
146	6H	*Cast*: Leee John (not Lee).
147	6K	*Cast*: Wendy Padbury played Zoe Heriot (not Herriot).
151	6P	*Cast*: Mike Mungarvan (not Mungarven).
156	6T	*Writer*: Eric Saward, uncredited.
158	6X	*Cast*: Hus Levent (not Levant).
159	6W	*Cast*: Nicholas Fawcett (not Farcett).
160	6Y	*Cast*: Add the following name: Neil Hallett (Maylin Ranis).
161	6Z	*Story*: Nekros (not Necros).
164	7C	*Cast*: Add the following name: Martin Weedon (Guard).
167	7D	*Cast*: Jacki Webb (not Jackie).
170	7G	*Story*: Svartos (not Spartos); Sabalom Glitz (not Sabalon).
172	7L	*Cast*: Richard D Sharp (not Richard); Annie Hulley (not Anne).
176	7N	*Cast*: Dorota Rae played Flight Lieutenant Lavel (not Pilot).
	7Q	*Cast*: Sylvia Syms (not Sims).

PAGE	STORY	CORRECTIONS
	7M	*Cast*: Cory Pulman (not Corey); Aaron Hanley (not Handley); Add the following name: Raymond Trickett (Ancient Haemovore); Transposed: Cy Town (Haemovore).
177	7P	*Writer*: Rona Munro (not Munroe); *Cast*: Julian Holloway played Sergeant Paterson (not Patterson); Will Barton (not William); Kate Eaton (not Eadon).